INTRODUCTION

Home for Christmas by Paige Winship Dooly
Stella Grant arrives in Christmas, Florida, content with her nomadic RV lifestyle and ready to tackle her next job as event planner for the town's Christmas festival. Brick Myers keeps busy with his contracting job, heading up the Christmas committee, and as a single dad. When festival plans throw the two together, Stella and Brick realize their lives are lacking in the relationship arena. Will the small town put a postmark of approval on their relationship before Stella leaves Christmas for good?

Merry Christmas, With Love by Darlene Franklin
War widow Randi Pearson enjoys sending Christmas cards postmarked from the Christmas, Florida, post office to men and women serving in the armed forces—until a retired major, Troy Brennan, shows up as a post office volunteer. Can Troy convince Randi to let go of the past and move into the future?

A Blessed Angel Came by Kathleen E. Kovach
Ever since the accident that claimed her father's life and left her sister in a wheelchair, Gabi Archer has retreated into herself. That is, until photographer David Preston challenges and intrigues her through their shared work at a nature park in Christmas, Florida. They secretly send cards to each other through the town's post office as a way to show their admiration. Can David draw Gabi out of her shell, or will his past cause her to withdraw further?

You're a Charmer, Mr. Grinch by Paula Moldenhauer
Retired police officer Rick Stanton dons a Grinch costume for the holidays and "patrols" Christmas, Florida, to promote the festivities. Everyone falls under his charm except the person he most wants to impress—postmaster Edie Hathaway. Rick wants to be loved for himself, not his secret. His silence confuses Edie, stirring up her painful past and threatening her secure future. The Grinch is stealing Edie's heart, but will Edie learn to trust him before he gives up on love?

POSTMARK CHRISTMAS

FOUR-IN-ONE COLLECTION

PAIGE WINSHIP DOOLY, DARLENE
FRANKLIN, KATHLEEN E. KOVACH,
AND PAULA MOLDENHAUER

BARBOUR
PUBLISHING

Print ISBN 978-1-61626-836-7

eBook Editions:
Adobe Digital Edition (.epub) 978-1-62029-098-9
Kindle and MobiPocket Edition (.prc) 978-1-62029-099-6

Scripture taken from the HOLY BIBLE, NEW INTERNATIONAL VERSION®. NIV®. Copyright © 1973, 1978, 1984, 2011 by Biblica, Inc.™ Used by permission. All rights reserved worldwide.

Published by Barbour Publishing, Inc., P.O. Box 719, Uhrichsville, OH 44683, www.barbourbooks.com

Our mission is to publish and distribute inspirational products offering exceptional value and biblical encouragement to the masses.

ecpa Member of the
Evangelical Christian
Publishers Association

Printed in the United States of America

Home for Christmas

Paige Winship Dooly

ACKNOWLEDGMENTS/DEDICATION

To my husband Troy. Thank you for all your love, support, patience, and encouragement—and for taking on so many of the never-ending household duties while I juggle this and all the other stuff that's always going on when I write. And Tessa, Cassidy, and Jetty—I love the way you jump in to help with the little girls and the house and everything else when I'm on deadline—and even when I'm not. I love and appreciate you all so much! Lena, Tempest and Ashton, your antics make me smile when I'm needing a break from work—and pretty much during every other moment of the day. Thanks for being such wonderful and adventurous little girls. I love you Josh, JT, and Dalton! I'm proud of the men you've become. And to Dalton's wife, Felicia—you make a wonderful addition to our family. I love you, and I thank you for blessing us with not one, but two precious grandsons to love on. I love you Dillion and Gabe!

Chapter 1

Stella pushed a strand of hair behind her ear and flexed her stiff fingers. Both hands were cramped from battling the temperamental steering wheel for the better part of the morning. She dared a quick glance at the map on her GPS—which she fondly referred to as "Roger"—before returning her eyes to the road. Only another half mile due west and she'd reach her destination. Finally. She'd been on the road the better part of the past week and wanted to settle in.

The shiny new device looked out of place on the dull gray dashboard of her ancient RV, but it had proven to be worth its weight in gold on this trip. She'd never been through this part of Florida before and couldn't imagine how she'd traveled all over the country without the useful gadget. They'd had a few instances of miscommunication, but for the most part, Roger hadn't steered her wrong. She giggled at her pun. *Steered her wrong*. Or was that a pun? It didn't really matter, she found it amusing. Hmmm. Perhaps she'd spent a little too much time on the road. Alone. She frowned. Definitely time to stop traveling. Human interaction would do her good. Or was it *well*? Human interaction would do her well? She frowned, debating.

The monotone male voice of the GPS interrupted and gave its next direction, telling her to hang a left and do a U-turn before heading slightly east and merging into the south lane on Colonial Drive before taking a quick right. She smiled, doing as instructed while Roger spouted off directions like a drill sergeant. She quipped out loud, "Why thank you, Roger. Whatever would I do without you?"

The silence she got in return made her wish for a travel companion—even a cat or dog would suffice and would beat talking to herself or a piece of electronics. Holiday melancholy threatened to overtake her. She shook it off. She didn't have much experience when it came to family holidays. As a young child, she'd moved around a lot, going from one divorced parent to the other. She'd been passed off to her aunt in her early teens and hadn't heard from either of her parents since. Her aunt died when Stella was sixteen, and after graduating high school, Stella hit the road. Family traditions, in her experience, had changed like the Midwestern weather. It was hard to miss what she'd never really had, but once in a while a certain family-oriented commercial or a holiday show would make her yearn for what could have been. Stella redirected her focus—again. Traffic. Traffic was always a safe topic to muse.

Traffic in Christmas, Florida, was sparse, just the way Stella preferred. She doubted the small town ever had much of an issue with rush-hour traffic, but today most everyone would be home enjoying their bountiful Thanksgiving dinners, surrounded by family and friends. The few cars here and there were probably in transit, heading from home to the location of their midday meal.

Stella frowned. The thought unexpectedly blindsided her and made her feel adrift and lonely without her own friends or family to celebrate with. What was wrong with her? She'd never minded traveling alone before. She preferred the solitary life she lived on the road, didn't she? She brushed the thought away and tried to focus on Roger's instructions.

The quick right had her turning into a narrow lane that led to the parking lot of the small Christmas, Florida, post office. She could see the post office to her left, but somehow, while lost in her musings, she'd missed the driveway that allowed her to enter the parking lot. Roger hadn't told her to make the final left turn—another instance to add to their minor list of miscommunications.

Stella slowed then stopped, peering at the narrow lane before her that meandered into a thicket of pine trees. She debated whether she should try to back the behemoth of an RV out of the trees and onto the right path, or whether she should continue forward until she found a good place to turn around.

Roger was spewing out warnings to turn around at the next possible intersection in order to get back on track.

"Better late than never," Stella muttered at the small box as she considered her options. The problem was, her gas tank read low and she didn't dare waste more fuel continuing on, just to find out she couldn't turn around anytime soon. She didn't know where the nearest gas station was, nor did she know how many miles she'd have to travel to find one before heading to the campground where she'd park her rig for the duration of her stay.

With a sigh, she leaned her right arm on her armrest and turned to look over her shoulder through the large back window. Visibility in reverse was rough to say the least. The engine roared in protest, but finally began to inch backward. She briefly considered turning around, but even if the trees that lined both sides of the road gave her enough space to do so, the soft sandy soil on either side of the lane prevented her from trying to do a three-point turn.

She backed slowly and caught herself veering a little to the left when the sharp sound of a nearby horn caused Stella to swerve hard and slam on her brakes. Pots and pans clanked as a cabinet door flew open. Cups and mugs tumbled onto the carpet as the heavy vehicle sank into the sand at the side of the road.

"Wonderful!" Stella clung to the steering wheel and buried her face on her arms. She'd been so close to settling in for the day. After the long week spent on the road while traveling from California to Florida, she was more than ready to hook up her hoses, plug in her electric cord, and plant her lawn chair in the sand. She'd even stopped at a convenience store and picked up a turkey sandwich and a bottle of cranberry juice in honor of the holiday. The new paperback novel sitting on her bed in the back called to her, promising the perfect ending to a previously nice day.

All that lay between her and that dream had been a quick check of her temporary post-office box in Christmas, Florida, to see if news of a future event-planning gig or any exciting mail had come in while she'd traveled to the area. A neighbor of her cousin forwarded her mail from Missouri, her only connection to "home." After checking the box, she'd planned to head down the road to locate the small campground where she'd arranged to park her RV—until now. Now she was stuck in the middle of nowhere with her ungainly vehicle listing to the right, stuck at the side of an isolated country road.

A sharp rap on her driver's window made her jump. A large Ford truck sat in the lane in front of her. The cab of the truck was empty. She stared for a moment at the friendly-looking man who motioned for her to put her window down. Brownish-blond curls at the nape of his neck gave him a laid-back air as wind-tousled locks tumbled across his forehead. Her heart took a similar tumble as his deep-blue eyes stared into hers and crinkled at the edges with his crooked smile. Friendly or not, he looked more like a rogue off the cover of one of her pirate novels than a respectable modern man coming to her aid. The combination sent mixed messages and warned her to keep up her guard.

She cracked the window an inch—wide enough that she could hear him, but not so wide that he could force his hand in and open the door to take advantage of her. A single woman in her position couldn't be too cautious.

"Uh. . ." His smile morphed into a frown as he surveyed the small opening in the window and then honed back in on her. He raised his voice so she could hear him. "Looks like you've gotten yourself into a bit of a predicament."

"I got myself into—?" Of all the nerve! "I was doing just fine until you honked your horn and scared the bejeebies out of me."

"I'm sorry to hear that. I just saw you veer toward the sand, and I wanted to warn you. So many out-of-towners don't realize how soft the shoulders are around here."

"Thank you. I think I've found that out firsthand."

Amusement shone from his eyes. "I apologize. I have a chain in the back of my truck. We can get you out in a jiffy."

"We?" Stella glanced around but didn't see anyone else with him. A shiver of apprehension ran through her. If someone else was with him, why wasn't the person out in the open where she could see him? She glanced over at her passenger door to make sure the lock was in place. It was, but had she locked the door behind the passenger seat? The one that led from outside into the kitchen area? Where was her phone? She felt around the console and pulled the device into her hand. She fingered the buttons for 911 and prepared to push the call button.

"We—my son and I." The man motioned beside him and back, and Stella leaned toward the window and looked down. A small boy, no more than six or seven years old, stood on the road next to him.

She blushed, glad he couldn't read her mind. "Oh. I'm sorry. I didn't see him down there."

The boy scowled, looking like a miniature of his dad. She obviously wasn't making brownie points with either of the males who had come to her rescue, even if the intended rescue had caused her dilemma in the first place. But it was obvious the man had meant well.

"I'll just get that chain then. If you don't mind my asking, are you heading up the lane? I noticed you were backing out when I startled you. I just need to know so I'll set you in the right direction."

Stella opened her door and slipped from the driver's seat. "I was actually heading to the post office to check my box, but I missed my turn."

"Gotcha. If you want to walk over and check it now, you have time. It'll take me a few minutes to get hooked up. I'll have to turn my truck around, and we'll go forward when I pull you out of the sand. Once you're centered on the road, I'll help guide you as you back into the parking lot."

"I appreciate it. And I think I'll do as you suggested and check my mail while I wait." She reached into the cab for her keys and locked the door before she closed it. She started for the red brick building.

"One more thing."

Stella stopped and turned to him.

"I should introduce myself." He held out his hand. "Brick Myers, and this is my son, Seth."

Her face heated and her heart sank. Brick Myers—the widowed man who'd hired her as the new event planner to work on the festival through the holidays. They'd made preliminary introductions through e-mail, but she hadn't expected the widower to be so young—or so handsome. What a first impression she must be making.

"Oh—wow." She closed her eyes for a minute then bit her lip and gave him a sheepish grin. She held out her hand and clasped his. "Stella Grant. Event planner extraordinaire."

"Stella! We didn't expect you until Sunday!"

"I decided to head on down so I could look over the layout of the town and the festival grounds during the holiday weekend. I figured that way I could finalize my festival plans and make any changes in my notes, and I'd be ready to jump right in on Monday."

He appraised her. "Are you always such a workaholic?"

"No. Well, yes, I guess I am." She hesitated. "But my last event was over, and I figured I might as well move on."

"Didn't you want to spend the holiday with family or friends?"

Now he was making her squirm. He might be her associate, but she didn't feel it was any of his business whether she spent the holiday with family, friends, or alone. She looked up to tell him just that, but his furrowed brow and the friendly concern in his cerulean-blue eyes caught her off guard. "I don't really have any family. And to be honest, with my constant travels, it's hard to keep up with old friends."

"But it's Thanksgiving." He truly seemed at a loss that she could possibly consider being alone on such a special day.

"I know, and it's fine. I promise you. I'm used to entertaining myself and being on my own."

Brick stared at her for another moment then glanced down at Seth and changed the subject. "Well, let's get you out of this sand, and we'll worry about dinner later."

Stella had no intention of worrying about dinner or anything else, but she acquiesced for the moment and headed for the post office. The short walk, though welcome after her long drive, was a waste of time—she didn't have a key. Her mind was obviously mush after the long trip.

She caught a glimpse of her reflection as she walked out the door. She cringed. She'd twisted her blond hair into a ponytail earlier in the day, and she hadn't bothered with makeup. She hadn't expected to meet anyone on the road. The campground hostess had called to let her know she was off duty. The woman had given Stella a code and instructions on how to get her paperwork from the lockbox, telling her they'd figure out fees and finalize the registration process after the holiday.

When she returned, Brick had turned his truck around and hooked his chain to her RV. He gave the chain a few tugs to make sure it was secure before motioning her inside the camper. It only took a moment for him to pull her out of the sand and center the RV on the road. He climbed out of the truck, and Seth jumped out on his heels. Stella stayed put and rolled her window down as they approached.

Brick walked over to her. "Listen, Seth and I were taking Thanksgiving dinners to some of the area shut-ins for my mom. It's sort of a yearly tradition she has. The home at the end of this lane was the last one on our list. We'd love it if you'd join us at our house for Thanksgiving dinner."

"I appreciate your thoughtfulness, but I couldn't. To be honest, I'm not a big fan of family occasions."

"Please—don't say no. My mom will have a conniption if I don't—"

"Is this really your house?" Seth interrupted. "Can I see inside? Daddy says you have a whole house squeezed in there!"

A mixture of mortification and amusement passed across Brick's face.

"Of course you can see inside." Stella hurried to say, "That is, as long as your father says it's okay."

Brick nodded.

"Come around to the other side, and I'll open the door for you."

Seth bounced his way around the front of the RV and out of sight. Brick laughed and followed. Stella opened the side door and motioned them in.

"Feel free to look around."

Seth's face filled with wonder as he took in the double bed at the back of the camper, the small bathroom next to it, and especially the overhead bunk above the driver and passenger seats at the front of the cab. She showed him how to climb up onto it.

"Awesome! This is so cool. I'd sleep here every night if I lived in one of these." Seth jumped back down onto the bench seat at the table and hopped to the floor. "Can I see inside your fridge?"

"Sure." Stella exchanged an amused glance with Brick.

Seth opened the refrigerator before Stella had a chance to remember what they'd see inside. "You sure don't have much food in here."

"I just got to town. I haven't had time to stock up yet."

Brick appraised her measly turkey sandwich and the bottle of cranberry juice and gave her a knowing look. "Stella. Please tell me that isn't your intended Thanksgiving dinner."

Stella grimaced and, with a shrug, nodded.

"As I was saying outside, my mom will have a fit if she finds out you're here and we didn't bring you home with us."

"I don't want to put you out."

"You aren't putting anyone out. My sister and mom will both be there, and they each make enough food for an army. We can even go over some of your festival notes after dinner if you want to."

"Well, we do need to discuss some of the final plans."

"See? It's a necessity."

"Please come over, Miss Stella! If you do, maybe Dad will let me ride in your house with you."

"Seth, don't pester Miss Stella."

"If I'm not putting anyone out by crashing your Thanksgiving dinner, I hardly think Seth riding along will rock my world."

"Does that mean yes?" Seth looked confused.

"It means yes, son." Brick headed for the door. "Hop up here and buckle the seat belt. I'll call ahead and let Gram know to set an extra plate. You're centered in the road now. I'm sure you'll have no problem backing into the opening of the post office over there"—he pointed— "and making your turn. After you get turned around, if you'll follow me, I'll lead the way to the house. I'm glad you're joining us, Stella."

✳

Stella was surprised to find out how much she enjoyed her afternoon with Brick's family. After a huge meal of turkey, dressing, sweet potatoes, and all the other trimmings, they cleared the table and played board games until late afternoon while Seth napped on the nearby couch. Everyone wanted dessert after the games were over, so the table was cleared yet again, and two large platters filled with slices of pie, pieces of cake, and cookies were placed in the middle, forming a sort of dessert buffet.

Stella tried to take it all in. "Wow. You must have been cooking all week. I'm sorry I didn't have anything to contribute."

"Nonsense," Rose, Brick's sister, waved her off. "Mom and I both love to bake, so we make the pies and cakes. Brick and Seth made the cookies. We give a lot of the goodies away, but we pull a few pieces of each for ourselves."

Stella turned to Brick in surprise. "You cook, too? Contractor by day, baker by night?"

"I guess it's something like that," Brick admitted. "I like to dabble in the kitchen. And as you've noticed we like to make extra of everything. That way we can settle in and relax for the rest of the holiday weekend."

"Sounds like a good plan." Stella knew they also made excess to share with the area's shut-ins and elderly. She suddenly felt homesick for a home that didn't exist. She hadn't realized until now how far she'd drawn away from anyone who cared about her or how much she'd missed by not having family to spend time with on important days like this. An unfamiliar longing to settle down and fit in somewhere suddenly enveloped her.

Uncomfortable with the emotion, she changed the subject. "I've been here for hours and we haven't discussed one item on our list of things to cover for the festival."

Brick's mouth twisted into a guilty grin. "It's late. We can discuss it tomorrow. I know you need to get settled for the night."

Stella glanced out at the diminishing sunlight. "I guess I do need to locate the RV park. I don't like to set up in the dark."

Brick looked at his mom then back at Stella. "We were kind of hoping you'd like to stay here. I mean, in your own rig, of course. It isn't much more than a hobby farm, but we have plenty of space. I have a garden hose you can hook up to your water system, and my shop has an electrical outlet that'll easily handle your electrical needs."

Stella started to argue before remembering her lack of future engagements. Staying at the Myers' would save her a good chunk of money. "Only if you'll let me reimburse you for any utilities I use."

"I'll make sure the committee covers your minimal expenses. On that note, I think we'll be fine discussing anything else in the morning. You can come for breakfast."

"No. You aren't feeding me again. Not after this smorgasbord. I won't be hungry for a week. I draw the line at free meals as a part of my board." All she could think about at the moment was falling into her bed in the RV for a long night's sleep. She was thrilled to know she didn't have to drive around town in the dark, looking for the RV park.

Brick's mom, Vivi, appeared at Stella's elbow. "Nonsense. We'll expect you in for breakfast whenever you wake up. Sleep in, though, and make up for all that travel. I'm always exhausted for a few days after a long trip—and from what I hear, your life has been one long trip after another."

It wouldn't be for much longer—not unless she got another event lined up soon. This was the first time in years that she didn't have several future events in the works when she started in on the present gig. But instead of feeling the panic she expected, a sense of peace fell over her. She couldn't help but wonder if Christmas, Florida, had something special in store for her future.

Chapter 2

Stella squinted against the bright sun that shone through the RV's large back window and tried to get her bearings. Ah yes, her first official morning in Christmas, Florida. Apparently, she'd been too tired to think about shutting the curtain when she came to bed the night before. And the stars, they'd been so bright and plentiful. She'd enjoyed watching them as she drifted off. Her previous gigs in Oregon and California had been too citified for the stars to show—the bright lights made it impossible to see them—and the overcast skies that were ever present where she'd stayed would have prevented stargazing even if the city lights would have allowed it.

The repetitive thud of a basketball hitting the pavement on the far side of the RV had Stella reaching for her robe. She moved into the tiny kitchen area, leaned over the table, and slid the side window open. "Up bright and early, aren't you?" she called out to Seth.

He frowned up at the sun then grinned at her. "It isn't really early, I don't think, but my dad said I couldn't wake you up so I thought I'd play ball while I waited."

"Oh." Stella glanced over at the clock and realized she'd slept half the morning away. "I'll be out in a few minutes."

Seth nodded, his focus already back on the ball in his hands. He bit his lip in concentration as he tried to dribble the ball with a steady rhythm.

Stella moved away from the window and dug through her drawers, pulling out the clothes she'd need. She hurried into her small bathroom and took a quick shower before readying herself for the day. She made a mental note to find a dump station to empty her gray water midweek as she wiped the steam off the small bathroom mirror. The mirror fogged back up. The blow dryer came in handy during situations like this. She pulled it from its station on the wall and blew the mirror clear of steam while alternately blowing her damp hair dry. After a brief perusal, she gathered the shoulder-length blond layers into a messy bun and left it at that. A quick application of mascara highlighted her green eyes enough for a casual day.

In her hurry to get out the door of the RV, she stumbled and practically fell into Brick's strong arms.

"Hey!" He chuckled as he steadied her. "I was coming to see if you needed anything, and here you fall into my arms. Not a bad way to start my morning."

"Morning?" Stella muttered, suddenly feeling the urge to fuss with her shirt hem. She smoothed the nonexistent wrinkles out of it. "I apparently slept half the day away. I'm so sorry. I don't know what to say."

Brick laughed. "Midmorning is hardly half the day. You must have needed the rest. It's a holiday, and no one minds that you caught up on some z's."

Seth rounded the corner of the RV and joined them. "What are z's, Daddy?"

"It's a phrase meaning 'sleep.' "

"Then why don't you just say sleep?"

"Good question." Brick tousled Seth's hair while Stella tried to hide her smile.

She watched as Brick noticed the ball hugged up against Seth's side.

He stayed Seth with a firm hand. "I hope you weren't out here bouncing the ball in hopes of waking Miss Stella?"

Seth's sheepish grin gave him away. "I didn't throw it against her house or anything. I just bounced."

"Well, I'm glad you were thoughtful enough not to do that."

"He didn't wake me." Stella hurried to explain. "I'm not used to such bright sun coming through my windows. When it reached a certain point, it shone right in. It's a nice way to wake up." She lowered her voice to a mumble. "I just wish it had wakened me about four hours earlier."

"No way." Brick jumped forward and snatched the ball from Seth's hands, heading for the basketball goal that stood sentry over the front of the double garage door.

"Hey!" Seth looked perplexed at his father's sudden move.

With Seth at his heels, Brick ran up to the goal, made a perfect hook shot, caught the ball on the rebound, and curved around for another shot.

Seth batted at his side. "No fair. You got a head start on me!"

Brick hesitated while sending Stella a sideways grin. The grin held a challenge. He looked at Seth and back to Stella.

"Oh no you don't." Stella waved her hands in front of her.

"Don't drag me into your squabbles."

Seth giggled.

"Scared?" Brick started toward her, tossing the ball from hand to hand.

"No. I'm not scared." Stella snorted. "I grew up at my aunt's where I lived with three male cousins."

"Then what's holding you back?" Brick was in her space. She stepped away from him. He moved closer. His blue eyes issued a deeper challenge.

"Nothing is holding me back. I just don't want to interfere with Seth's game—like you are."

Seth's giggle made it clear he wasn't a bit bothered by his father's interference in his play.

Brick held his ground.

"Oh fine." Stella stood a moment, appraising him with crossed arms before jumping into action, snatching the ball from a surprised Brick's partially upraised arms and ducking under them to shoot her own perfect hook shot.

"Woo-hoo!" Seth bellowed as he chased the ball. "Did you *see* that, Dad? She stoled the ball right away from you and ran off to make a shot. Did you *see* her?"

"I saw her, son." Brick laughed. "Guess she put me in my place, huh?"

"She did. I'm going to tell Gram. That was awesome!" Seth ran off with the ball.

Stella moved to fall into step with Brick. They walked toward the house at a leisurely pace.

"I thought you said you didn't have any family."

"I don't. Not really. Not anymore." She said the words

matter-of-factly, trying to act like they didn't bother her, but she didn't fool Brick.

He stopped to look at her, concern marring his good looks. "What happened to them?"

"My aunt died when I was sixteen. My oldest cousin, Jeff, had already left home—he got in a fatal car wreck a year later. My other two cousins acted as my guardians after we lost my aunt, but as soon as I turned eighteen, Andrew went into the military. He'd wanted to go when he turned eighteen but stuck around for me. He was killed in the line of duty during his second tour."

"Wow, I'm sorry."

They walked in silence for a few minutes. They were nearing the back door, and Stella could smell the enticing aroma of bacon. She inhaled deeply.

"That leaves one more cousin."

"Yes, my middle cousin, Clay. He's still around, but he joined up when we lost Andrew. He said it was his duty to follow Andy's dream and to serve in his place. He's stayed safe, but he spends most of his time overseas. We keep in touch online and through letters—which is the main reason I arrange for post-office boxes in each town I work in. Our neighbor watches over the house and takes care of the mail—but with our work schedules, we're rarely in the same place at the same time."

"I'm glad you have him."

"Me, too." She smiled up at him. "We're all we have. I think we both try extra hard to keep that bond intact, but it's hard to get together with our careers."

"I can see that." He opened the screen door and motioned for her to enter. "Where do you go next?"

Stella walked over to the sink and washed her hands. "I'm not sure."

Brick joined her at the sink. "Mom put a plate in the oven for you. It should be warm. You have a seat, and I'll bring it to you."

"I can get it."

"I know, but I want to do it. You'll be so busy for the next few weeks that it's the least I can do." He placed the plate on the table and hurried over to pick up a metal carousel that contained small containers of coffee. "What flavor do you want?"

Stella glanced at her choices and picked her favorite. He popped the small cup into place in the fancy coffee machine and leaned against the counter as he waited for it to percolate. The mouthwatering aroma of french vanilla coffee filled the room. He carried her cup over to her and went back to make his own.

"This is wonderful! You can pick a different flavor each time?"

"It was a splurge last Christmas. We love it."

He brought his finished coffee and joined her at the table.

"I really am sorry I slept so late. I know we have things to do."

"Not really. You were coming in Sunday, remember? These are all bonus days."

"I don't want to interfere with your family plans."

"We don't have any—other than taking each day as it comes."

She buttered her biscuit. "Do you mind if I pray over my breakfast?"

"Not at all." He sat quietly while she said a silent prayer. After she raised her head, he resumed his line of questioning. "So, you aren't sure where the next gig will be?"

"Right. I really don't know. This is the first time in years that

I've not had two or three jobs lined up after the present one."

"Hmm. Maybe God's telling you to slow down."

"Maybe." She took a bite of bacon. "I'm not sure my bank account would agree, though."

"If you're supposed to slow down, the pieces will fall into place as you need them to."

"True. Speaking of. . ." She reached over for the jam. "What pieces need to fall into place for the festival?"

"All of them." He laughed. "I'd like to show you the grounds as soon as you finish eating. We'll head over to the festival site when you're ready."

She wiped her lips with her napkin and scooted her chair away from the table. "I'm ready now."

"Perfect." He took her plate and coffee mug before she could reach for them, rinsed both, and placed them in the dishwasher along with his, a thoughtful gesture which she appreciated.

He turned to her. "We can take my truck if you don't mind. I have some supplies to pick up on our way home."

Seth met them in the driveway and begged to come along.

Brick motioned him into the middle seat. He held the door for Stella and slammed it shut before walking around to the driver's side. Vivi waved them off.

Brick drove a few blocks before pulling into a vacant lot. "It doesn't look like much, but I'm sure you'll have it transformed in no time at all."

"No pressure there." Stella climbed down from the truck, Seth hot on her heels. "I see the ice rink's been delivered."

"In what seems like a million pieces, yes. It came in Wednesday. We'll start work on it Monday." He put his hands on his hips as he surveyed the area. "I can't say I've ever built an ice rink before."

"Especially in Florida, hmm?" Stella couldn't wait to get the rink up and going. She'd used portable rinks in other locations but always in cold locales. "The locals are going to love this."

"I agree."

"I have a crew coming in to set the rink up. You won't really have to do anything." Stella started walking around the field. "I wanted to capture the essence of Christmas, the traditional activities, as much as possible."

"We appreciate it. The kids—and their parents for that matter—will love dressing up to skate, even if the temperatures are warmer."

"I can imagine."

Brick grew quiet, letting Stella take it all in.

"I think we'll put the booths over there—do we have access to electricity?"

"Yes, the city will run power lines to the booth area."

"So my location will work—the power lines are near there."

"Right."

"The skating rink should take center stage, don't you think? So maybe booths on the far left"—she motioned to each area as she spoke—"and the rink in the far back edge of the property, and the community stage to the far right?"

Brick studied the layout. "What about putting the booths on both edges, far left and far right, and putting the rink and stage side by side in the back center? That leaves plenty of space for mingling in the front and middle. Parking will be in the next field over, behind that line of trees."

"That could work. What's your reasoning?"

His crooked smile softened his playful grimace. "Balance."

She laughed. "Ah, a bit of OCD coming into play?"

"Something like that." He smirked. "I just think that'll help the flow, and it'll give better placement to the vendors."

"Who's the expert on this anyway?" Stella laughed. "Maybe you should consider making event planning a career."

"No thanks. I enjoy carpentry just fine, thank you very much."

"Well, you're good at planning." She started walking the area. "If we put craft vendors at the front of both sides, the shoppers will end up at the food tents. Your plan works well because the festival-goers will be ready to snack after all that shopping. Too many choices can make it harder to narrow things down. If they snack on one side and then mosey their way past the rink and stage to the other side, they'll be hungry again and will be ready for the food tents on the far side."

"Sounds feasible to me, boss." Brick walked over to the truck and pulled out a measuring tape and small flags so they could mark off the booth spaces. The skating rink would fit perfectly between the stage and booths.

"I've arranged for horse and carriage rides. Do we have enough space for the carriage to load up here in front? The lines will be long. It would be nice if they could drift into the center area and visit while they wait."

Brick surveyed the space with a critical eye. "I think that'll work. Seems to me the horse could pull around the circumference of the field—out behind the rink and stage—then pull up here again for the next load. It would be perfect."

"I'm meeting with the horse people on Monday morning.

I'll have them look over the route so they can give any input on whether or not it'll suit them. I think we'll be fine, though."

They walked toward the rink.

"How's the rink stay cold?" Seth ran up to join them. He'd been exploring and running around the field. "Ice melts."

"That's a very smart thing to think about, Seth." Stella led him over to the stack of supplies. "The ice has sensors under it that'll tell the refrigeration system when to work. It'll stay frozen even in the hottest weather."

"What if it rains?"

"You have great questions!" Stella liked the curious boy. "The rink works just fine in the rain, even in the hot sun, but to be on the safe side, we're putting a huge tent over it. The festival visitors can skate even if the weather is bad. There'll be sides that drop down, too, in case of wind or cold."

"Same with the craft booths and food tents," Brick interjected. "We'll have huge tents over them, too. This time of year it's a toss-up whether it'll be hot or cold, rainy or clear. We're trying to plan for every contingency."

"Makes sense to be prepared." Stella checked over her notes. "I need to start calling people. You know, to answer last-minute questions, collect fees, discuss booth placement—though everyone should be assigned their booth numbers by now. All those final details that ensure everyone will be ready to set up."

She flipped through her papers. "I also need to finalize the event times for the stage. I have a mix of dancers, the talent show, and vocal groups who'll all be performing at various times."

"So all I have to focus on is helping to get the tents and rink set up—as needed—and helping with the booth and vendor setup?"

"Looks that way. The vendors are responsible for their own tables and backdrops. We just need to make sure they have access to electricity for their lights and such. The rink people will help with the rink when we're ready." She frowned. "Unless something else comes up that we haven't covered?"

"I think someone mentioned a snow machine? We'll need an area for that."

"I'll make note and we'll see how much space they want."

"I'm here to help with anything you need." Brick motioned Seth back toward the truck and the happy-go-lucky boy skipped his way over to the vehicle.

Stella usually worked with a large committee when setting up events. She'd done most of the preplanning on the road and felt confident that she'd covered all her bases. She appreciated having Brick by her side. She had no doubt that he would work hard to make sure things went smoothly.

Chapter 3

Sunday morning dawned sunny and bright, just like the previous two days. Whereas they'd lounged around for the most part on Saturday, Sunday was reserved for worship. Stella usually spent her Sunday morning quiet time in her RV, studying and praying alone, but Brick and his family had a church service right there at their home, and Stella couldn't wait to take part in it. She didn't have many chances for worship and fellowship with all her travel.

"We started the church with just a few families, but when we outgrew the homes we met in, we moved services over to our place," Brick had told her the night before. "We have them outside when the weather is nice, and in the larger outbuilding when it rains."

Stella had looked over at the large structure he pointed toward. It looked like a multipurpose building. "Seems like a nice setup."

"It is. I think you'll like the people."

"I'm sure I will. Do I need to dress up?"

"Nope. Not unless you want to. We're laid-back here."

"Good. I'll dress casual." Which was a good thing since she

hadn't brought anything really fancy with her. She had one set of formal clothes for dress-up events on the road but didn't have space for in-between dressy clothes.

Stella had a couple of hours before church but decided to get a head start on her day. She dressed quickly and went inside the house to eat. Vivi had a breakfast casserole warming in the oven, a nice touch that allowed everyone to eat as they awakened.

"Did you pass Brick on your way in?" Vivi asked as she breezed into the room. "He left a few minutes ago to collect the chairs for the service."

"No, I didn't see him." Stella dumped a large spoonful of egg and sausage casserole on her plate and glanced over at Vivi. "Would you like for me to serve you up a piece while I have it out of the oven? It smells heavenly."

"No thanks. I already ate."

Stella placed the casserole back in the oven and headed for the table.

Vivi joined her. "Brick had to go out to the storage building to get the chairs. You must have just missed him."

"I'll catch up to him in a few. I want to help him set the chairs up."

"He won't let you. That son of mine likes to do for himself."

"Well, it's high time he learns to accept help. I can be stubborn when I want to be."

"I can imagine." Vivi laughed. "I like your style, Stella. Keep him on his toes. He needs it."

Seth skidded into the kitchen. "Is Daddy already outside setting things up? I told him to wake me!"

"As you do every week." Vivi picked up her coffee mug and

placed it in the dishwasher. "And what does your dad always tell you?"

Seth sighed. "He always says he wants me to get my sleep, that when I wake up I can go out to help him."

Vivi patted him on the head, retrieved the casserole and scooped out a portion for Seth, and placed his breakfast in front of him. "See? Eat up and you can head out."

Seth's shoulders sagged. "He'll have it all finished by then. He always does."

Stella mussed his hair. "How 'bout this, Seth? I'll head out and slow him down."

Seth giggled. "You'd do that for me?"

"Of course I would. We can't let your dad have all the fun, now can we?"

"Nope." He giggled as he took a huge bite of his eggs.

"Slow down, Seth." Vivi admonished. "Chew the food or you'll choke and won't get to help your daddy at all."

"Yes'm." Seth answered, but he continued to shovel in the food as Stella slipped out the door.

She found Brick in the garden, just outside her RV. "Do you want me to move this thing? Park it behind the storage building or something?"

"Why would you need to do that?" He answered without looking at her. He continued to unstack chairs and place them one by one into rows.

"It kind of ruins the décor out here. The garden looks so pretty. The chairs make it look like a wedding. My RV kind of messes up the image."

Brick stopped working for a moment, standing with his hands

on his hips. The sun shone into his eyes and he squinted against it as he looked at her. "Nah. No one's going to care. Everyone parks all over as it is. I'm telling you, we're laid-back here." He grinned and picked up another chair and set it into place.

"Then let me help you set up."

"I have it under control."

"It wouldn't kill you to let me earn my keep, you know. The least I can do is set some chairs into place."

"You sound like Seth."

"I got it from Seth—in the kitchen. He was lamenting the fact that you never let him help and you don't wake him when he asks."

"Um-hmm."

"It seems important to him, Brick."

"It does, huh?" He stopped again to study her.

"He wants to help you out. I don't want to overstep, but I told him I'd come out and slow you down so he would have something to do."

"You told him that?" Brick glanced at the house.

Seth slammed out the screen door and hurried across the back deck. "Hold him off, Stella! I'm almost there."

Brick laughed. "She's doing a good job of it, Seth."

"Yeah!" Seth's whoop carried across the yard.

"I guess I get so caught up in getting everything done that I haven't noticed how important it is that he helps. Thanks for that, Stella."

Seth's eyes shone with excitement as he slammed into Brick's leg. Brick grimaced and steadied him.

"How about Stella unstacks the chairs and places them here by the cart; I'll carry them where they need to go; and Seth, you'll open them and put them into place."

"Sure, Dad! I can do that." Seth fisted his hands on his hips, feet slightly apart, and looked like a perfect miniature of his father.

It was all Stella could do not to laugh. He was so cute!

Brick turned to Stella and mouthed *thank you*.

She grinned in reply.

They worked as a team and had everything ready in short order.

"We usually have around a hundred people, but with a lot of them out of town for the holiday, it'll probably be closer to half that." Brick looked at Stella. "I'll get more chairs if and when we need them. I'm going to run in and freshen up. I'll be back out in a moment. Seth, come with me and wash your face and hands. Everyone should be arriving soon."

"I'll go in the RV and do the same. I'll grab my Bible and meet you all out here."

"Save us a seat."

"Will do." Stella headed into the RV, excited about the service. She hadn't been to a church service with friends in years. The thought stopped her short. She wasn't with friends now, was she? The realization that Brick, Seth, Vivi, and Rose already felt like dear friends flowed over her like a calming river. She'd been in Christmas, Florida, for less than seventy-two hours, but already she felt a connection with the family she was staying with that she'd not felt with anyone else in a long, long time. Desperation or destiny?

Again she realized how adrift she'd become since losing her aunt and cousins. She quickly went through the routine of touching up her lip gloss, blush, and mascara and hurried back outside into the brilliant Florida sunshine. The desire to put down roots overwhelmed her. She was falling in love with the tiny town of Christmas. And she had to admit, she also really liked the kind man who'd hired her for this job.

❄

Stella met Pastor Seely, a friendly man in his midforties, when he arrived with his wife and teen daughters. She chatted with them for a few minutes then headed forward to save five seats near the temporary stage. She settled in to wait for Brick, Vivi, Rose, and Seth.

Rose arrived in a flurry of greetings and made her way to the front to settle in beside Stella. "I was excited to get such a great parking space until I realized I'll be hemmed in until dinner with all the other cars that'll be coming in behind me!"

Stella laughed. "I thought you stayed through dinner anyway."

"Hmm—good point." Rose grinned. "Mom has a habit of snagging me for the day now that you mention it. I'm usually running late, so I'm not used to the repercussions of arriving early. Now I see why Pastor Seely always parks so far away."

"Um-hum." Stella craned her neck over the guests, trying to locate Brick.

"Looking for anyone in particular?" Rose asked in a teasing tone. She nudged Stella with her elbow.

"Just making sure I don't save the seats if your family decides to sit somewhere else." Stella's flush gave her away. Rose raised an eyebrow. "Okay, fine. Since I only know about four people in town, and one of the four is sitting next to me, I guess it's kind of obvious."

"For the record, I think my brother likes you, too."

"Rose! We've only just met."

"I know," Rose shrugged. "But I know my brother, and I can tell he enjoys your company. That's all."

Stella reached over to clasp Rose's hand. "I enjoy his, too. In fact, I've enjoyed all of your company. You and your family have been wonderful about taking me in during a family holiday and making me feel welcome the past three days. I appreciate it more than you know."

"Our pleasure. We used to celebrate with the whole family—grandparents, uncles and aunts, cousins, my father, Brick's wife—but things are quieter now. I think we all miss the chaos that comes from celebrating with a large family. Your presence helped round things out a bit, made things more exciting."

"I don't know, there's something to be said about a small, intimate gathering, too." Stella thought back to her handful of Thanksgivings with her aunt and cousins.

"True."

They sat in silence for a few moments, each lost in her own thoughts.

Stella didn't have any experience at the large group celebrations, but she could imagine it would be fun. "Do you mind my asking what happened to make you stop celebrating as a group?"

"Everyone grew up and started their own families. My cousins all came from large families, so as they started to have kids, I guess they found it easier to celebrate at their own parents's houses. We just drifted away. Our group was smaller with just Brick and I. Brick married, brought Lisa into the fold, and they had Seth. I was engaged to a great guy and it looked like our family was blooming, but then Lisa got sick and passed away and my fiancé was transferred overseas. I didn't feel I could marry and leave the family at such a hard time, and Johnny and I drifted apart. He was upset that I wouldn't go with him, but I think deep down he understood. At least I hope he did."

"Have you tried to get in touch with him now that things have settled down?"

It was Rose's turn to blush. "As a matter of fact, I have. I've sent him a card with the traditional 'Christmas, Florida,' postmark every year since and—while I haven't even had a chance to tell Mom or Brick yet—Johnny wrote yesterday that he is coming home for the holidays, and he wants to get together."

Stella smiled. "Maybe it'll be a season for second chances! You'll have to have him take you to the festival, skate a few romantic laps around the rink. The festival will be magical. Love will be in the air."

"Stella, stop!" Rose playfully glanced over her shoulder to see if anyone was listening. "I wouldn't have pegged you as a romantic. What about you. . .do you plan on taking a few laps with my brother?"

"That would be a great idea, if I could stand up on skates."

"I bet Brick can entice you to give it a go."

"I doubt it. But I think it could work for you."

"Like I said, deep down you're a romantic."

"Stranger things have happened." Stella nudged Rose with her shoulder. "You never know."

The air moved beside Stella, and Brick leaned around her to peer at Rose. "Stella's a romantic? What did I miss, sis? Fill me in."

Mortified, Stella pushed him back toward his seat and away

from Rose's. "It's nothing. Really."

"It most definitely doesn't sound like *nothing* to me." He leaned behind her. "Psst. Rose. Tell me about Stella's romantic streak. C'mon, there's nothing like a little presermon gossip."

"Sorry, bro, you should have come out earlier if you wanted to catch the gossip. You're on your own when it comes to finding out about Stella's romantic side."

"*Rose!*" Stella hissed. Never had she been so happy to see a pastor step up to the pulpit.

They opened with prayer, but Stella had a hard time concentrating with Brick sitting so close to her side, especially on the heels of the conversation just before the service started. It didn't help that his woodsy cologne drifted her way on the gentle breeze, or that his deep chuckle sent a tingle through her each time Pastor Seely said something funny. Something felt entirely too right about sitting in the midst of the family in the balmy Florida sun.

They stood to sing and their voices carried through the mid-morning air. The scene was perfect in its simplicity. After warm greetings, they settled in for the sermon.

Pastor Seely stepped to the front. "Thanksgiving provides a wonderful time for family and friends to reconnect, a chance for us to count our blessings and offer up prayers of thankfulness for all that we have. It's a time to look forward to the coming season of Christmas, when we celebrate the birth of our Savior.

"Americans tend to cut themselves off from each other in this day and age—we rely more and more on electronic devices to keep us connected." He held up the electronic reader he had in his hands. Everyone laughed. "I'm not saying this is a completely bad thing. I use my reader for sermon notes, and I have several versions of the Bible in here. . . ."

Stella had a sense that the pastor was saddened by the fact that everyone was so caught up in electronics, even as he tempered his words with humor.

"But when long-distance relationships and electronic communications replace good-ole face-to-face fellowship, disconnect quickly follows."

He'd just described Stella's life to a *T*. Was she disconnected? Who was she kidding—of course she was disconnected. She was about as disconnected as a person could get. It was too hard to try to stay in touch with people she met and worked with for a few weeks at a time before moving on. There were too many to count, and they all knew they most likely wouldn't ever see each other again, so she really had no coworkers. That left her with her cousin Clay, whom she hadn't seen in person in several years, and their neighbor back home, Agnes, whom she talked to by phone on a monthly basis. Her life was sadly lacking in the relationship department.

She squirmed. Brick glanced over at her. Did he also see the pastor's description in her? She had no roots, no firm foundation. She'd built her house upon the sand. Any strong wind or storm could blow her off her foundation. She had no strong roots to hold her steady in a storm.

"You okay?" Brick whispered.

"As well as I can be when any ole wind can blow me clean away." She retorted.

Confusion rolled across Brick's features. "Are we listening to the same sermon?"

"Yes. My mind grasps things and runs with them." She whispered back.

"I can see that."

A matronly woman in front of them glanced over her shoulder to peer at them with a chastising frown.

Brick raised a hand in acknowledgement and apology.

Stella mouthed *sorry* to him. He grinned, and she fought the inappropriate urge to giggle. Rose elbowed her, but when Stella looked her way, Rose seemed on the verge of giggling herself. Seth leaned around Vivi, his expression curious. Vivi shook her head at him, sighed, and rolled her eyes. Stella would have some 'splainin' to do after service.

"Let's bow our heads in prayer. Take a few moments for personal prayer, and then I'll close."

The congregation bowed their heads.

Lord, forgive my mind for wandering, but in my defense, it wandered based on Pastor Seely's sermon. His words spoke to me and caused me concern about my own disconnect. I want to be connected. If You brought me to Christmas, Florida, for more than a work gig, please show me Your plans and make them clear to me. Help me find my way. Thank You, Lord. In Jesus' name, Amen.

Stella had a physical home she could go back to. Clay had made it clear the home was as much hers as it was his, but she always felt the family place belonged to him. Her sense of camaraderie with Brick and Rose fell away as she realized how truly alone she was.

God was with her, of course He was, but she couldn't help but wish for the warmth of human companions. People who would hurt with her, cry with her, rejoice in victories with her. Why these emotions were hitting here in Christmas, she didn't know.

She believed God had a plan and purpose for everyone on

earth, and she knew He had one for her, but she hadn't felt like she'd ever found it. She loved her career, but lately the travel hadn't been as much fun. She assumed the Myers' warmth had something to do with her emotions and feelings of loneliness. It highlighted the coldness in her own life.

The other places she'd gone, she'd kept people at arm's length. This time she'd come in on Thanksgiving, and the kind family had reached out and drawn her in. She didn't think it was a coincidence. Her priorities were changing—she wanted more from life.

Chapter 4

Stella looked up from her conversation with the skating rink foreman late Friday morning and saw Brick picking his way around the various tents, trucks, ropes, and supplies as he made his way in her direction. His arrival made her smile. They'd eaten most meals together the previous week, and he'd gone over her notes each evening, helping her plan the event. She treasured the time they spent together.

His face lit up when he noticed her watching him. "You're a sight for sore eyes!"

"So are you."

"I haven't seen anyone but my construction crew all morning. Nothing like staring at big burly men for hours."

Stella pretended to shudder. "Sounds horrible."

"It was. But things look way better over here." He grinned.

"Glad to hear it, but on that note, it isn't quitting time yet. What brings you over to the chaos?"

"We finished the Mastelli house. Since it's Friday, I figured I'd give the crew the rest of the day off and head over here for the afternoon and see if I could pitch in. Can you use another set of hands?"

Stella's heart soared. "Can we ever! Things are crazy around here. The rink needs some physical labor for the final touches, but half the crew didn't show. There are some glitches in scheduling with the performances—several of the groups have conflicts and want things changed around. I've explained that each performance I change has a snowball effect on the others, but they are adamant that they have to be moved or they can't perform. Several of the vendors want to switch to different locations. You know"—she rolled her eyes—"just the usual pre-event pandemonium. And need I remind you the event starts *tomorrow?*"

"How do you stay sane?" Brick shook his head, but his eyes held admiration. "I can pitch in with the rink. If you'll let me take a peek at the clipboard, I'll see if I can give a new eye to the scheduling and vendor changes."

"Have at it." Stella thrust the clipboard into his outreached hand. "I'm ready for a break."

"I have sandwiches in the truck. Let's go to lunch, and we'll look everything over while we eat. You'll come back refreshed. Are you hungry?"

"Famished."

"You should have kept the truck. Then you could have run out for lunch."

"And let you miss out on the afternoon's fun? No way!"

"You could have come to pick me up."

A small smile formed on Stella's lips as they walked to his vehicle. She imagined this was what marriage felt like. Brick had insisted that he drive Stella back and forth to the field, dropping her off in the morning and picking her up at night. He stated, rightfully so, that it would be too hard for her to unhook the hose and electricity on the RV and drive to the field, then find a place to park where she'd be out of the way and could get in and out easily.

While Stella would have preferred to have her RV on-site so she could get away during breaks for a moment of quiet, she did like the ease of Brick's pickup and drop-off service.

Brick left the windows down, and a slight breeze filled the cab as they shared a light lunch of sandwiches and chips and drank from cold bottles of soda.

"This is nice." Stella sighed. "I usually take my lunch under one of the trees, but someone always finds me with another dire need that can't seem to wait until I'm finished."

"Well, I guarantee they'll leave you alone during your breaks with me on the job."

She watched as one of the townspeople approached Brick's side of the truck. "Hey Brick. Stella in there?"

Obviously—she was sitting in full view of the man.

"Yes she is, but she's eating lunch and won't be available for another fifteen minutes."

"I just have a quick question for her."

"Not gonna happen. Let the lady eat in peace. We'll find you as soon as we're finished here."

"Fair enough." The man turned around and headed the other way.

"Thanks." Stella popped the last bite into her mouth and dusted the crumbs out the window. "I guess I could've talked to him, though, since I'm finished."

"Not if we want to go over these schedules. The festival isn't going to collapse if someone has to wait fifteen minutes to talk to you."

"Good point."

Stella flipped open the clipboard and showed Brick the conflicts. He perused the papers, made a few quick changes, and asked her how they looked. She'd spent the better part of an hour doing the same and couldn't get her mind to figure out the best solution. It probably had something to do with the seven people who had interrupted while she was trying to think.

"You make it look so easy."

"No, I'm just analyzing it from a fresh point of view. Sometimes that helps."

"Then take a peek at the vendor issues and see if you can figure them out." She showed him the pages. "This one's legit—the vendor asked for a double space and only has one, so we need to move him or move his neighbor so he'll get the space he needs."

Brick leaned close. His aftershave tickled her senses. "Show me the others."

"Um." Stella forced herself to concentrate. "This one here and that one over there want to be by each other. They're mother and daughter and forgot to ask for adjoining booths. We have three more that don't like the locations due to personal preference."

Brick made notes as she spoke, and before she knew it, the situation was fixed.

She pumped her fist in the air. "That's it. You're amazing. I'm taking you on the road with me from now on."

He glanced up at her, amused. "You are, huh?"

"Oh—that didn't come out the way I meant. At all. I so didn't mean—" She gulped. "That sounded totally wrong."

"No worries. I know what you meant."

"You do?"

His face was inches away from hers. His blue eyes twinkled with laughter. She wondered what it would feel like to lean forward and brush her lips against his. He stared at her lips. Was he wondering the same thing?

"I do."

Wonder about kissing me? Yes! Stella flushed, wondering if he'd read her mind. Then she remembered the question she'd just asked him. "Oh, you do understand."

"Yes." His face crinkled and his eyes flashed with humor. "Isn't that what we were talking about?"

"Sure. Um. Yeah. Well, I guess we'd better get back out there then. Our fifteen minutes are up."

He stared at her a moment longer then nodded. "Alrighty then. I'll head on over to the rink and offer up my services."

"I'll see you in a bit."

"By the way—tonight is pizza night. Be thinking about what kind of pizza you want to make for dinner."

"Pizza night?"

"Seth and I make dinner on Friday nights. We always come up with new creations for Mom and Rose. Tonight we'll let you join in the fun, so you need to come up with something."

"Okay." She grinned. Pizza night in Brick and Seth's company sounded like a fun way to spend the evening.

Stella hurried off to tell the vendors and performers about the changes, glad to have her plate swept clean of those decisions. Brick had a wonderful head for details and would be an asset to any business, on the road or not.

She flushed. She couldn't believe she'd inadvertently insinuated she wanted to take him on the road with her! At least he hadn't given her a hard time over the slip. Hopefully he wouldn't bring it up again.

❄

"Here we go, Seth." Brick placed his shopping bag on the counter and waved his son over. He winked at Stella, causing her heart to stutter. "Ready for our newest creation?"

"Yes, sir!" Seth sped across the kitchen floor in stocking-clad feet and slid to a stop at Brick's side. "What kinds are we making tonight?"

"You and I are making barbecue chicken pizza."

Stella waggled her eyebrows at him. "And I'm making a sloppy joe pizza."

"Sloppy joe?" Seth looked up at Brick.

Brick shrugged.

"You know, just like the sandwiches?" Stella explained. "It'll have sloppy joe sauce mixed with hamburger—I'll put that on the crust—and then I'll top it with lots of shredded cheddar cheese. You can eat it with dill pickles if you want."

"Sounds good to me," Brick said.

"It actually sounds kind of gross." Seth wrinkled his nose.

"It isn't. It's *actually* very good."

"That's right—don't knock it until you've tried it, bud." Brick nudged Seth with his hip. "Sloppy joe pizza might end up being a new favorite."

Seth didn't look convinced. "I don't think so."

Stella gathered her ingredients and took them to the counter. "Is this a competition? Do we have some kind of voting process when it comes to the finished project?"

"We haven't in the past, but now's as good a time as any to start the tradition."

"What tradition?" Vivi asked as she walked into the kitchen.

"A new Christmas tradition. We're starting a Christmas pizza bake-off."

"Sounds fun." She walked to Stella's side. "What will we be voting on?"

"Let's see." Brick was quiet as he contemplated her question. "How about uniqueness, taste, and presentation."

"What's oo-neek-ness?" Seth asked.

"Uniqueness. That means different or special compared to other similar items."

Seth glanced Stella's way. "Then she'll probably win for that. Her pizza is oo-neek for sure."

"Call me when it's time for the judging," Vivi said. "This will be fun." Her laughter lingered behind as she walked out of the kitchen.

Brick grinned at Stella over Seth's head. "We'll give Stella a run for her money with taste."

Seth smiled up at him.

Stella didn't miss the challenge. "Seth, I have a thought. If you want to join my team, I have an idea for presentation that I think will win the competition hands down."

"Okay. Bye Dad."

"Wait—just like that?"

"Yep. I wanna be on the winning team."

"How do you know Stella's team will win?"

"She just said she would."

"Oh. Then you two take the counter, and I'll stay over here

at the table. We'll have thirty minutes to make our creations. No peeking at the other team's creation."

"We'll be so busy we won't think to peek, right Seth?"

"Right Stella." He hurried to the sink to wash his hands.

Stella busied herself with gathering her ingredients. Brick made a great show of clanking his pans and ingredients around his table. Pizza dough mix clouded the air as he dumped it in his mixing bowl.

Stella shook her head over the mess he was making.

"You aren't supposed to be peeking, Stella," Seth admonished.

Brick snickered.

"I'm not. Your dad is trying to get our attention with his theatrics."

"What *theatrics*?" Brick sneezed. "I'm just working over here."

"By making all that noise? The drama is distracting."

"Now I'm doing drama?"

Seth's giggle egged Stella on.

"Brick, you can continue with your one-man show while we quietly plot our winning dishes. How's that sound, Seth?"

Seth nodded his head with exuberance then lowered his voice to a whisper. "How are we gonna beat him, Stella? My dad makes really good pizzas."

"Watch and learn, grasshopper."

"Grasshopper? I'm not a grasshopper." Seth giggled again.

"It's from a movie called—oh never mind." Stella motioned for Seth to stir the dough while she checked the hamburger she'd put on the stove. She opened a can of sloppy joe sauce and poured it over the browned meat and let it simmer.

When the dough was well blended, they split it between their two pans.

"Here's where we'll get the winning points for presentation," Stella whispered. She pushed the dough around on the first pan, shaping it while Seth watched.

"A Christmas tree?" Seth asked. "We're making a Christmas tree pizza?"

"Shhh." Stella glanced at Brick, but he wasn't paying them any attention. "Yes. A Christmas tree-shaped pizza will win hands down, don't you think?"

He nodded.

"And we're making two Christmas tree-shaped pizzas."

"You're so cool, Stella. I'm glad I'm on your team." He threw his arms around her in an exuberant hug.

"I'm glad, too, Seth." Stella's eyes misted over at the unexpected show of affection from the little boy. She could get used to hugs like that. "I'll put the sauce on the traditional pizza and you can spread it around, and then we'll decorate it."

"What are we using for decorations?"

"Sprinkle the cheese over the sauce, and I'll show you."

Seth carefully placed the cheese on top of the sauce.

Stella pulled out round pieces of pepperoni for "ornaments." They cut up small pieces of green pepper to sprinkle on for color. Seth meticulously decorated while Stella threw together their other pizza.

"I tell you what"—Stella glanced over at Brick—"I'll take credit for the sloppy joe pizza, your dad will take credit for his, and you take credit for the red-and-green Christmas tree."

"Okay, but you'll have to decorate yours with pickles so you have a decent chance. I think I'm going to beat you both, though."

"I kind of have a feeling you will, but that's okay," Stella said.

"As long as I get a piece of the winning entry."

"You can have all the pieces you want," Seth assured.

Stella popped both pizzas in the lower oven then slipped out of the kitchen and peeked around the corner while Seth supervised Brick as he placed his pizza in the upper oven. He held the pan high, keeping his creation out of Seth's line of vision.

"No peeking at ours, Dad."

"I won't peek. Unlike other adults in the room."

"Busted." Stella walked around the corner. "I was just making sure you didn't peek at Seth's secret entry."

"Secret entry?" Brick's eyes widened, and Seth nodded.

"I have my own team now. We're all three competing against each other."

Brick feigned a deep sigh. "Then I doubt my super duper barbecue chicken pizza has a chance."

"It's okay, Dad. I'm sure someone will eat it after ours is gone."

"Thanks, son."

The timers went off within minutes of Rose's arrival from work. "Something smells good in here!"

"A lot of somethings smell good in here," Brick agreed. "You have a minute to relax, Rose, while we finish up in the kitchen."

"Then I'll make myself scarce while I go wash my hands." Rose left the room.

Stella busied herself pulling the pizzas from the oven while Brick and Seth set the table. She set the pizzas on the counter, starting with Seth's festive tree, then adding Brick's overloaded round barbecue chicken pizza that set her mouth to watering, and ending the lineup with her own Christmas tree-shaped pizza. A few minutes later, Vivi and Rose joined them.

Brick explained the rules of voting and stepped out of the way.

Vivi and Rose studied the lineup of pizza pies.

"Oh look, Mom. Christmas trees! How fun." Rose clasped her hands beneath her chin. "I wouldn't have ever thought to try that."

"It was Stella's idea. She let me decorate the pepperoni one." Seth bounced around between them.

Vivi motioned toward Brick's pizza. "I'm sorry to say, whoever made the traditional round pizza—Brick—is already out of the running. While it'll hold its own for taste, it loses on uniqueness and presentation."

"I concur," Rose said.

"Now wait just a minute!" Brick interrupted. "First of all, how do you know the round one is mine? You're jumping to conclusions."

"Is it yours?" Rose raised an eyebrow.

"Well, yes. But that's beside the point."

"And what's the point, big brother?"

"I could still win on taste."

"But you've already lost on presentation and uniqueness."

"Which are terms that technically mean the same thing and should probably count as one category."

"Hmm, good point." Rose looked over at Stella. "Who came up with the rules?"

Vivi, Stella, and Seth all looked pointedly at Brick.

"So you came up with the three separate categories, but now that the vote is going against you, you're saying you want to change to two categories."

"To give myself a better chance!" The corner of his mouth tilted up with humor. "Okay. Not when you put it that way."

"Can we continue this competition then?"

"Yes ma'am."

Rose and Vivi studied the remaining two pizzas. Seth bounced with anticipation. The women cut off pieces of each pizza to sample. They whispered as they contemplated the final winner.

Seth reached over and placed his small hand in Stella's and held it tight. Stella saw Brick's face soften with emotion as he took in the scene.

"The judges have made their decision," Vivi said.

Rose cleared her throat. Stella smiled at the realization that Brick wasn't the only theatrical person in the family.

"Though the pizzas both have a wonderful flavor—and we're partial to the sloppy joe pizza, Stella—we have to say the taste of the pepperoni pizza, coupled with the Christmas tree shape and careful placement of decorations makes it a winner in presentation, which also makes it stand out as most unique. The winning pizza is the one created by Seth!"

Seth whooped with excitement.

"Winner gets first piece." Brick stepped forward to cut the pizzas. "Congratulations, Seth."

"Thanks, Daddy."

Brick placed a large piece of the winning pizza on Seth's plate, followed by smaller pieces of the other two.

"I think I'll have one of each, too," Stella said. "I've worked up an appetite."

The other two women requested the same. Stella loved the feeling of camaraderie and her inclusion in the warmth of the family kitchen.

Brick served up pieces of each for everyone, and they settled at the table. Though the atmosphere was light, Stella couldn't help but notice that Brick grew more silent as the meal wore on, as though he'd distanced himself from the group in some small way. A frown creased his forehead as he watched Seth interact with Stella.

Stella tried to catch Brick's eye, but he carefully evaded her glances. She wasn't sure what had changed, but something had placed a wedge in their camaraderie.

Chapter 5

Brick hated that his change of mood had ended the fun meal on a sour note, but he couldn't help it. The more he watched Seth interact with Stella, the more he realized how attached the boy had become to the flighty woman. If he dug deep, he had to admit that he, too, had become attached in the week he'd known her. Stella had a way of lighting up the area with her presence. Her elfish smile and the perky enthusiasm in her sparkly green eyes made everything a bit more festive. Inside or out, the day seemed brighter just because she was a part of it. But the fact was, neither he nor Seth had room for a gypsy in their lives—even one as pretty and full of life as Stella. He needed to pull away and set an example for his son. He needed to create a distance between the pretty event planner and his family.

"I'll be outside," he said as he headed through the door. Though no one else commented, he could tell everyone had noticed his silence. Seth was on his heels as he bounded down the back steps.

"Where are we going, Dad?"

"Nowhere in particular, bud. I just needed some fresh air."

He heard his mother and Rose shooing Stella from the kitchen. Great. They always insisted on cleaning up the leftovers after he and Seth made dinner, and they were continuing the routine by sending Stella his way. The back door opened and closed. It was hard enough to think straight and figure out how to create distance when she wasn't around, but with her standing in front of him, smiling her charming smile, it would be impossible.

He turned to see Stella's silhouette as she slowly made her way down the steps and headed in their direction. She wasn't smiling. She seemed hesitant—as if she wasn't sure she'd be welcome. Another wonderful effect caused by his dour mood.

She started to speak, but then her gaze rested on Seth and her eyes softened. "Looks like you two are enjoying some father-son time. I think I'll turn in early. I'll see you both in the morning."

Her eyes held questions, but she was too polite to ask them in front of Seth.

Brick couldn't let the evening end on such a negative note. "Wait. There's something we need to do." The words flew out of his mouth before he could fully think them through. All he knew was, he wanted to wipe away her doubt and confusion and make everything better before they parted for the night. A tiny voice whispered in his ear. *Dude, you've got it bad for the lady. You're falling hard. You're in deep!* Brick shook the warning off. "I mean, there's something we need to do—if you have time."

"There is?" Her eyes brightened. "Of course I have the time. I was only planning to read."

Brick turned to his son. "Seth, run back inside and tell Gram you can have a small bowl of ice cream. After you've eaten it, you can watch the new DVD I laid on the entertainment center, okay?"

"Which one did you get? Is it the one we talked about the other day?" Seth was already heading for the door.

"You can look once you get inside." Brick felt his smile returning. It was hard to stay morose with Stella and Seth around. "Tell Gram we'll be back in a couple of hours."

"So where are we going?" Stella's eyes still reflected her confusion, but some of the brightness had returned. "I thought we were home for the night."

Home. He liked the way the word sounded when she used it in collaboration with *we*. He pushed the thought aside, not wanting his previous mood to prevail. "I've just thought of something we need to check out."

Stella shrugged and followed Brick to his truck. He held the door for her and helped her in before walking around to his side and climbing in beside her. As he swung the truck around to head down the drive, Stella touched his arm. Warmth from her hand seared his arm.

He glanced over at her.

"Do you mind if we swing by the post office real quick? I forgot to go by on our way home. My mind was on pizzas and the competition."

Brick hadn't missed the fact that Stella made frequent stops at the post office a daily routine. She was such a regular at the place that she knew the staff—both permanent employees and temporary Christmas workers—on a first-name basis. At one point she even mentioned asking the postmaster, Edie Hathaway, if something was wrong with her paperwork, but Edie said everything was up to par.

Stella said she was watching for correspondence from her

forwarded mail that would tell her what job to go to next. But Brick couldn't help but wonder if she was looking for something else, a note from someone special. Someone else she'd met on a previous job maybe. For all he knew, she could have a whole string of men she'd attached to during her travels, though the minute the thought crossed his mind, he dismissed it. Stella didn't seem like the type to keep a string of men on the line. He chided himself. His thoughts were all over the place at the moment.

"Sure. We can stop by." Brick pulled into the parking lot and waited while she ran inside.

She returned empty-handed. "Nothing."

Now *her* mood was heavy. And he had just the thing in mind to pick them both up. He pulled back out on the highway.

"We're going back to the festival grounds?" Stella said as he maneuvered the car into a parking spot. "Didn't we just leave here a couple of hours ago?"

"Yes, but the difference is, by now everyone should have wrapped up their preparations and we'll have the place to ourselves."

Stella was staring at him like he'd lost his mind.

"Don't you see? We can test everything out tonight, so we'll know things are ready for tomorrow."

"I guess that's true. But I figured we'd go in early and just do it tomorrow before the event starts."

"Good plan, but tomorrow doesn't allow us time to fix any serious problems."

"This late in the game, serious problems better have been avoided by the team."

"True enough." Brick laughed. "Guess we're about to find out."

He'd parked by the master switch. He made great pomp and ceremony as he flipped the switch. Stella stood close by, shaking her head at his antics.

"Well? What do you think?"

"Um, I think it's really bright for starters." Stella shaded her eyes with her hand. Her features brightened with a smile. "But it is festive, don't you think?"

Brick had to agree. Strings of white lights surrounded the outside perimeter of the festival grounds, giving the inner area a party feel. One area even had a tunnel of lights for people to walk through. Large spotlights lit up the stage and ice rink. Smaller lights lit the interiors of the tents.

Stella laughed and held out her hands as small "snowflakes" fell down upon their heads. "These are great!"

"What are they?" Brick rubbed his thumb over a few of the flakes on his hand.

"Soap flakes. Bubbles. They look real coming down, don't they?"

"They do. The kids will love them."

"Wait until they see the snow play area. They'll get to make snowballs, snow angels, and snowmen."

"Amazing." Brick walked around and surveyed the grounds. As they walked he made minimal changes, tweaking the angle of this light or adjusting the tautness of a tent support. Each time he cleared an area, he turned out the lights so they didn't waste electricity.

The last stop was the ice rink.

"Doesn't it look nice?" Stella sighed. "I assume most people around here haven't had much experience with ice-skating, right?"

"I think you can safely say it'll be a major treat for the locals."

Brick's eyes lit up like a child looking over a ride at an amusement park as he surveyed the shiny sheet of ice that lay before them.

"Wait—are you one of them?"

He tilted his head her way, his eyebrow raised. "*One of them?*"

"You know, one of those Southern boys who's never skated on ice before."

"How about this?" He grabbed Stella by the hand. "Why don't we take a spin on the ice, and I'll show you exactly what this Southern boy can do."

"I don't think so." Stella dug in her heels and pulled back.

"Why not?" Brick challenged. "Surely you've been on ice before at one of your many events."

"I never have time. I'm always so busy setting things up—the only reason I have this downtime tonight is because you've been so wonderful about helping out and troubleshooting the glitches for me."

"That's just wrong. You should always get a chance to play in the worlds you create. You go to all this work, planning these events, and never take the time to savor the moment and enjoy?"

"I'm usually scheduled back-to-back for the next event. This is the first time I've faced this situation. The first time I haven't had several jobs lined up waiting after I finish the previous one."

His bubble burst. He didn't want her to leave. He found himself wishing she'd never hear of another event to go to. He asked God for forgiveness. He didn't want to make her suffer for his gain.

"So if you had another job lined up, when would you pull out?"

"As early as day after tomorrow. Sunday. After I made sure everything worked out over the weekend, I'd have to leave for the next place."

"But in this case, you don't have another event laid out? So you're free to stay through Christmas and enjoy?"

"I guess I am."

Brick tried to contain his joy. His bonus time with Stella was stressful from her viewpoint. He'd have to tread carefully with his emotions. And he'd have to figure out how to balance his excitement over her staying with his concern that she'd break his and Seth's hearts when she moved on. He handed her a pair of skates.

She eyed them with distaste and took them from him with two fingers. They dangled from her outstretched hand. "I don't have the slightest clue how to put these things on."

Brick didn't even try to hide his amusement. He led her to one of the benches that lined the outer wall of the tent. "Sit."

She sent him a challenging glare.

"Sit, please?"

"Well, since you asked so nicely. . ." She sat.

"You folks are out late tonight." Stella jumped as a rotund security guard's booming voice preceded him around the tent flap. "Rick Stanton's heading up security for the volunteers tonight. He saw you drive up and suggested I come over and say howdy." He popped the last bite of a doughnut in his mouth and licked the remnants of jelly from his fingers.

"Good to know you're on the job, Lucas." Brick glanced up at Stella as he loosened the laces on her skate. Her amusement mirrored his. The man had taken his sweet time getting to the tent. Brick fussed with the laces, slid the boot on her foot, pulled the laces into place, and focused on Stella as he finished tightening her skate. "How's that feel?"

"Tight. Foreign. And like I'm about to make a fool of myself by falling on my face."

Brick couldn't help but laugh out loud. "I won't let you fall."

Stella snorted. "Until I take you down with me. You haven't seen me on ice, have you? There's a reason I take the long way around—through the entire South—to get to my northern gigs. I don't like ice under my tires, and I don't like it much better under my feet."

"So you're saying the RV you drive doesn't do too well in snowy conditions?"

"Well, there's that, too, yes. But more importantly, ice and I don't get along well unless it's in my drink."

"Let's see what I can do to change that opinion." Brick made quick work of tying his skates. He pulled Stella to her feet.

She wobbled. "This isn't a good idea. If I break something, I'll be up a creek."

"You won't break anything. Trust me. How can you do this for a living and not want to give it a try?"

"I don't do ice rinks for a living. I don't skate for a living. I plan events. Varied, random, mostly wonderful events. Skating rinks are few and far between. I've never skated before. Remember? And like I just said, I have this issue with going to the next event in a cast."

"So this is the perfect time. See the silver lining? You don't have another gig lined up. You have time to heal before you have to leave. And you have people who care about you to take care of you while you heal—not that you're going to fall."

"Very inspiring, Brick. You should consider a job as a life coach with sentiments like that." The sarcasm rolled off her tongue.

The security guard guffawed. "I'll leave you two to your fun. As much as I'd like to stay and watch, I have a job to do. Call if you need me to summon an ambulance or anything." His final comment ended in a snort.

"Lucas, you aren't helping." Brick waved him out of the tent. He turned his attention back to Stella. "Have you ever roller-skated?"

"When I was a child, yes. *Years* ago."

"The balance is a bit different, but if you can skate on wheels, you'll pick up skating on ice in no time. All you have to do is take that first step. Hold on to me. Hold on to the wall—whatever feels most comfortable. Get your balance. You'll be moving along in no time."

"Moving along isn't the problem. Standing isn't the problem. Falling is. I don't like to fall."

"No one does. So don't fall."

"I'm going out on the ice on two tiny bars of steel. Does that seem practical? That doesn't sound like a very smart way to avoid falling to me."

"I'm here. I'll catch you if you fall. Give me a chance."

He'd like nothing better than a chance to catch her in his arms. For someone who'd just given himself a pep talk on letting go and pulling away, he sure wasn't listening.

Brick didn't want to listen. The lights inside the tent were romantic; the moment felt magical. He felt like two conflicting voices were whispering in his ears, and he wanted to brush off the negative one and toss it across the ice. For now, for this moment, he wanted to enjoy the time he had with Stella.

Stella moved forward.

"Wait!"

She froze. "What?"

"You have to take off your blade guards. They protect the skates off the ice, but you don't want to skate in them."

"Oh." She blushed and lifted her foot.

Brick slipped the guard off the blade and repeated the process on the other foot. "Now you're ready to roll."

"I can see me doing just that. Rolling across the ice on my stomach. On my back. Feet first. Head first. Hitting the wall on the far side."

"You're a nut, you know that?" Brick shook his head.

Stella stepped onto the ice. She wobbled but stayed upright. Brick hurried to join her, not sure if he should offer a hand. Desire to be near her overrode his aversion to rejection, and he reached out to take her hand. She smiled at him with relief-filled eyes, and she clung to his hand with a death grip.

"How am I doing?"

"Amazingly well. You're still standing. If I didn't know better, I'd think you were conning me about not being able to skate."

She wobbled and grabbed his arm. He let her. He pulled her close and wrapped his arm around her waist.

"Thanks."

"For making you come out on the ice?"

"That and for being here for me. You've been so kind and thoughtful—from the moment I drove in Thanksgiving morning and you invited me home to spend time with your family until tonight when you forced me to do something I've always wanted to do but was scared to face on my own."

Brick felt like a heel. Here he was, telling himself to back off and figure out how to put distance between them, and she was so happy to have been accepted into his world. Later he'd have to figure out how to right all the wrongs so everyone came out happy in the end. For now he just wanted to glide along the ice with this woman at his side.

❄

"Slowly push forward with one foot, put your weight on the front foot, and balance on that one. Then do the same and stroke with the other foot."

Stella did as Brick said. She wobbled at first, but soon her strokes became more confident, more steady, and her outlook became more positive. Slow music drifted to them from the speakers just outside the rink, the melody soft and romantic.

"Do you hear that?" Stella motioned to the speakers in the corners of the rink.

"I do, but I'm not sure how it was activated."

"Lucas." They voiced in unison.

Stella strained to place the tune.

"I'll be home for Christmas," Brick quietly sang in her ear as they drifted along. "You can plan on me." His voice was deep and sure.

Stella had another deep desire to be "home" for Christmas. She didn't want to travel alone anymore. She wanted to settle in and have family and community. Christmas, Florida, was the first town that had called to her so clearly. But was it possible to plunk down so suddenly and put down roots?

Brick continued to sing, his baritone notes making her smile.

"I didn't know you could sing." Stella stopped to look at him.

"I'd imagine there are a lot of things you don't know about me," Brick teased. "We haven't known each other all that long."

"Good point." She found herself wondering what else she'd learn about him if she stayed in town longer. With no future gig, she had to make a plan. Her original thought was to return to the family home, catch up with her neighbor/secretary, and regroup from there, but the holiday loomed lonely with no one at the house to celebrate with. Again she wondered about the possibility of staying in Christmas, at least until the holidays were over.

The thought lifted her mood and she moved forward, picking up her pace. Her feet found their rhythm, and she felt as if she were flying around the rink. She loved the feel of moving over the ice with the cool air blowing her face.

"You're a natural!" Brick called from the other side of the rink.

Stella didn't know about that, but she did love the sensation of moving across the ice.

"Now try to swing around backwards and see how much easier that is."

Stella's laugh ricocheted off the walls of the tent. "Yeah, right. You do want to see me bounce, don't you?"

"You aren't going to bounce." Brick slid to a stop just ahead of her. His blades threw ice against her legs.

"Where did you learn to skate like that?"

"Here and there." He grinned. "I went to college up north. I spent some time on a hockey league."

"Oh a hockey league, just like that."

"Yeah. . .why not?"

"You don't grow up in Florida, head north for college, and then one day just decide, 'Hey, I think I'll become a hockey player.' "

He considered her words. "Uh, yeah. Pretty much. My roommate and a bunch of the other guys in the dorm played, and it looked like a good time."

"Skating around chasing a little puck and hitting each other with sticks—a way good time I'm sure." She snickered.

"It was. Or rather, it was once I learned to actually stand up on these things." He lifted a foot and twisted it her way. She glanced down and almost tripped. "That's how I earned the nickname 'Torpedo.' I'd fly across the rink, taking out everything in my path, until I either crashed into the wall on the other side or crashed into another player."

"Nice hockey style." She noticed he'd spun around backward. "I'm sure the other players loved it."

"The players on my team sure did." He grinned. He held out his hands. "Come on, turn around and join me."

"You make it look so easy."

"I find going backward is easier than going forward."

"You and a bunch of other people in this world."

"Very true. Though I wasn't talking about regressing in life." He grasped her upper arms and slowly swung her around in a half circle. "Let's see how it works for you."

Stella stumbled and clutched his arm. Her fingers tingled at the contact.

"Point your toes out, heels closer together. It'll make you spin in a circle."

She tried it, and he spun her slowly around. "You're right. It works!"

"Of course it does. I told you. I won't lead you astray. Now, put your feet side by side. Toes together, heels together."

"Okay. And now I'm going backward. But I'm not doing it on my own momentum."

"Not yet, but you will. Feel the rhythm—just like you did when you went forward. One foot then the other foot. There you go. Keep going."

She got the rhythm. "Um, Brick, we're heading toward the corner of the rink."

"Do you trust me?"

"I do." She looked into his kind blue eyes and knew she meant it. "Tell me what to do."

"Balance on your right foot and lift your left foot, crossing it over the right. Set it down, careful not to trip, put your weight on that foot then lift your right foot and put it back in place."

Brick held tight to her arms, which allowed her to focus fully on following his directions. She felt like she was following orders from Roger, her GPS, when he spewed them out on the highway. The result in this case was a gentle glide that carried her at an angle as they curved around the edge of the rink.

"I did it! You're right, it's so much smoother than going forward around the corners."

"You'll take the corners better as time goes by. The more you practice, the more skating will become second nature to you."

"Time." She sighed. "Something we don't have much of, at least when it comes to the ice."

"I bet we can find ice in other places even if it isn't here."

"Maybe so, Brick."

They skated to the opening and stepped off the ice. They put on their skate guards and walked over to the bench.

Stella untied her boots and slid them from her feet. "And I thought my feet ached after I got off work today. Those skates give a whole new meaning to aching feet!"

"I didn't even think of that. I'm sorry." Brick took her sock-clad foot in his hands and massaged her arches. "I've forgotten how bad skating can make your feet and ankles hurt when you first start out."

"So it gets better?"

"Some." His sheepish grin said otherwise. He massaged her other foot and motioned for her to put her shoes on. "That'll help a bit. If you can, soak your feet in hot water for a few minutes when you get home. If you have Epsom salts, throw them in. I'm sure Mom has some at the house if you don't have them in the RV. As a matter of fact, if you want a soak in the tub at the house, feel free. You deserve a bubble bath while you read after the past few weeks you've had. Take over the guest room for the night. I'm sure Mom won't mind. She leaves it made up in case we get unexpected guests."

A bubble bath. What a luxury! She couldn't think of the last one she'd taken. Even when she stayed in hotels, she had such a tight schedule it didn't leave room for anything but falling into bed for a night's sleep before hitting the ground running the next morning. She probably hadn't had one since she'd left her aunt's home years ago. What a nice man Brick was, to think to offer such a thing.

She studied Brick through lowered lashes as they headed from the rink's tent. Lucas waved them off as they walked to the truck. Stella felt like she was limping, but sore feet or not, she wouldn't have changed this day for anything.

Chapter 6

Brick looked around until he spotted Stella. She was over by the ice rink, watching over the skaters. He'd spent the better part of the evening troubleshooting for her. Stella flitted from booth to booth, sampling food, chatting with crafters, and watching the tiny dancers as they performed on stage.

His mother was somewhere in the mess of guests, being dragged around by Seth. They'd planned to meet up later in the evening so he and Stella could spend time with Seth and Vivi could take a break and meet up with her own friends.

He snagged a cup of hot cocoa and headed Stella's way. Instead of backing off as he'd told himself to do, he'd fallen in love with the planner.

"I see Stella right over there." A booming voice called out from over Brick's shoulder. "I'll get her for you."

Brick spun around, nearly losing his grip on the foam cup. "Just a minute, partner. Stella's getting her first breather of the evening. Is there something I can help you with?"

The man frowned, his gaze seeking out Stella's. She was lost in thought and didn't notice him. "The guys and I wanted a picture

71

with her. She's worked really hard on this, and we want to get a picture before she moves on."

Brick didn't see why any man needed a picture of Stella. Well, he knew *why*. She was gorgeous. But he didn't like the thought of other men taking pictures of her at all. "Look, I understand you want the picture, but look at her. She hasn't had a moment to herself in two weeks. Do you really want to break this moment of silence for her?"

"No, I guess not." The man's shoulders drooped as he made his way back to his friends.

No doubt Stella had made some friends in the time she'd been here. He figured it was the same way everywhere else she worked. She probably left a trail of broken hearts in her wake when she moved on, and even more incredible, she probably never even knew it.

He hadn't wanted the other man to break into Stella's contemplative mood, but he didn't think she'd mind if he entered her space. He came bearing chocolate. "Thirsty?"

❄

Stella glanced away from the rink and accepted the cup of hot cocoa from Brick. She couldn't believe the difference a week made in the atmosphere of the festival. The first weekend had been a resounding success. For the most part, things had gone without a hitch. A few last-minute changes had to be dealt with, which was typical for an event of this size, but the issues were few and far between compared to some of the other events she'd planned. The weekdays had lighter crowds, but tonight, the second Saturday, the festival was packed with people.

"Has it really been a week since you took me skating?" Stella asked as Brick walked up to join her. She rested her arms on the wall of the rink and watched the skaters as they whirled around in circles. "It's packed out there."

"It's really been a week. A lot's happened since then, hasn't it?" He faced her, leaning an arm casually on the wall beside her. He joined her in her perusal of skaters.

Stella's hand flew to her mouth as a young skater slammed into the boy in front of her, knocking him off his feet. "Oh, I'm so glad I'm not out there right now."

"Really?" Brick shifted his pose. "I'd planned on asking you to take a spin."

"Maybe when it clears out, say, around midnight?" Stella giggled as she took a sip of cocoa. "There's no way you're getting me out there in that madhouse to make a fool of myself, even with my crazy good skating skills."

"You were pretty good."

"I was joking."

"I'm not."

She liked that she knew many of the people that made up the mad swirl of skating figures. Every so often one of the skaters would wave or would call out a greeting to her. She liked that, too. She'd given lots of thought over the past week to the idea of staying in town permanently, but she hadn't really talked about it with Brick.

Stella could feel Brick studying her. He reached out to touch her arm. "You're growing serious. What are you thinking about?"

She glanced around their secluded area of the rink. No one stood within earshot.

"I was wondering—if I did continue to stay through the holiday—would you be okay with us spending more time together? Maybe we could—you know—get to know each other better."

Brick's eyes lit up, but he quickly shuttered them. She couldn't read Brick's expression as he released her arm and moved slightly away.

Stella's heart dropped as he withdrew.

Stella gave him space, slowly following Brick as he made his way around the edge of the rink, walking just ahead of her. She tossed her empty cup into a nearby trash can.

"Let's take this outside." Brick's long-legged pace left her breathless as she tried to keep up. He finally slowed near the farthest corner of lights but remained with his back to her, his stance rigid, his hands stuffed in his jeans pockets.

Fake snow fell around them and landed on their shoulders and hair. Joyful Christmas music belted out from the speaker over their head.

"What is it, Brick? Did I say something wrong? Please tell me." She moved into his line of vision and splayed her hands. "I don't have to stay, not with your family anyway. I can keep my distance if you'd rather."

Had she misread his feelings for her that badly? She thought he'd felt the same things she had. The connection that had started the moment he'd invited her to Thanksgiving dinner. The chemistry that made her constantly aware of him—even when he wasn't with her.

His face was a mask of frustration. "You didn't say anything wrong. Not really. And I'm sorry that I'm making you feel bad as I wrestle with this. It isn't anything you've done, Stella. It's just that the more time we've spent together, the more I've realized how much Seth is falling in love with you. He adores you and it scares me. He hasn't been this animated and happy since he lost his mother."

Stella tried to understand. "But isn't that a good thing? She's been gone for a while now. . . . Surely you want him to move on?"

The gentle breeze blew his hair. He looked so handsome with the contrast of the snowflakes resting against the golden strands.

"I don't mean that I want him mourning her forever, Stell. I'm just concerned that he's growing too attached to you too quickly. He's finally opening up, and I don't know what it'll do to him when you have to move on. I don't want him to have a setback."

"Oh." The lone word hung in the early evening air. She sighed, deflated. "So by staying longer, I put off the inevitable." Brick was right; if she got another call, she would have to move on. Her chosen career required it. And when she moved on, a certain little boy she'd quickly grown to love would be heartbroken. She'd leave a hole in their family, short as her time with them had been. If she was honest with herself, she'd leave with a matching hole in her own heart. Even though she'd only known the family for a short period of time, she'd fallen hard for them, too.

Hardworking Brick. Vivacious Vivi. Friendly Rose. And the little boy with the big heart, Seth.

"It was so awful when we lost Lisa. Seth cried for her all the time. We thought he was getting better, and then we received his grades. He'd always loved school, but his teacher said he wouldn't engage, wouldn't cooperate; he was grieving too deeply." Brick turned to Stella. "I sent for Mom, and she moved in with us and started homeschooling him. He meets with other students throughout the week for play dates and activities so he can connect with friends again, and he's doing so much better. I can't watch him shut down again when you leave. I can't risk that we lose him again like we did back then."

"I had no idea. I mean, I know he homeschooled, but I didn't know the reason why. I don't want to be responsible for hurting him." Tears threatened the back of Stella's eyelids. She turned away from Brick and blinked the tears away. She didn't want to say good-bye. She didn't want to move on to a lonely place where she didn't know anyone. The Myers family had changed her life, too, in the short time she'd been with them. But she knew she couldn't risk staying and messing with Seth's adjustment unless she was sure Christmas was the place she wanted to settle into. The little guy had been through enough.

Is this it, Lord? The moment we've been talking about? Is this where I give it all up and dig my roots deep and leave it up to You to take care of me?

Stella realized she'd known all along what God was trying to tell her. He'd been working on her heart ever since she'd arrived in Christmas, Florida. She'd been trying too hard to make it on her own. She'd had God in her life but hadn't given God control of her life. Just as Brick was trying to shield Seth from the hurt of loving and losing people dear to him, she'd been doing the same for herself. It was hard to grieve losing someone you didn't let in.

"Stella." Brick's voice was soft, gentle.

He laid a hand on her shoulder.

Stella closed her eyes, not daring to look at him. "I get it, Brick. I understand so clearly what you're doing for Seth, because I've been doing it for myself far too long."

Brick looked confused. "Doing what?"

"Guarding my heart. Closing off from everyone around me so I don't hurt again if I lose anyone else."

"And you think that's what I'm doing with Seth?"

"You've pretty much said the same. But you're doing it out of a father's love. I've been doing it in rebellion. I've even closed myself off from God when it comes to listening to His gentle voice. He's been telling me from the moment I arrived that this would be a special place for me. He wants me to stay, Brick."

Brick smiled. "Interesting. I like where you're going with this."

"I don't fully know what He has in store for us, but I do know that no matter what happens between us, I'll always be there for Seth. I won't leave him if he needs me nearby. If it helps, I'll move to the campground at once. Do you think that'll help give a clearer line to Seth about our friendship?"

"I don't want you to leave, Stella." Brick caressed her arm. "I don't want you to leave Christmas or the farm. And I agree; I've felt all along that maybe this lull in your career is God's way of telling you to slow down and see what He has next."

She studied him as he waited for her response.

She took a moment to contemplate what he'd said. She stepped outside the lighted area, onto the path the horse-drawn carriages followed. Brick fell into a rhythm beside her. They walked a few moments as she thought about the sermon they'd heard right after she'd arrived, remembered her scattered thoughts on putting down roots and staying in one place. The idea completely appealed to her. She'd stay. Peace drifted over her like a cloak.

"What will I do for a job?"

"I don't know." Brick's eyes filled with hope. "What would

you want to do?"

Stella's foot twisted in a rut and she stumbled. Brick's arm steadied her. He held on even after she'd gained her balance. "I've never really thought about other options. Not in a long time. I fell into a job as an event planner when I left high school. I worked with the company for seven years. I only left because the owner sold out and the new owners were bringing in their own crew. That's when I struck out on my own. I'd made a lot of connections and figured I could make it work. I've been doing this ever since—I guess it's been three years now."

"Your life sounds like a whirlwind. Everyone needs a time of rest at some point. Maybe this is your time. If you settle in here and stay in the RV on our land or in the guest room in the house, would you have enough to live on for a while? Until you can decide the next step in your career?"

"I don't know. I've never liked to spend too much time in one place. This is the first time I've considered slowing down. I like to stay busy."

"Because when you slow down, you realize how alone you truly are?"

"I'm not—" She glanced at him, and his eyes dared her to say it.

"You're not alone?"

She knew she couldn't tell him that. Though they'd only known each other a short time, he knew her too well when it came to some things.

"Okay, so I don't like to feel lonely. Who does?" She wrapped her arms around her stomach. "Every time I try to put down roots, I lose the people I love. My parents. My aunt. My cousins."

"We're not going anywhere, Stell." Brick swung around in front of her and took her by her arms. "I won't lie—I do worry about Seth getting too attached, but please stay here in Christmas—at *least* through the holidays. Pray about God's plan for your life and His direction for your career. Think about what you'd like to do next, or what you'd like to do if you put down those roots and decide to stay in one place. If the idea unsettles you too badly by the New Year, you'll know it isn't God's plan."

"But I think it is His plan. I can be an event planner here, too." She quipped. "There are still weddings, corporate events, other towns nearby."

"I could use some help at the office—you know, while you build your client list. Mindless things like filing, organizing, answering the phone. You'd have time to think. My receptionist had a baby right before you arrived and called the other day to say she doesn't feel she can come back after her leave is up. And again, your expenses would be low if you stayed on at our place."

"Well, it would be easier to work with you and build our relationship if we're near each other."

"I agree. So it's settled?"

"Yes, I do believe it's settled." Joy swirled around her like the drifting snowflakes. The only difference was, her joy was real.

Brick stood in the moonlight, his blue eyes sparkling in the reflection of the many lights, even though they were surrounded by darkness on the outside of the perimeter. The gaiety of laughter carried to them from the festival-goers, but they were alone in their dark corner of the world.

"You know. . .you do realize that if you get a call for a faraway event, you can always take it from here, home base."

"I can, can't I? This doesn't have to be the end."

"And if things continue to develop between us—I know it's early to be talking about this, and I know we need time—we could always hit the road with you if things work out. Seth home-schools, remember?"

"You'd do that?"

"I'd love to. I think it sounds like a blast. Seth and Mom would love to see the country. I have a good crew when it comes to my workers. I can take time off here and there when I need to. And if we were to marry, Mom would love to have the house to herself now and then."

Did he really mention *marriage*? Her heart swelled. "It seems we're on the same wavelength concerning, well, everything. And I love the idea of keeping some of the events. Maybe just the ones nearby for now. Later, as things work out between us, we could consider gigs farther away."

Brick moved closer and reached up to cup her cheek. "I want you to know I'm here for you, Stella. I won't let you fall, on or off the ice."

"I know you'll keep me safe, Brick." Stella stepped into his embrace. A tear rolled down her face as she wrapped her arms around him and rested her cheek against his chest.

He held her close.

They stood together in the darkness, staring out over the festival that had brought them together.

"I've finally come home for Christmas."

"Welcome home, Stell."

"Thank you." She lifted her face, ready to meet his kiss.

Paige Winship Dooly is the author of over a dozen books and novellas. She enjoys living in the coastal Deep South with her family, after having grown up in the sometimes extremely cold Midwest. She is happily married to her high school sweetheart and loves their life of adventure in a full house with six homeschooled children and two dogs.

MERRY CHRISTMAS, WITH LOVE

Darlene Franklin

DEDICATION

My mother once said, "Christian writers are the greatest."
Robin Patchen proved the truth of that by helping me make
the changes in the copyedit while I was in the hospital. I have
enjoyed getting to know you outside of our monthly meetings.

Chapter 1

Randi Pearson moistened the flap and closed the card envelope. If she left now, a brisk walk would bring her to the post office shortly after closing time. After she dropped off her cards, she hoped to catch her mother, postmaster Edie Hathaway, before she left work.

The walk plus the cool November air cleared Randi's mind and refreshed her body and spirit. As she moved along, she hummed "The Twelve Days of Christmas." By the time she had reached her destination, she was on day nine. Was it nine lords a-leaping or nine ladies dancing?

As usual, cars lined up by the mailboxes along the street entrance. A dozen vehicles remained in the parking lot, more than she expected. The post office had closed five minutes ago. The outer door remained open for patrons to reach their mailboxes, but the lobby was deserted and the inner door locked. Randi slid her cards down the mail chute and opened her cell phone.

"Edie speaking." Her mother answered after a single ring.

"Mom, what's going on? Why are all those cars in the parking lot?"

"Randi! Glad you could make it. Give me a minute." A moment later her mother appeared at the door. "Our volunteers completed their training today. We're having a reception to get to know each other. Come on back and let me introduce you."

Randi clicked her tongue against her teeth. Almost two decades had passed since she was one of those volunteers herself, eager to spread Christmas cheer through the volume of cards that came through the post office. "Lead the way."

A dozen people circulated in the conference room. Randi saw several familiar faces.

A couple she remembered from her own days as a volunteer, faithful helpers who came year after year. Others she knew from church, work, and local businesses. A few were strangers to her, seasonal workers who came only for the Christmas season. Among the new faces, one caught her attention. A man, perhaps forty, with hair outgrowing a buzz cut, held his back ramrod straight. Most women would respond to his handsome face, strong jaw, and clear, blue eyes. Not Randi. First a military wife, then a widow, she had no interest in repeating the experience.

"Come along, let me introduce you." Mom clapped her hands together and the room quieted. "This is my top elf and first daughter, Randi Pearson."

Laughter rippled around the room.

"Pleased to meet you." Randi smiled. Lowering her voice, she said, "A few new faces this year."

"Let's mingle." Mom headed straight for the blue-eyed stranger. "Major Brennan just retired from the army, and he decided to spend his first Christmas as a civilian with us. Isn't that marvelous?"

Major Brennan? Randi's worst fears were realized.

—MERRY CHRISTMAS, WITH LOVE—

❄

Major Troy Brennan, retired, surveyed the group of volunteers—earnest, bright-eyed, hardworking, most of them would thrive in a military environment.

The postmaster—she insisted they call her Edie—headed in his direction with her daughter but stopped by the refreshment table. The younger woman ladled a cup of red punch. He considered her beneath lowered lids. She fit the profile of the woman he sought, but so had half a dozen others he had glimpsed since his arrival in town. Perhaps today was the day he would hear from his correspondent of five years, giving him a time and a place to meet.

Edie tapped on a glass with a fork. "Let's take a few moments now to get to know each other—what part of the country you hail from, why you volunteered for this duty, what your favorite Christmas memory is."

Randi set down her cup of punch, a faint red mustache evident on her upper lip. "I'll start. Of course I grew up here, and I've been in and out of the post office all my life. I could hardly wait until I was old enough to work here myself. I stamped Merry Christmas on thousands of cards over the five years that I volunteered. And that is one of my favorite Christmas memories."

Applause broke out among the gathering, and she bowed. "Then I decided that it was time to let others enjoy the same experience."

Continuing around the circle, each one shared their story: a retired schoolteacher, a stay-at-home mother, a college student. . . . Troy didn't want to reveal his real reason for coming to Christmas, not until he heard from Aranda.

"What about you, Major?"

He almost missed his turn. "I am Troy Brennan—recently retired after twenty years of active service with the army."

"Thank you for your service, Major." Edie pressed his hand warmly.

Renewed applause followed her remark, and he nodded his head in acknowledgment while preparing his remarks. "As Edie has indicated, I was a major in the United States Army. I heard about the amazing service that the town of Christmas offers to postal customers and decided this was a perfect place to readjust to civilian life while I consider my future options."

"Welcome to Christmas, Major." Edie beamed. "We hope you like it so much that you decide to make this your permanent home."

"Perhaps. We'll see which way God directs."

As the introductions continued, Troy listened with interest. They would work in close quarters for the next several weeks. God put him here for a reason, one that could differ from Troy's goal. As much as Troy wanted to keep his eye on PO Box 1, he forced himself to pay attention to the conversation flowing around him.

A pimply-faced teen who had identified himself as a first-time volunteer asked him about his time in the military. "You must have seen some fighting." His eyes gleamed, ready to grab a rifle and take his spot at the front. His comment came during a lull in conversation.

"Yes." Troy didn't elaborate; not many veterans he knew did. Only fellow soldiers could understand, and they rarely cared to discuss their experiences.

"Major Brennan might not have been involved in combat at all." Randi spoke over her shoulder as she refilled the punch bowl. "The army has bases all over the world. He might not have done anything more interesting that maintain a fleet of cars in Heidelberg, Germany." She winked at Troy.

"Mechanics can't be majors." The boy scoffed before confusion overtook his face. "Or can they?"

"Soldiers are all kinds of things—engineers, lawyers, chaplains, bunches of things. But me, I was just an ordinary foot soldier." He smiled. "Are you considering a career in the military?"

"Maybe." The boy turned bright red.

"If you like, we can talk about it later." The military would make a man out of this boy. It had transformed Troy when he wasn't much older than the kid. He headed for the punch bowl.

"You were in Afghanistan." Randi made it a statement, not a question.

He nodded agreement. How did she know? "Yes, I was. And now I'm more than glad to be out."

"Welcome home." A shadow of sadness sped through her eyes. "The town of Christmas has been welcoming our soldiers since the days of the old fort. Military and the Orlando attractions—and golf and sun and surf. Plus more ordinary things like construction and manufacturing. All kinds of things draw people here. Have you decided what you want to do in your postmilitary career?"

"Not yet. God is leading me one step at a time." He couldn't look for work until he knew where he would spend the rest of his life.

With a smile on her face, she shook her head. "It's unsettling when that happens, isn't it?"

"Perhaps if you take me on a tour of the town, God will show me what's next." What made him say that? He was in Christmas to meet one woman—and one woman only.

An enigmatic smile played across her mouth. "I'll get back to you about that. Welcome to Christmas, Major." With that dismissal, she headed out.

"Troy, please." He addressed her departing back. Her less-than-enthusiastic answer chilled his interest, and he glanced out the window to the row of mailboxes. He wondered when he could slip away from this get-together.

❄

Randi had to leave before Troy took her breath away. She had never swooned over a handsome man, and she didn't intend to start now. Throwing her empty cup in the trash can, she headed for the door.

"Wait a minute." Her mother hurried after her. "I have your mail out front. Let me go with you." They whisked through the door. Once it shut, Mom asked, "What's going on?"

"Michael." Randi let out a long breath. "Nothing new. We can talk about it later. I didn't realize today was the volunteers' first day."

They paused in front of the post-office box that Nativity Community Church rented. Edie handed her the top two envelopes. "These are for you." She held on to the cards. "What did Michael do this time?"

"It doesn't matter." Randi shook her head. "I just wanted to blow off steam." She took the envelopes from her mother's hand.

"I'm always surprised when they write back." As she slipped them into her purse, she glanced up and saw Troy looking down the hallway in their direction. "I'll see you later." She hugged her mother and headed to the street.

Since she had lingered at the post office longer than she intended, she hurried to get home on time. If Michael returned to an empty house, he might use it as an excuse to head out again. Ever since his sixteenth birthday two years ago, he had played tug-of-war over every aspect of their lives. So many times she had wondered if things would have been better if he had a father in his life.

Randi walked home. Every block was familiar from her childhood. After several years away, she had moved back when Mike's unit shipped overseas in the wake of September 11. She and Michael still lived in the same rental house, a cement box built in the post-World War II building boom. In some ways their family clock had stopped on the day they received the news that Mike was killed in action.

The motion-activated outdoor light came on as she approached the front door, but no light gleamed through the windows. If Michael was at home, he had holed himself up in the back bedroom. She closed her eyes and counted to ten, sending up a prayer for patience and wisdom.

She opened the door, her ears straining for sounds of Michael's presence. The house had the hollow feeling of an empty space. She walked from room to room and verified that her son wasn't home.

In case Michael had left a message, she checked the notepad on the fridge and voice mail on her home phone. If he had called her cell, she would have caught it. "Oh, Michael."

Head spinning, Randi considered what step she should take next.

Chapter 2

Troy pushed back from the table. He had enjoyed every bite of the home-cooked meal.

"Are you sure I can't tempt you with another slice of pie?" Faith Draper, wife of Troy's longtime buddy Will, started to slide another slab onto his plate.

Troy threw up his hands. "No more, please. I surrender. I want to keep my fighting weight."

"If you're successful in your search for your mystery woman, you'll be packing on the pounds before you know it." Will patted his middle, where an inner tube had formed. "Every pound, packed on with love." He grabbed for his wife, and she tumbled into his arms.

"You don't have to remind me of the advantages of married life." Troy began clearing the dishes.

Will's cell rang, and he flipped it open. "It's Michael."

"Not again." Faith shook her head.

Will shrugged. Lifting the phone to his ear, he headed in the direction of his study.

"Someone in the youth group?" Troy guessed.

"He's going through a bad spell. He's a senior, almost ready to graduate, but he's as lost as most eighteen-year-olds."

Troy nodded. "Some of us take longer than others."

Will came back. "It's a good thing you cooked extra food tonight. He's headed over here."

"I *always* cook extra. I never know when we might be feeding an extra mouth—or two or three." She dished the remaining key lime pie onto individual serving plates and wrapped them in plastic.

A loudly idling car pulled into the driveway, and a six-foot-tall beanpole climbed out of the driver's seat. All arms and legs, not yet comfortable with his size, looking so thin that a stiff breeze could blow him over. He reminded Troy a lot of himself at that age.

"Should I go ahead and leave?" Troy didn't belong in a situation where the youth spilled his heart out to his youth minister. Worse, his presence might discourage him from opening up.

"Nah. He just wants to hang out with us." Will opened the door to their front closet, and a ball bounced onto the floor. "How would you like to shoot some hoops?"

"Outside, in the middle of November." Troy shook his head. "Winter in Florida."

"Football, basketball, whatever, he'll give you a run for your money. Michael is talented."

"Faith said he's a senior. Is he looking at a college scholarship?"

"That's part of the problem." Will tossed the basketball to Troy. "He didn't try out. He's not interested in the discipline required for high school ball."

"That's too bad."

"Come on out and meet the miscreant." Will's smile took the

sting out of the words.

"Should I call his mother?" Faith appeared at the door to the kitchen, a frilly red apron tied around her waist.

Will paused with his hand on the doorknob. "Give us half an hour, unless she calls here first."

Faith flashed the okay sign and returned to the kitchen.

"Hey, Michael, want to shoot some hoops? Or do you want to eat first? Key lime pie for dessert."

The boy's face lit up at the mention of dessert, but he grabbed the basketball and feinted for the basketball hoop. "I gotta work up an appetite first."

Troy tossed the ball to him. "I'm Troy, a friend of Will's. Are you ready for some two-on-one?"

For answer, Michael moved to the hoop. Troy blocked his approach.

"I'm Michael." He dodged around Troy and heaved the ball through the hoop. Troy caught the rebound and made a jump shot, his fingers brushing the bottom of the net. Adrenaline kicked in, and his muscles stretched effortlessly.

After a quarter of an hour, Troy and Will had matched the kid point for point, and they were down to the final point.

Michael dribbled the ball between his legs, his eyes darting between the two men. "Two against one, and I'm still beating you." He taunted them.

"Wait till you're our age." Will darted forward but Michael evaded him. He ran for the basket and threw it up, catching the rebound when his shot missed.

A white sedan parked on the street in front of the house. "Merry Christmas" was painted on the hood of the car, with a wreath separating the two words. Troy shook his head. It reminded him of the General Lee in the old TV show, *The Dukes of Hazard.* Michael took advantage of the distraction to drive past Will and Troy and make the final basket.

"Twenty-one points! I won." Michael pumped his fist in the air and tucked the ball beneath his arm. He swiveled, ready to dunk the ball one last time, when he noticed the car waiting at the curb. "You called my mom."

Will clapped his hand on Michael's shoulder. "She called here."

The car door opened and a shapely stockinged leg dangled from the edge before her head popped into sight. It only took a few seconds for her identity to register—Randi Pearson, his boss's daughter.

❄

Randi stayed rooted to the tarmac as she surveyed the Drapers' front lawn. What was Troy Brennan doing here?

Will trotted toward her. "Have you had supper yet?"

Supper. After the night she'd had, she'd settle for fast food, again. If judged by attention to her family's diet, she'd be convicted. "I'll scrounge something together."

"Nonsense. Faith fixed enough to feed the whole youth group. She loves to share. Besides, Michael has worked up an appetite."

Michael came out of the garage, sans basketball.

She might as well offer a peace branch. "What do you want to do?"

He looked at the ground. "It sure smells good in the kitchen."

"Then we will accept the invitation." She glanced at Troy,

who was smiling. What was funny about the situation?

Will came between them. "Randi, I'd like to introduce you to my good friend, Troy Brennan."

"We've already met." Troy's smile widened. "She came by the post office earlier." He nodded at Randi. "It's a pleasant surprise to run into you twice on the same day."

Michael's face took on a resigned expression. He had trouble forging his own identity—with the postmaster for his grandmother, a high school guidance counselor for a mother, and a military hero for his father. If only his efforts weren't earning him the moniker of "troublemaker."

Troy simply said, "Your son is quite the basketball player. He beat the two of us straight up."

A small smile played around Michael's lips. "It's not hard to beat a couple of old geezers."

"Hey, be careful who you're calling an old geezer." Will's wounded expression made Randi laugh.

Her decision to eat a meal faltered when she noticed the two place settings on the table. "You've already eaten." She took a step back.

Troy swept past her into the kitchen and poured himself a cup of coffee. "I'll join you. Faith promised me a second piece of key lime pie."

Soon the five of them were seated at the table. Michael didn't talk as he dove into the piles of food. She wouldn't attempt to pry any answers out of him in this setting. He had the silent treatment down to an art form.

"You were in the army for twenty years?" Since Troy was new to town, she should be friendly.

He nodded his head and lined his napkin up with the plate then chuckled. "Hard to undo the habits of half a lifetime."

What a charming smile. His mouth sneaked out of its serious lines and lifted as if against his will. Maybe stealth defined his nature.

"Tell her why you came to Christmas. It's so romantic." Faith grinned. A teakettle whistled on the stove, and she took down a tin of holiday-flavored teas. Randi picked out a bag filled with peppermint-flavored leaves. How would Troy answer?

Pink suffused the major's face. "There is a lady here who has been sending me Christmas cards for the past five years. I'm hoping to meet her."

"Like I said. Isn't that romantic?" Faith beamed.

Randi scrambled for an intelligent response. "That's interesting." She cleared her throat. "I do that myself. Send cards to servicemen."

"She must have sent something special, for you to come all the way here to find her," Faith said.

What would it take to get Faith to stop pursuing the subject? Randi had finished her meal, but Michael had taken a third helping of potatoes and gravy. He was as eager to delay leaving as she was anxious to get home. Her eyes drifted in Troy's direction.

A dreamy look blinked from his eyes. "We've exchanged a few letters. I don't know how to explain it."

"No need." Will leaned back in his chair. "When God brings that special someone across your path, you're helpless." He laid his hand on top of Faith's, squeezing it. "I'm a solid piece of mush where you're concerned."

The Drapers had married in their midthirties, shortly after

—MERRY CHRISTMAS, WITH LOVE—

Will became youth pastor at Nativity Community Church. The honeymoon glow hadn't faded yet. Their age exemplified the wisdom of waiting for the right mate. But Faith had the typical newlywed's attitude of wanting to fix everyone else up. She might push Randi into Troy's path, if he weren't searching for his elusive correspondent.

At last Michael allowed Faith to take his plate in exchange for a slice of pie, with a cup of hot strong tea. Let him finish. Soon. Before someone asked questions that would reveal it all.

"Tell Randi what you know about this woman." Faith turned to Randi. "It's like a detective story. He has to unravel the clues to find her."

Hurry up, Michael. His crumb-by-crumb enjoyment of the pie delayed the inevitable departure.

"I first got a Christmas card from her six years ago, and we started writing each other once a month or so. She said she was a military widow—"

"Randi lost her husband in Iraq." Will pulled his chair closer to Faith.

Michael's fork paused in midair. Although he wouldn't admit it, he missed the presence of his father in his life.

"I'm sorry to hear that." Troy's simple words of sympathy brought a tickle of tears to Randi's eyes.

"I wrote back, and, well, I came to look forward to her letters as much as Christmas morning."

Two bites remained of Michael's pie.

"Do you have her address? She must have put something on the envelopes." Faith plowed ahead.

Troy shook his head. "No help there. She used a post-office box."

"What's her name?"

Michael pressed the last of the graham cracker crumbs onto his fork.

"She only gave me the initial of her last name. She signed all the cards the same way: 'Merry Christmas, with love, Aranda H.'"

Michael's head snapped up, his eyes widening, and Randi feared he would blurt out the truth. Then he retreated into his shell, and she let out her breath. She needed to leave, before one of them revealed her secret.

"That's an interesting story." Randi offered a neutral response. "But now we need to head home." She prayed her son wouldn't put up an argument.

Instead of argument, he used his best manners. "Thank you for the supper, Mrs. Draper. See you at church, Pastor Will." He held back his questions until they both climbed into the front seat of her car.

"Who is that guy, and why is he looking for you?"

Chapter 3

Randi eased the car into traffic while she considered her answer. "As far as I know, he's exactly who he says he is. An army officer who retired after giving twenty years of his life to service."

"But Aranda H. That's you, right? Unless there's another Aranda Hathaway here in Christmas?"

Randi chewed the inside of her lip. When she had received Troy's letter announcing his intention to come for a visit, she hoped he would change his mind. The letter refusing his visit remained unwritten, since she had been as helpless then to think of an answer as she was now.

At length she spoke. "Yes, it's me. He's one of the hundreds of soldiers I've sent cards to over the years."

"And he wrote back."

"A lot of them do." She wouldn't tell him how Troy's letters had struck a chord in her as well. Sharing her struggles with a man serving at the opposite end of the globe had given her a false sense of security. Then he had to go and ruin it by showing up in Christmas.

"So why didn't you tell him you are Aranda H.?"

Randi couldn't tell if disapproval or curiosity drove his question. "He's still a stranger. I don't think it's wise."

"Somebody else might tell him." Mike grabbed a bottle of water from the fridge. "Pastor Will says he'll be helping with the youth group."

The post office, the youth group—how could Randi avoid Troy if he showed up everywhere she went?

❄

Troy stretched his legs as far as he could under the table. At the post office, every letter had to be stamped with the "Merry Christmas" seal on the day it was dropped at the post office. After an already long day, Edie brought back three more buckets. "This is all for today, folks."

Stifling a groan, Troy flexed his right hand several times. Anyone who stamped envelopes for a living must suffer from carpal tunnel syndrome. Perhaps he'd develop a rhythm before long.

Edie noticed the motion and laughed. "Don't worry. It gets easier. Of course, the volume of cards increases as well. Our volunteers strive hard for the privilege of working for nothing."

The work kept them so busy that Troy had yet to get a good look at whoever used post-office box 1. As soon as he left, he would head to the Drapers' home for the youth planning meeting tonight. He shook his head. His own fault, for offering to help as soon as Will mentioned the need.

"I figured you would." His friend had laughed at him.

Troy ran the stamp over the envelope in front of him. A bill. He prayed for both the business and the payer. If he lifted each letter up to the Lord, he'd keep focused on what was important.

With a prayer for the people each envelope represented, Troy finished the day's work in better spirits. Again he glanced toward the post-office box he was keeping an eye on. Will came in—he had offered to drive Troy to avoid the crush of traffic near the post office—and checked the box. Troy frowned. He thought he had pinpointed the location of the box, but so far he had seen at least three different people check it. He was foolish to think he'd be able to find Aranda H. that way.

Troy stamped the last envelopes in his basket at the same time the others finished. Gathering the metered mail from the outboxes, he headed for the mail bins.

Edie took the envelopes from him. "How was your first day?"

"I didn't know stamping mail was such hard work."

She laughed. "Perhaps I should bring ointment tomorrow. Feel free to get up and move around. You're not chained to that desk." She sorted through the latest stack, quickly tossing them in various bins faster than his eye could keep up. "I'll see you bright and early tomorrow morning, then."

Minutes later, Troy climbed into Will's car.

"I had an underhanded reason for picking you up tonight." Will pulled into the traffic.

White lights outlined candy canes down the main street. Troy was amazed at how much earlier stores began advertising for Christmas every time he returned home, but maybe in a town called Christmas, they celebrated all year long.

"I guessed as much. What's up?"

"The youth group is meeting tonight. How does pizza sound for supper?" Will flashed white teeth.

Troy pretended to groan. "It's my own fault. I did offer to help."

"Tonight is a planning meeting for their booth at the Christmas festival. At least that's what we call it." Will found an opening in the left lane and charged ahead. "Although they do more eating than planning. They toss out all kinds of impossible ideas, like having the quarterback from the Buccaneers come to open the festival. That, or have Justin Bieber perform in concert."

Troy laughed. "That would bring in extra business. So, what can I do to help?"

"You're handy with building things. I figure you can give us guidance as to what's realistic and how to go about getting it done."

"I can do that."

Will stopped by the pizza parlor for a stack of pizzas—pepperoni, pepperoni, and more pepperoni, with a side of plain cheese, as Will put it—and headed for the church.

"Are there any other adult sponsors?"

"Randi Pearson." Will zipped around the car in front of him.

"Randi? How does Michael feel about it?"

"She's worked with the youth group for years. She showed me the ropes when we started here." He glanced at Troy. "She's a guidance counselor at the high school. She's good with kids."

"Just not with her own son?" Troy shook his head. "I guess she's not the first." As they pulled into the church parking lot, he said, "If I weren't here looking for the woman I hope will be my bride, I would accuse you of trying to set me up. Are there any other single women over the age of eighteen who are coming tonight?"

"No. And as much as Faith and I would like to see you happily married, it wouldn't be with Randi. She's as determined to remain single as anyone I've ever met."

Troy wasted a thought wondering why before he climbed out and grabbed the bags of pop. Randi's distinctive car pulled in a couple of spaces down. Michael slouched out of the passenger side and headed for the gym door without looking at his mother. Troy followed him inside.

A couple of guys were already shooting hoops in the gym. Troy spotted Faith in the kitchen. She grabbed a bowl and poured in a bag of ice chips. Randi joined her, scooping ice into plastic cups.

Troy poured out pop after Randi added the ice. Will disappeared to the church office to make copies and then set up a table in front of a whiteboard where he wrote *Christmas Festival* in bold red letters, underlined it twice, and added two exclamation points.

This was Troy's first Christmas stateside in five years. He had spent more holidays in dry desert heat than he cared to remember. Bring it on, all of it: schmaltzy decorations and canned music, kids on Santa Claus's lap, and stores crowded with the latest and best gift ideas. His eyes strayed to Randi and his lips twitched. If he could find Aranda, he'd ask her to show him the best places in town. He couldn't afford to get involved with anyone else. As in combat, focus on the mission's objectives.

By now, about thirty youth jostled around the tables. They cleaned out the pizza boxes like ants carrying away picnic food. Randi brought out a new box, and Troy grabbed two slices. She winked at him. "We still have two pizza pies in back. Take as much as you want."

He signaled okay with his thumb and looked for a place at the table. Michael sat with a pack of boys, nowhere near his mother. Troy had to smile. Like any other teenager, he probably found her presence embarrassing. Grabbing one chair, Troy patted the one next to him and invited Randi to join him.

An expression of—what? Annoyance? Distrust?—raced across her face before she nodded. "Of course."

Will took a final bite of pizza then stood. "Next summer, we're heading to Kentucky to hold Vacation Bible School for a week."

Cheers erupted from the group. "Yeah, mon." Michael droned in a fake Jamaican accent.

"We'll need at least a thousand more dollars this year than last to do everything we want to." A pointer emphasized the words written on the white board. "And our booth at the Christmas festival always gets us off to a good start. But some of you said you'd like to try something new, besides the bake sale and crafts we usually sell. Yes, Maribel?"

One of the girls, wearing clunky glasses, stood and pulled another girl to her feet beside her.

"My folks took me skiing last year."

"The ski trip again?"

Maribel ignored the good-natured jab. "Chelsea, tell them about it."

The girl beside her looked like a cheerleader waiting for the Friday night football game. Her voice projected enough enthusiasm to get the stadium to their feet. When she opened her mouth, melody came out. "Chestnuts roasting on an open fire, Jack Frost nipping on your nose." Switching to speech, a girlish high soprano, she said, "Maribel told me all about these little stalls where they sold hot cocoa and marshmallows and roasted chestnuts, and I thought it sounded like such fun."

"People who pay a dollar for three cookies might pay five dollars for three chestnuts." Maribel argued like the captain of the debate team.

"'Cause it sounds so Christmassy," said Chelsea.

"How do you roast them? They won't let us have an 'open fire.'"

"Traditionally chestnuts were roasted over an open fire, but it's also possible to roast them on a stove top, so that's what we'll do." Maribel's answer turned into a lecture. "We need to buy marrons—that's a kind of chestnut—and soak them in water, and put them in a roasting pan with holes in the bottom." She continued, knowing the answers to all their questions.

Randi shook her head. Troy leaned in close. "What is it?"

"Oh, I tried roasted chestnuts before. I wasn't that impressed. But it's a creative idea."

Will spoke up again. "I hear there's going to be an ice-skating rink. And a cold-weather treat might sound perfect after someone has just gone ice-skating."

"It would be even better if we could have real snow." Michael grinned. "Too bad we live in Florida."

"We could all pray for a freak snowstorm," Will challenged.

"That's not necessary." Troy stood. "I know someone who can lend us a snow machine."

Chapter 4

F or real?" Surprised, Michael forgot his usual disdain. "He'd let us borrow it?"

A hint of a grin fluttered around Troy's mouth. "Sure."

Will raised a cautionary hand. "Let's talk about this. We'd probably need to get permission from the planning committee."

"I promise that won't be a problem." Randi loved the idea of a snow machine.

Maribel lifted a hand. "I've read that it's really easy. It's a great idea, Michael. *Perfect* for roasted chestnuts and hot chocolate."

A gentle pink colored Michael's cheeks at her words, as if he were a gangly freshman unused to a girl's interest. This was interesting. Hadn't she heard Michael call Maribel a Goody Two-shoes? Randi better keep her hands off the situation. That would scare Michael away from a truly nice girl.

"I'm pretty sure my friend would loan us the machine for free. I'll call him when I get home tonight. If he says yes, and it's what we all want to do, I can go up there on my next day off to pick it up."

The youth started rolling the ball with his offer.

"I saw a snow pavilion on one of those reality shows, about a place in Saudi Arabia where you can go skiing inside and build a snowman. Could we do something like that?"

Randi pictured local children stumbling through snow in short sleeves. The grin on Troy's face suggested he was envisioning the same scenario. "Then they'll be plenty cold enough for some of that hot chocolate."

"We'd have to rent more space, maybe for a tent," Maribel suggested.

The kids continued to toss out ideas. Will was good at letting the kids lead, only stepping in when they needed a little nudge in the right direction.

"I'll check on the cost of the supplies." Michael was more eager than any of the kids to bring the snow machine to Christmas. "Will people pay enough for us to make money?"

Randi kept her smile of approval to herself. "Do you remember when we went to one of those snow castles when your father was stationed in Germany? It was a lot of fun. Worth the money." She glanced at Will. "You'll want to do some extra publicity."

"I'll work on that." Chelsea piped up.

When the meeting broke up, all but one slice of pizza was eaten, and all the kids were high-fiving each other. Some estimated how much money a snow booth would raise. All were as excited as kids at the first snow of the year, more excited, since it would be the first snow many of them had ever experienced. She had never seen snow before Mike was posted in Germany. She and Michael had spent hours building a snow family. Did he even remember?

None of it would have happened if Troy hadn't mentioned his friend's machine. She should find some way to thank him.

Her mother called later that night. "How did the meeting go?"

Randi explained about the snow and winter fun the youth had planned.

"What a wonderful idea." After that, conversation moved on to their Thanksgiving plans. "I'm thinking about asking Troy to join us." Her mother frequently invited Christmas orphans to share their holidays.

Randi stalled. "He might already have other plans. . . ." She didn't trust her mother to keep quiet about the identity of Aranda H.

"If he does, we'll invite him over sometime during December. I wonder if he prefers turkey or ham, or maybe even a good roast beef. Some people like beef for Thanksgiving, although it seems strange to me."

"He's eaten canteen rations for years, I'm sure he'll like whatever you serve." Randi interrupted before her mother mentioned every variation on the Thanksgiving menu. She decided to tackle the problematic question head-on. "Has Troy mentioned his reason for coming to Christmas to you?"

"So you know." The ensuing silence shouted as loudly as her mother's previous chatter did. After several seconds, she said, "He's looking for Aranda H."

"You haven't told him anything, have you?"

"Nooo." The drawn-out syllable told Randi how much her silence cost her mother. "Why haven't you?"

"I'm not interested in a boyfriend. Even saying it sounds weird. I'm too old to date. I'm not in high school anymore."

"Nonsense. You're never too old for love."

This coming from the woman who had resisted suitors ever since her husband had deserted them more than twenty years ago?

"I'm not comfortable with this man hunting me down."

"From what I've seen, he's a perfect gentleman. I'm not saying you should run to the courthouse for a wedding license tomorrow, but give him a chance."

"I will, as long as you promise not to reveal my identity. Promise?"

Her mother drew a deep breath. "I promise. For now."

That was the best Randi could hope for.

❄

Troy pushed back from the dinner table, still filled with a cornucopia of culinary delights. "That was. . .amazing." Too many years of Thanksgiving meals as imagined by Uncle Sam made him doubly appreciative of a menu that allowed for some individuality.

"Are you ready for some football?" Michael did an amazing imitation of Hank Williams Jr.

Troy groaned. "Give an old man a few minutes. If you want to watch football, I'm your man."

"Do I get to play?" Randi had tied a brown apron adorned with a brilliant display of fall leaves around her waist. "Don't look so surprised." She flashed a grin. "Since we have more ladies than men in this family, I usually act as a running back." She twisted her body in imitation of the Heisman Trophy.

Troy raised an eyebrow. "I'll have you know that before I retired, I was the reigning running back of football in the desert. So watch out."

Eight people sat scattered around the living room. A couple of other post office orphans were there, as well as some young adults temping at the resorts in nearby Orlando. Troy hung back until everyone else had grabbed a seat. Randi joined him. "So which team do you usually watch? The Lions or the Cowboys?"

Troy shrugged. "Whichever one was playing when I wasn't on duty. I guess, overall, the Cowboys. In some ways they still are America's team."

"Well, grab yourself another slice of pie and find a seat. Rest up, 'cause I'm warning you that my team is going to win our game."

"Then I'll have to be sure I'm on your team."

"I wouldn't count on that. Michael might demand you join him." Merriment sparkled in her eyes.

That would give him a chance to get to know the kid better, but he'd rather spend time with the kid's mother. What business did he have looking for the elusive Aranda H. if he was distracted by the first single woman he met in Christmas? He shook the idea away. "Then we'll have to let the captains decide."

Troy took a seat in time to see the opening kickoff. When he looked around for Randi, he found her in the kitchen. Of course she was washing dishes. She was the hostess. He half rose out of his seat then sank back down for the most American of all Thanksgiving traditions—televised football.

Michael parked himself with the men, but he stayed busy texting on his phone.

"I thought you liked football," Troy said.

Michael glanced up. "The Patriots are my team. I don't care about the Lions."

"The Patriots, huh? That's a long way away from Christmas."

"My father was based at Fort Devens before the war started. He took me to a couple of games." A vulnerable looked flashed through the boy's eyes.

"It must have been tough, losing your dad."

Michael shrugged thin shoulders. "It was a long time ago. It's no big deal."

Time didn't always soften the blow, but Troy left his observation unspoken. Michael returned to texting.

By halftime, the Lions led by two touchdowns, and the competition had turned into a yawner. To avoid falling asleep like an old man, Troy made a circuit of the house. Aside from the Thanksgiving decorations around the dining room table, Christmas had overtaken the house. He wandered down the hall, admiring the multitude of needlepoint designs. They represented hours of work, all for one short season every year. He bent in closer. Each picture was dated and signed, starting the same year he had first heard from Aranda. He wondered if Randi had lost her husband that same year.

Boxes were piled atop a table covered with a pine-green table-cloth, in preparation for some holiday project. Perhaps Randi spearheaded a gift-giving charity at church. In addition to helping with the youth group? He doubted it. Leaning over so he could see inside the boxes, he found Christmas cards, ten full boxes. A printed list of names and addresses sat atop. Glancing at the list, he noticed they all belonged to men and women serving overseas. He ran his finger down the list but didn't recognize any of the names. What were the chances Aranda H. was part of the same outreach? These ten boxes amounted to a tiny percentage, compared to the volume of cards passing through the post office on a daily basis, not to mention the number of people in the military.

A bedroom door opened and Randi exited. She had changed her dressy Thanksgiving sweater for a faded blue-and-red sweatshirt emblazoned with the Patriots' logo. "Game time."

He gestured to the table with the Christmas cards. "This looks like serious business."

Pink flashed in her cheeks. "We like to do our bit to support our troops."

"The cards are welcome. A kind word from home goes a long way in the sand. A picture of a snowy night causes the temperature inside the tent to drop by twenty degrees." A question about Aranda stuck in his throat. If she knew anything, she would have spoken up when Faith brought up the subject.

She tucked her hands beneath her armpits. "I enjoy doing it. It's fun to pick out cards without worrying about being politically correct. A gentle witness." A smile accompanied that statement. "When I think about young soldiers Michael's age out there, so far from family—I want to encourage them."

She opened the door to a hall closet filled with neatly stacked supplies. One basket held a variety of sports equipment, and she dug out a football. "Let's go."

In the living room, Edie was making plans. "Ten people. That makes five on a team."

Angie, one of the college-age volunteers, counted on folded fingers. "I see eleven people."

"I don't play," Edie said.

Michael slipped an arm around her shoulders. "But Grandma,

everybody has to play. That's what you always say." Genuine affection broke through his habitual cynicism.

"Everybody except me. I'm the hostess, so I get to break my own rules. Besides, no one wants my creaky old body on their team. I'll cheer from the sidelines."

Randi tossed the football to Michael, who caught it single-handed. "Now we count off one, two, around the circle. I'm a one."

To his chagrin, that made Troy a two. So was Michael, however, and maybe that was best.

"Guys, a reminder that this is flag football. No NFL tackles, no matter how much you cheered for the Lions today." Randi walked around the circle, passing out blue and yellow rags. "Whoever reaches three touchdowns first will win."

The degree of organization told Troy this was a tradition in the Hathaway household. He tied his yellow band to the back loop of his jeans. "Blue team, prepare to meet your doom."

Chapter 5

A snowball sailed past Randi, reminding her of the Thanksgiving Day football game. Randi straightened her back. Cool air whistled through her blouse and she shivered. "This is amazing."

Troy reappeared from behind the machine. Snow clung to his shoes as he walked across the tent, one leg slipping slightly. He corrected his balance with the instincts of a natural athlete. "I hope we have enough." He had worked up a sweat—despite the fact that they kept the room air-conditioned to prevent the snow from melting prematurely. "The sign looks good."

After Faith volunteered to roast chestnuts and prepare hot chocolate, Randi had stepped in to do the signage. "Too bad we couldn't have done more publicity. I hope word of mouth will bring folks in the longer the festival goes on." For something as simple as the outline of a snowman and a snow fort, it had taken a lot of care and time. Once finished, she advertised online, in the newspaper, as well as the signs at the booth. They had accomplished a lot in the ten days since Troy had confirmed his friend would loan them his machine.

Will came in with several members of the youth group,

Maribel and Michael among them. "Look at this, our own winter wonderland. Let's give a round of applause to Troy for making it possible."

Applause, not as enthusiastic as Randi expected, broke out. Instead, the boys headed straight for the snow and grabbed fistfuls with their bare hands. She ducked as one sailed in her direction.

A wide grin split Troy's face. Beside him, Will had already bent over. Randi grabbed Faith's arm. "We better move out of the line of fire."

After a few minutes of intense horseplay, Will called it to a halt. He dusted off his hands. "That's enough. We need to leave some snow for our customers."

Fallen faces suggested they hadn't thought about that result.

"No harm done." Troy's deep voice boomed out. "What's the fun of having your own snow machine if you don't get to enjoy it?"

The tent flap opened, and a young man appeared with a large red bag on his arm. "Did you folks order pizza?"

"Pizza! Yay!" Michael led the charge on the boxes.

Pizza, again. Randi longed for an occasional change—lasagna or Chinese or something.

"Does anyone want any hot cocoa? We have plenty." Faith tugged her sweater close. "It's chilly in here."

"I'll take you up on that offer." The girls followed Faith to the booth. Maribel began singing, "I'm dreaming of a white Christmas."

"Just like the ones I used to know." Randi joined the song. "It is lovely, isn't it?"

"It's the first time I've ever had a snowball fight." Cheerleader

Chelsea grinned. "Makes the hot cocoa taste that much better."

"So maybe our cocoa sales will go up. Maybe we can go on two mission trips. Or stay longer." Maribel bounced on the heels of her feet. "Can I try a chestnut?"

Smiling, Faith handed them each a single chestnut, and Randi almost dropped the burning nugget. Chelsea popped hers in her mouth then spit it back out. "Ouch."

Maribel blew on hers before biting into it. "Hmm. Interesting. I like pecans better."

"A true Southerner." Randi took a dainty bite. Not bad. Maybe using marron chestnuts gave it that nutty, sweet flavor. "It's a good contrast with the hot cocoa." By the time they finished the cocoa, her insides had warmed enough to venture back inside the snow pavilion.

While the girls were outside, the boys had finished spreading the snow over the floor, but Randi noticed with interest that Troy had started up the snow machine again. Through the canvas she could hear children's excited voices, and she realized with a start that only fifteen minutes remained until their pavilion opened.

Most of the youth group had come out for the first night of the festival. From now until the end of the festival, they would take turns working the tent and booth in shifts. Although the festival ran all week long, the youth would open the snow pavilion on weekends only. Troy was there, of course, keeping an eye on his friend's machine.

On Sunday evening, she would host the Christmas cookie and card party at her house. Between the festival, school events, and students struggling with the holidays, she seldom had a minute to herself for the entire month of December. Next year, since

Michael would be out of high school, she might take a season off.

Michael. She hadn't seen him since the snowball fight before the pavilion opened. He had disappeared, as had his friend Jack. Those two could get into trouble quicker than a rabbit had babies. He was scheduled to work in the morning. She might not see him again until the Sunday party.

Troy joked with the families as they came through the pavilion. He was good with the children, especially for a man without young ones of his own. She should have expected it, after she had seen him interact with the youth.

He caught her studying him during a short lull. Grinning, he packed a ball of loose snow and threw it at her so that it fell apart before it arrived. She reached down to make one of her own, but the girls returned. Shrugging, she dropped the snow onto the ground. His mouth moved in a silent word—*later.*

❄

So far, retirement kept Troy busier than his days in the service. Between the post office and the youth group, he had little time left to locate the elusive Aranda.

Friday night, he had gone straight from work to the snow pavilion, not arriving to his temporary rooms until after midnight. Saturday was filled with chores like laundry and shopping before heading to the festival for the rest of the day. This morning he had gone to church, and this evening, he was going to Randi's home. to help the youth with their annual Christmas card party.

The party offered promise. Perhaps Aranda would attend and reveal herself in some way. Even if she didn't, he could encourage some lonely soldier serving his country in the same way he had been encouraged.

After his years in the military, his civilian wardrobe was simple, a matter of mix and match. He pulled out a green sweater festooned with pine trees from between sheets of tissue paper. Ordinarily he wouldn't wear it until later in December, but he wanted to break it out early this year. He couldn't resist the urge to dress up for no one except Randi and a bunch of teenagers. In this town, he could find a dozen holiday-themed shirts and sweaters if he wanted to. He might even buy one festooned with palm trees.

Since his hair had grown out from the military buzz cut, he tried combing it this way and that. Nothing looked right, so he gave it up as impossible and slicked it back. Silly to get so concerned about his appearance. If that was his focus, he should put on his dress uniform. Women always loved a man in uniform, people said, and he had seen appreciative gleams often enough to know the truth of the statement.

He glanced down at his green sweater and grinned. He couldn't get away from army green, even for Christmas.

Randi's house was located on a quiet side street not far from the post office. Several cars that he recognized had parked in front. He pulled his rental car across the street—he needed to buy a car as soon as he had settled on a permanent home, maybe right here in Christmas. A single strand of lights adorned the eaves of Randi's house, and a tree filled the front window. The yard looked neat, well maintained. How she managed that, with a full-time job, a growing child, and volunteer work with church, amazed him.

Michael climbed in his car as Troy approached. He waved him down. "You're not staying?"

A scowl appeared on Michael's face. "I don't do Christmas cookies and cards. Besides, I haven't seen my friends all weekend."

At least the kid said good-bye before he pulled away.

Randi opened the door before Troy could knock. Her eyes followed the departing car, but all she said was, "Merry Christmas! Come on in." Her eyes took in his sweater, and he was glad he had taken time to dress up.

Christmas carols overlaid with happy chatter greeted him as he came in. He was enjoying his time with the youth of Nativity Community Church. Around them, he forgot some of the memories seared into his brain by war and shed some of the extra years they had added to him. Even if he didn't meet up with Aranda, Troy was glad he had come to Christmas. With his future plans uncertain, perhaps he should try something that involved working with kids.

Several folding tables crowded the living room, each with two or three kids in chairs munching on cookies. Faith and Will had already arrived. "How can I help?"

"We're making work for you, I'm afraid." Randi grinned. "Or someone at the post office. It's fairly simple. We send cards to all the servicemen involved with our church in some way, and then we use lists to send to others as well."

Tall boxes adorned each table. "How many cards do you send out?"

"We started ten years ago with fifty." She giggled self-consciously. "Now it's closer to a thousand, until we run out of cards or time."

Troy arched an eyebrow. "That's an expensive proposition."

"Not really." She shrugged. "People at church give us their

left-over cards. They include stamps with the envelopes. Other people donate money for cards and postage. We mostly just do the work."

Troy picked up a box and leafed through it. Different-sized envelopes with festive stamps filled the space. "I've received a few of these cards, but I never realized how much work was involved." He peeked at a couple of the cards. Some featured funny verses, some winter snow scenes, and some religious. "Are they all different?"

"We have a lot of different designs. We don't like to send the same card to everyone in the same platoon. It seems less personal. The only thing we insist on is that they say 'Merry Christmas' and not 'Happy Holidays'." She turned a concerned face in his direction. "Did that ever bother anyone that you know of?"

Troy thought about it and shook his head. "People were so happy to hear from home, they appreciated the gesture. Some years they decorated the barracks with the cards everyone received."

"Good." She smiled. "Ready to get started?"

"Point me in the right direction." He nodded a greeting at Will and Faith and took a seat next to Maribel. Randi joined them a few minutes later.

"Hey there, Troy." The serious young woman reached for a clipboard with a sheaf of pages and handed him a page with a box of cards. "Here's all you need to get started."

"How do you sign them? Return address?"

"That's up to you. You can sign them from the church if you want to. And you can use PO Box 1 for the return address."

That fact piqued Troy's interest. They used PO Box 1 for the return address?

The same address Aranda H. used in her cards?

His eyes narrowed, settling on Randi. Was it possible. . . ?

If so, why hadn't she introduced herself to him?

Chapter 6

Randi riffled through the stack of papers in front of her at the table. Where was the list of her regular contacts, Major Troy Brennan among them? Opening her mouth, she started to ask. But what if Troy had the list she sought? He'd be sure to ask questions. No, she'd have to find out a different way.

After she checked her list again, she peeked at the pages the others at her table were working on. Troy's hand curled over his sheet, like a student making sure no one could copy his answers. Relaxing the tension in her jaw, she made herself smile and stood. "I need to check something in my office."

A quick glance at the other tables didn't reveal the list. She almost cried with relief when she powered on her computer monitor and discovered the document, set up for print. Grabbing the sheet from the print tray, she tore it into shreds and threw it away.

"So, this is where you keep the brains of the house?"

At the sound of Troy's voice, she jumped in front of the computer and reached back to turn off the monitor. "The brains?" The shakiness of her voice must betray her anxiety.

"If you were in the kitchen, I'd call it the heart. But the computer holds everything we used to store in our heads—or at least our desks." He surveyed the room from wall to wall, and Randi suspected he missed nothing. "Just one small file cabinet. You've taken the paperless viewpoint to heart."

"I try. We lived in some tight space in base housing, and I learned how to make every inch count." The printer spat out a page.

Troy glanced at the printer. "More names?"

"Soldiers I've connected with over the years." His eyebrow raised. Had she revealed too much? "I want to make sure we aren't duplicating names." She lifted the page from the printer, ran her eyes down the page. For some reason the printer had made two copies. "We're not." She laid it facedown on the desktop.

Troy's attention wandered to the books on her shelf. "An interesting assortment: Daniel Silva. . .Karen Kingsbury. . ." He leaned forward. "And quite a collection of John MacDonald's works. I'm impressed."

"MacDonald's character Travis McGee is a Florida icon."

He flashed a grin at her then laid his hand on a haphazard pile of well-worn books. He sifted through the titles. "Aha! I have found your secret passion. *A Christmas Carol, The Best Christmas Pageant Ever,* even *Deck the Halls* by Mary Higgins Clark." He shook his head. "Anyone who lives in a town called Christmas must either love the holiday or grow cynical. You, my dear Randi, most definitely belong in the first group."

"Did the ten-foot tree in the living room give you a hint?" She opened her arms wide. "I confess, I'm hopelessly sentimental about the holiday. And I read my favorite books every year. Mom is the biggest believer in the Christmas spirit that there is. She's a large part of what made the Christmas card traffic what it is."

"Trees, cards, carols, all that was missing was the snow." Troy nodded his head in satisfaction. "And now I've taken care of that."

Her laughter rang out, loud enough to be heard in the living room. "Thank you so much for that. I think everyone at the high school plans on making a run through the snow pavilion before the festival is over. You've given them a chance to experience a traditional Christmas."

Troy placed a hand over his heart. " 'I'm dreaming of a white Christmas.' Bob Wallace, reporting for Christmas duty." He topped off the line with a salute. "Good old Bing Crosby combining patriotism and white Christmases in one tuneful package."

"The song that always brings tears to my eyes is 'I'll Be Home for Christmas.' So many soldier boys, both then and now, never came home for Christmas." She blinked back tears, transported back to that first Christmas after Mike's death.

He moved closer. "Your husband?"

Unable to speak, she nodded. "He died the day after Thanksgiving. Twelve years ago. I've moved on, but. . ."

"This time of year is always hard." His eyes darkened in understanding. "Dreaming of Mom, home, apple pie—and snow—helped keep me sane. I've received Christmas cards from folks back home, like you're sending out tonight. They meant a lot." Those darkened eyes looked at her directly. "On behalf of everyone serving our country, I want to say thank you." He inched forward, close enough to invade her personal space, where she had to look up to meet his eyes. Kissing close.

Heat pushed into her cheeks. Backing away, she cleared her

throat. "You're welcome." The doorbell rang as she was searching for a reason to escape. "I wonder who that could be." She almost ran for the front door.

❄

Troy watched her departure with interest, like a rabbit diving into its hole when a fox grew near. The more time he spent with Randi Pearson, the more he suspected she was the Aranda H. he was seeking. Aranda could shorten to Randi, and the initial H could stand for Hathaway, her maiden name. In addition to that, something about the way she spoke, her passions that came through, ran parallel to what he had discovered of Aranda from their letters.

But if Randi was Aranda, why hadn't she admitted to the connection?

How could he confirm his suspicion? His eyes lit on a calendar, Monday circled in red for "last date for yearbook pictures!"

Yearbooks, of course. The next time he had a chance during the day, he'd visit the high school. He went back to the main room, but Randi wasn't there.

The front door was closed. A little concerned, he peeked through the window. Randi was talking with a police officer. Compelled, he opened the door.

Two police officers stood on either side of a sullen Michael. The male officer, about Troy's age with a similar buzz cut, was talking with Randi in low tones. He stopped speaking when he saw Troy.

Michael saw him at the same time and twisted away from Troy's gaze. He fixed him with his sternest look. The kid could use the discipline of basic training. "Can I help with anything, Officer?"

Randi swiveled to see who was speaking. "Troy. . ." Her voice hovered between shame and plea, demanding and hopeless, all at the same time.

"Are you the father?" A petite Latina barely tall enough to meet the height requirement asked.

"Just a friend of the family." The possibility ran across Troy's mind. The boy would benefit from a father figure in his life.

The young officer, whose name tag read M. GUTIERREZ, returned her attention to Randi and Michael. "We're releasing him into your custody, Mrs. Pearson. And you"—the look Miss Gutierrez leveled on Michael could have stopped a stampeding buffalo in its tracks—"consider yourself warned. You won't get off so easy the next time."

The hunch of Michael's shoulders would look heroic and menacing on a football field. In the moonlit dark, he looked exactly like what he was, a scared boy learning to be a man. At the moment he probably felt like a complete failure. Troy's heart went out to him.

Randi's mouth was stretched in a straight line, and the breath vapors escaping in the chill air could have been steam rising from the fire steeped within her. She looked up at Michael, the boy grown too big to take over her knee and spank.

Aranda had mentioned a teenage son, but she had kept the details of raising a child on her own to herself.

Her mouth twisted, opened, shut, and then opened again. "I feel like locking you in your room and throwing away the key." She managed a shaky laugh. "But that wouldn't accomplish anything. And the youth group is here addressing Christmas cards. I don't want to ruin their fun. But after they leave, we'll talk with Pastor Will. You'll be doing some community service, at the very least."

"Whatever." Michael shuffled inside.

Randi looked at the closed door, pain written in sharp lines on her face. Troy lifted his foot to take a step forward, hesitated, and then walked to her side. "A bad night, huh?"

She lifted watery eyes to meet his. "I don't know what to do with him. Nothing I've tried works. And now the police are involved. . . ."

"Look, I know we only met a few weeks ago." *Unless you're Aranda*. "And I don't have any children. But I like Michael. Community service sounds like a good idea. Will is pretty busy these days, but I have some free time. I'd be happy to work with him, if that's all right with you."

"Are you staying in Christmas after the holiday season is over?" She colored a little. "I know it's none of my business, but I don't want you starting something you can't finish."

"I haven't decided yet. I keep hoping I'll find Aranda." *Please tell me you're the woman I'm looking for*. "We still have four weeks until the New Year. A lot can happen before then. Give me a chance." Why he felt compelled to help Michael, Troy couldn't say. But God was pushing him in that direction.

Randi looked at him a long moment, as if she were weighing him in the balance. "Why don't you meet with Michael and Will and me? And now I'd better get back inside before he escapes again."

He laid a gentle hand on her forearm when she reached for the doorknob. "Thank you."

She turned questioning eyes at him. "I should be thanking you."

"For trusting me with your son. Your most prized possession, so to speak."

"I can't think of anyone better qualified. And I mean it." The tremulous smile she turned on him made him ready to launch a crusade to save her son, to win her heart, whether she was Aranda H. or not.

One thing he knew for certain: God had a reason for him to be in Christmas at Christmastime.

Chapter 7

Edie agreed to Troy's request for an extended lunch hour on Tuesday. Once through the doors, he slipped back to his own high school days, when he was neither athletic enough to be a jock nor smart enough to be a nerd. Only God's grace kept him from making a mess out of his life. The Christmas high school suffered from the same overwrought teenage smell, the silent halls filling with noise loud enough to endanger hearing when the class bell sounded.

The library seemed like the best place to find yearbooks, so he located a map of the school. He needed to go up the stairs and down a long hallway to the right. The guidance offices were to the left; he'd check in with Randi later to set up times for working with Michael.

Troy moved with the flow of the crowd, earning a curious glance from a boy who didn't look old enough to be out of elementary school. They got younger all the time. One girl carried a stack of books with a flute case dangling from her arm, her nose stuck in a book as she walked down the hall. How did she avoid running into anything? She turned into the doorway where Troy expected to find the library.

When he entered the room, the girl had set her books down behind the circulation desk and was booting up the computer. He approached the desk, but she ignored him.

Smiling to himself, he decided to look for the yearbooks on his own. After a few minutes, he found a bookcase with volumes stretching back for the past forty years. Estimating Randi's age to be close to his own, Troy took out volumes from a five-year span and found a seat on a chair that would have worked in a living room. A boy sat on a nearby chair, chin nodding in sleep. He probably belonged in class, but if the girl at the front desk could ignore him, so could Troy.

Opening the first book, he paged through it without finding anything. How much had Randi changed in the past two decades? Still trim, her hair was its original blond as far as he could determine, he expected her to be recognizable. In case "H" wasn't her last initial, he scanned all the pictures. The faces, pop culture references, hair styles, and fashions all looked familiar from his own high school days. Strange how dated they looked now.

When he reached the *H*'s, he slowed down. Three pictures in, Randi's face stared up at him. He scanned the details. Activities: volunteer work at a local children's shelter, debate team, class secretary. His eyebrows rose at that detail. Future plans: college at Florida State; marriage to the marine of her dreams, Mike Pearson; a career in social work.

At last he forced himself to look at the name under Randi's photo: Aranda Hathaway.

He had all the proof he needed. Randi Pearson and Aranda H. were the same person. For some reason, she didn't want him to know.

Until she told him to leave, he would seek to court Ms. Randi Pearson.

❄

"She's in Spanish class now." Will had called Randi, trying to get in touch with Maribel. "I'll get a message to her." She picked up the phone but decided she'd like a change from her desk. She stood and walked through the nearly empty halls, enjoying the chance to stretch her legs. She waited by the door until the bell rang and stopped Maribel on the way out. "Will asked me to get you a message. Can you give him a call at church, during your lunch?"

"Sure!" Maribel stopped by her locker for her trumpet—band practice. "The snow pavilion has been so neat. Everybody's talking about it."

"That's great." Randi spotted Troy, his face breaking into a smile the moment he saw the two of them. Before she had a chance to question his presence, he had reached them. "Maribel, Randi." Although he greeted both of them, he had eyes only for Randi.

"Hey, Troy." The bell rang. Maribel shut the door to her locker. "Gotta run. I'm going to be late for band." She walked down the hall, blond hair bouncing on her shoulders, cell phone pinned to her ear.

"How do they get any learning done, when everybody has one of those contraptions at their fingertips these days?"

"The same way they always did. With dedicated teachers, ingenious ways to engage students, some students who want to learn, and some who resist. And Maribel is one of the former.

She's doing well." She turned to Troy. "But what are you doing here?"

"I wanted to see you, of course." When he grinned like that, she smiled along with him. "Edie gave me extra time for my noon break. I thought we could finalize plans for Michael's community service, and then maybe we can catch some lunch?"

His attention gave her a fit of giggles. Covering her mouth with her hand, she stifled the mirth. "I have to be back in the office before long, but you're welcome to join me in the teachers' lounge. I'd be happy to share my tuna salad with you."

"Sounds delightful." He fell into step beside her.

A couple of kids glanced at Troy a second time, but she didn't assign any meaning to it. He exuded authority, the kind that would tickle the antennae of the guilty to think "cop" or "security guard." A few feet past the guidance offices, she opened the door to the teachers' lounge. Inside, attention sharpened. Belatedly Randi wondered if she had just started the rumor regarding her and Troy. The flush warming her cheeks wouldn't help, but no one asked. The physics teacher stood and offered them his table. "I'm finished. I want to grade some tests before next period."

Randi claimed the space with her file folder then headed for the fridge. "Coffee's free, or you can get pop from the machine."

"Coffee sounds good." Troy studied the snack machine.

She found an unused plate over the sink and divided her banana in half and added half of her sandwich. "It's not much, but. . ."

He tossed a couple of bags of chips onto the table. "Ah, but it's fresh, and the company can't be beat." He held her chair. "We'll talk about Michael later. When we have a little more privacy." He spoke in low tones, matching the quiet murmur in the room.

Sometimes the staff lounge rang with laughter, but other times, like today, people withdrew into their private worlds, rebuilding strength to face the afternoon. Students and staff alike grew on edge the closer the winter break approached. "I have an appointment right after lunch today, but if you want to schedule an appointment. . ."

"Or we could talk about it someplace else. Maybe over dinner?"

Troy was asking her on a date. Wasn't he? She blinked while her brain scrambled for an answer. In the years since Mike's death, she'd dated a few men, but the experience left her drained. In fact, her husband was the only man she'd let close to her since her father had deserted her as a teenager.

There was no future with Troy. He would be gone by the time the New Year rolled around. What harm could it do to share a dinner and discuss what to do about Michael? She'd be fine as long as she remembered they were colleagues, two people who cared about her son's future, nothing more.

He waited for her answer, undisturbed by her delay in answering.

"Dinner sounds nice."

He relaxed, and she realized he was more nervous than he appeared. "Does tonight work?"

She frowned. "I'm supposed to make some phone calls for church. . . ." Her voice trailed away. She shouldn't put him off. She could find an excuse every night of the week. "I'll do that another night. Tonight sounds good." The bell rang. "Sorry. I've got to go."

"I'll take care of the trash." He swept the debris into her lunch sack. "I'll pick you up at seven."

What had she just agreed to? She had nothing to wear.

Randi felt like she was a fifteen-year-old going out on her first date all over again.

❄

Troy convinced Randi to go on a second date with him on Saturday evening, after a morning and afternoon at the Festival. Their dinner on Monday night had lingered until close to midnight, conversation leaping their relationship forward in hours instead of what might otherwise have taken weeks. Knowing Randi and Aranda were the same person cleared the way for his heart.

When Randi agreed to another date, Troy felt better than he had in years. He would have taken her out Tuesday, Wednesday, and every night in between. Two problems stood in the way: he didn't think Randi would agree, and they both had other time commitments.

One commitment he enjoyed was the time he spent with Michael. They had spent two afternoons grooming the church grounds, trimming the bushes, and watering the grass. Troy watched him work, snapping a reminder when he slacked. He still needed supervision, but he arrived on time and worked hard. Unfortunately, the same friend Randi had said was a troublemaker picked him up afterward on both days. Michael was treading water, nothing more, no significant changes. Troy continued to pray about the situation.

He had seen Randi a few times since Monday, of course. She stopped by the post office on the days he wasn't working with

Michael. Troy allowed himself to imagine she wanted to see him, if only for a few seconds. A smile broke out on her face, and she waved when she saw him in the workroom.

The closer the days grew to Christmas, the more hours the volunteers worked. Edie warned the hardest days would come after the fifteenth. With practice, Troy became faster, processing more cards in less time, so he hoped it wouldn't get too bad.

After the first weekend in the snow, when Troy's hands had grown numb from the cold several times, he ordered hand warmers. He wondered if the first weekend would have dulled some of the interest. Instead, interest had increased. When he arrived to crank up the snow machine, lines had already formed.

The first family in line had brought a large bag full of hats, scarves, mittens, and other snowman-making equipment. They had enough to clothe an entire snow family. The sight brought back memories of Troy's Oklahoma childhood; the rare snow days numbered among his favorite holidays, although his mother might disagree. He wouldn't mind joining the family and putting his old expertise to work.

"Hey there." Randi approached, waving. A pretty blue beret rested on her head with a matching scarf tied artfully around her neck. Glancing around for Michael, Troy spotted him down the block with a group from the church, as far away from his mother as possible. At least he had shown up; changing his attitude would come with time.

Unlike the adults, Michael hadn't brought winter gear, nor had most of the other youth. Troy suspected he might have to order more hand warmers before next week.

Within fifteen minutes of opening the pavilion, Troy had

given out all the hand warmers. The afternoon flew by, the line longer when Will and Faith took over than at the beginning of the day. Randi gave Troy a thumbs-up sign as she helped bundle up a new family headed for the snowball area. Once he had handed off the next group to Will, he went outside before he was drawn into helping someone else.

While waiting for Randi, Troy scanned the field for Michael. He searched his mind for what the kid was wearing. A black T-shirt, he decided, with some kind of tasteless logo on the back. Why did a kid with so much going for him insist on reaching only the lowest expectations? Many teens followed the pattern: Whatever mattered most to parents, their children flirted with the opposite behavior. Will insisted most of them came back full circle to share their parents' values, tweaked a little. He pointed out that even Jesus had tested Mary and Joseph when they went to the temple.

If Troy pursued a relationship with Randi, he would become a father overnight. Did he feel up to the challenge? Would a high schooler on the verge of adulthood accept him in that role? Until he met Michael in person, he hadn't understood the difficulties facing him as a stepfather.

Down the line of booths, in front of a stall where they could ring the bottle, a group of black-garbed kids loitered. Michael was in their midst. Some younger children who had engaged in a lively snowball fight inside the pavilion an hour earlier came up behind them, headed for the game.

Michael's friend Jack blocked the path. The smallest of the girls backed away, hanging behind one of the boys. The biggest and bravest of the younger boys tried to run around the teens, but the teens circled the children.

Troy had seen enough. He headed their way, his pace increasing with each step. He hoped his approach would discourage a direct confrontation. Though not in uniform, Troy knew how to make his presence felt. By the time he had closed half the distance, the ringleader of the teens noticed him, and they melted away. Troy arrived seconds later.

"Thanks, mister!"

"Are you guys okay?" Troy ignored the adrenaline pumping through his veins, urging him to pursue the gang.

"We're cool." With the teens gone, the biggest boy asserted his dominance.

"Find your parents. Do you know where they are?"

One by one each child nodded. They scattered, and Troy watched until he was certain of their safety. By the time they were settled, he had lost sight of Michael.

"There you are." Randi called from in front of the pavilion.

Slowly Troy turned.

Should he tell Michael's mother about what her son was up to?

Chapter 8

Randi didn't need any of her finely tuned emotional sensors to know something was troubling Troy. When she spotted him down the street, he had transformed from the fairly easygoing man she had come to know to a soldier tensed for battle. But as she watched, he relaxed his stance. Another thing to consider with an ex-soldier: did he suffer from PTSD? Many veterans dealt with some kind of stress, even those who made a successful return to civilian life.

"Let me drop off my coat." Troy helped Randi remove her coat, and she tossed it in the front seat of her car. She exchanged her jacket for a sweater. When he held the sweater out to her, she shook her head. "Just around my shoulders." His hands landed lightly on her shoulders, warming her where they touched.

"If you don't mind, I thought we would walk to the restaurant."

Randi glanced in the direction Troy pointed, toward the center of town. Festival revelers lined the sidewalks, and street parking was blocked off. "Good idea." She fingered the cotton-wool blend of her slacks. "I'm not dressed for that venue."

Troy turned his attention on her, all warmth and appreciation in his eyes. "You look fine to me. I, for one, would enjoy something besides pizza and burgers for supper."

Her laughter rang out. "So true. I worry I'll turn into a slice of pizza, pointed at the top and broad at the bottom." She put her hand over her mouth. Had she really just said that?

Throwing his head back, he laughed. "You'll never resemble a slice of pizza. Perhaps an apple core. . ." His face reddened.

"Thank you. I think." Randi thought about an apple core and decided it was a unique way to say she had an hourglass, Barbie-like figure. What every guy dreamed of, and what every woman despaired of having. Heat flamed her face, until she expected the red spots on her cheeks matched Troy's.

They looked at each other and started laughing. "Okay. If I'm an apple core, then you're a. . ." She narrowed her eyes, thoughts deserting her. "Maybe you're the slice of pizza. Broad in the shoulders, narrow at the hips. . ." Her face grew even warmer. She was describing him in terms one might apply to a male model. She wished she could see him in his uniform. He would strike a handsome figure.

"Let's stop talking about food. I'm getting hungry." His eyes laughed, and she relaxed. He hadn't taken offense at her description. "And here is the restaurant."

Since the hour was early, they had the restaurant largely to themselves. Troy scanned the menu. "What do you recommend?"

"I don't think I've been here before." *Never.* Even the appetizers cost twelve dollars, and a hamburger went for twenty. "What do you like?"

"It's been quite a while since I had a good steak. I learned to appreciate lamb and lentils, but nothing beats steak and potatoes."

After a quick study of the menu, he chose the most expensive item, a surf and turf combo.

With the least expensive item running into double digits, Randi decided to throw caution to the wind. She settled on a risotto appetizer followed by lobster for a main course. The waiter offered them the wine list, and Randi was pleased when Troy politely refused. They both settled for sparkling water. Even that felt ridiculously indulgent.

While they waited for their appetizers, Troy steepled his hands. "I've enjoyed spending time with you away from the youth group. They're great, and Will is doing a terrific job, but. . .a little goes a long way."

"Like wasabi." They had discussed some of their food preferences on Monday night.

The waiter appeared with their appetizers. Troy speared a scallop and slowly chewed, making appreciative noises. After he finished, he said, "So, Edie is your mother. Do you have any brothers or sisters?"

"It depends."

Confusion crossed his face. "Isn't that a yes or no question?"

"I have half-brothers somewhere. After Dad deserted us, we learned he had another family somewhere up in the panhandle. But I've never met them and don't have any interest in finding them."

"Your father left you?"

She set down her fork. "It's not something I like to talk about."

"I didn't mean to pry." He addressed himself to a second scallop. "As for my family. My parents still live in Yukon, Oklahoma."

"Siblings?" She turned his questions back on him.

"One sister. She lives near the folks."

"Did you enter the service right after high school?"

"I went to college for a year. Unfortunately I majored more in partying than in my studies, and I lost my scholarship." He shrugged. "My father gave me a choice: join the army or come home and work on the farm." After he chewed the scallop, he followed it with a drink of water. "What about you? You must have gone to college, working as a guidance counselor like you do."

"I earned both bachelor's and master's degrees. It took a long time between Mike's transfers and the baby. I finally graduated the May before September 11." Promise had filled those months, Michael ready to start school, Mike stationed in Alabama. Then Mike shipped out. . . Randi didn't like thinking about those dark days.

"And then things changed." Troy understood.

"I was looking for a job, and Mom told me about an opening here in Christmas. One thing led to another. I've had no reason to regret it. And having Mom around has been a lifesaver."

The waiter removed their appetizer plates and replaced the basket of cheddar biscuits. "Your entrees will be ready shortly."

After he left, Troy continued their conversation. "It must have been tough, widowed and with a young son to raise."

She shrugged. "It happens." It was a risk all military families accepted as part of the conditions of service.

"But until it happens to you, you don't know what it's like." Compassion shone from his eyes.

"God is faithful. He gave me good people to help me through. But I can't help wondering"—she swallowed some of the water and licked her lips—"if Michael would have gotten into so much trouble if his dad had been around."

Troy didn't offer any easy answers. "Perhaps, but he has to make his own choices. And you've done a good job with him. He understands the difference between right and wrong."

The conversation flowed back and forth between them while they enjoyed their entrees. Randi refused a desert, but Troy insisted on sharing his cheesecake with her. More than three hours passed by the time they finished and he walked her back to her car.

"Thank you for a lovely evening, Randi." Troy bent over her, bringing her even closer. "Let's do it again. Soon." He closed the distance, capturing her lips with his.

❄

Fool. A man supposedly searching for the elusive Aranda H. had no good reason to date Randi Pearson, let alone kiss her. Not without telling her he knew her identity.

Not to mention allowing juvenile delinquent bullies to escape his grasp. Troy had to talk with Michael. Half a dozen times during the evening, he started to tell Randi about the scene he had witnessed, but something held him back. He might not tell her, unless Michael failed to show up for the agreed-upon community service.

After wrestling in prayer about the situation, Troy managed to put it out of mind during Sunday worship until their next appointment. He had arranged to work early hours three days a week so he could meet up with Michael after school. On Monday, he ducked out of the post office at three on the dot and drove for the snow pavilion. Michael was scheduled to clean up after the weekend's festivities.

Michael wasn't there when Troy arrived. If he didn't show up, Troy would have to clean the pavilion by himself. He was walking the perimeter, making sure the tent was still securely anchored to the ground when Michael found him.

"Hey."

Take it slow. Troy finished checking the patch of tent before straightening. "You're here. Good. Let's go see how bad it is inside."

"I noticed some trash by the entrance."

"I've got trash bags in my car."

Michael worked with a will, a silent apology for his behavior on Saturday night. They finished cleaning, inside and out, in short order, leaving forty-five minutes of service time. Rather than heading back to the church, Troy decided to have a serious discussion with Michael at a neutral setting.

He avoided the restaurant where he had dined with Randi; few teenagers would appreciate the fine cuisine. Debating, he headed for a coffee shop. Maybe the promise of coffee would imply trust in Michael's maturity.

Michael surprised him by ordering peppermint cocoa. "They only have this at Christmastime."

Troy ordered a pumpkin spice latte at an inflated price. One sip told him it wasn't worth the money. "I should have got one of those as well."

"Pumpkin pie is okay on the plate. But I don't like drinking it."

Was that a joke? Troy allowed himself a small smile. He drew two shortbread cookies from their sheath and handed one to Michael. One bite melted in his mouth.

He had avoided the touchy subject as long as possible. "About Saturday night."

Michael pushed his chair back. "I. . .We. . ."

"You and your friends aren't a gang, not into drugs and violence and all that. But you're headed that way. One strong squall will blow you in that direction."

"They're just guys I pal around with. People who don't expect me to be perfect."

Michael wasn't a PK, a preacher's kid, but in some ways he had it worse: war hero's son. Mother a guidance counselor, a professional at helping troubled teens. Grandmother the postmaster of the town. Probably had attended church every week since his birth. "You have a lot to live up to."

Michael snorted then buried his nose in the cup. The silence between them stretched. Michael stirred the cocoa with a candy cane. "Are you going to tell my Mom?"

Troy made himself take a long swallow of the latte. "What do you want to do with your future, Michael?"

The question sidestepped the issues of guilt and expectations. With luck, it would open Michael's eyes to consequences and possibilities. "Because I think you want more out of life than scaring little kids out of their spending money."

Red flooded his cheeks at Troy's rebuke.

Troy tapped his fingers on the table. Should he make the suggestion? Risk angering the woman he hoped to marry? Looking at Michael's despairing, lost expression, he knew he must.

"It wasn't all that long ago when I fought my father at every turn. I couldn't wait to leave the farm."

Michael's expression suggested he didn't quite believe it.

"I know. I've changed. God changed me. One thing made the biggest difference in changing me from an angry farm boy to a man with the world to choose from."

Michael finished the cocoa and set down the cup. "The army."

Troy nodded. "Have you ever considered enlisting?"

Chapter 9

Knowing Troy was watching out for Michael made the Christmas season much easier for Randi. The jangle of her cell phone and ringing of the doorbell no longer caused her heart to jump into her throat with worry. She didn't have any more free time, but she was so much more relaxed, she seemed to get twice as much done.

Tonight she would tackle her remaining Christmas cards, ones that she wanted to include a personal note with. The night of the Christmas card party, when the police arrived on her doorstep with Michael, she hadn't accomplished much at all. Feeling more at ease now, she decided to finish the task.

The third name down was a familiar one: Major Troy Brennan. Would he think it strange if he *didn't* receive a card from Aranda H.? Should she send him two cards, one from Randi Pearson, the postmaster's daughter whom he had dated a few times? As well as one from Aranda H.?

No. By Christmas she would have had enough time to make up her mind about Troy. She wanted to like him, to welcome his courtship. She liked and trusted him more than she did any man she had met since Mike's death. But he hadn't given her any hint of his future plans. She had moved enough with Mike; she didn't want to leave her hometown, her family, Mom as she grew older. She wanted to provide a stable home base for Michael as well, whatever his plans after high school.

At Randi's urging, Michael had completed an application for the local community college. The sloppy job he did on the form betrayed his lack of real interest.

Maybe Troy was waiting to make a commitment until he had found Aranda H. And Randi/Aranda was waiting for a commitment from him before revealing herself. What a mess.

Randi dug through the assorted cards, looking for the right one. Three quarters of the cards featured a biblical scene, a clear but simple explanation of the Gospel, impersonal but appropriate for anyone. Now that she knew Troy, others caught her eye. One showed Santa waterskiing behind a boat filled with Christmas toys—so very Floridian. A sentimental card with a World War II theme said "I'll be home for Christmas." That brought their earlier conversation to mind. The problem was it might reveal the personal connection that had grown between them over the past few weeks. In the end, she chose one of the Holy family with a verse about connecting with friends and family.

She addressed the card without signing it and added a religious stamp. Folding the flap over, she set it in the outgoing mail holder on her desk. The minute hand read half-past seven. She was glad she had leftover chicken meat to throw together in a quick meal.

The front door rattled. Michael must have returned.

"Mom?" he called from the front room.

"Randi?" The first time Troy came in with Michael had

surprised Randi. After all, Michael wasn't a preschooler who might get lost between the street and the front door. Randi decided Troy's sense of responsibility ran in hyperdrive, above and beyond his commitment to supervise Michael's community service.

On those occasions, Troy hadn't lingered. Tonight he removed his coat and added it to the coatrack, next to Michael's letter jacket. Troy laid a hand on Michael's shoulder, man-to-man style.

"You two look like you've had a day of it."

"He did a great job, cleaning up from the festival," Troy boasted, as proud as if Michael had served a thousand hot meals to the homeless on Christmas Day. "In fact, he's doing so well, he could probably get a job doing odd jobs around the church when he's done."

Michael didn't bolt for the door at that statement. Would wonders never cease?

"Come sit at the kitchen table, while I start on supper." Randi pulled the cubed chicken out of the freezer. Hot, hearty soup went with winter weather. She decided on chicken tortilla, easy to fix and one of Michael's favorites.

Michael sat in his chair backwards, staring at the floor. Both waited in unnerving silence while she chopped onion and garlic.

"Something is up." She stirred vegetables into the chicken broth. "Out with it."

"Mom." Michael lifted his gaze from the floor and turned the chair around so he was facing the right direction.

His demeanor alarmed her more than his silence. Turning down the burner, she joined the men at the table. Michael managed to meet her eyes. Troy sat back, staying neutral.

"I did something today. Something I'm proud of." He bit off

the last word. He wasn't talking about something that would land him in the county jail, but that left a lot of ground. "I enlisted in the army today."

Randi stared without speaking. Troy stood and turned off the stove before rejoining them at the table.

Swallowing, she broke the silence. "You did what?"

"That's not all." Michael didn't repeat his incredulous words. "Since I'm already eighteen, and I've got all the credits I need to graduate, I'm leaving once I finish this semester. I'm bored here, Mom. You keep telling me I need to grow up. Well, I think this is the way to do it."

Randi had always held up Mike as a good role model, but the military was his life, not hers. She had never suggested their son should follow in his footsteps. She focused on Troy. "Did you put him up to this?"

❄

Inside, Troy flinched at the anger in Randi's voice. She sounded betrayed, disappointed.

"I told him some of the mistakes I made when I was his age and how joining the army turned my life around."

"And that gave you the right to tell my son what to do?"

"He didn't tell me, Mom. I did something else stupid."

Good, he's decided to tell his mother about what happened. Troy didn't want to betray his confidence, but she needed to know about it.

"What else did you do? Steal an iPod this time?" The police had caught him shoplifting a CD from his favorite rock group.

"Mom!" The universal cry of the unjustly accused. He

grabbed a can of Coke from the fridge. "It was something different. I was with my friends."

"You mean Jack Spader? That bunch?"

Michael kept his eyes averted from Troy. *Good, kid. No taking the easy way out.*

"Yeah, them. They—we—started roughing some young kids."

A little color leached from Randi's face. "You were bullying small children. Oh, Michael."

He shrunk at her evident disappointment.

"What happened?"

Troy decided it was time to speak up. "I left the pavilion a few minutes before you did, and I saw what was going down. I convinced them of the error of their ways."

Randi's gaze swung from Troy to Michael and back again.

"I have to thank you. Again. It's like you have Michael on a special GPS tracker that alerts you when he's in trouble."

Troy struggled to keep from chuckling. It was clear that Randi didn't find it funny. "God made our paths cross at a few important times, that's all."

"Like today, when he signed up for the army?" She crossed her arms over her chest and glared at Michael. "Do you know when you'll leave?"

"Not yet, but it might be soon."

"I'll be home for Christmas." She sang the single line like a low howl. "Fix yourselves bologna sandwiches if you're hungry." Standing, she disappeared down the hallway in the direction of her bedroom.

A dejected Michael sat at the table. Troy felt like he had trampled on sacred ground, where he didn't belong. The least he could do was finish fixing the meal. Ah, she had tacked a recipe card on the fridge with a magnet. He tasted the broth and decided she had already sprinkled in spices. After he added chicken, he spread tortilla strips on a baking sheet to crisp them and grated Mexican cheese into a bowl. As the soup bubbled, his mouth watered.

"Monday night football?" He asked Michael, who was busy studying the material the recruiting officer had given to him.

"I guess. None of the Florida teams are playing."

"We were just glad to watch American football, no matter what teams were playing." Troy shrugged. "If you like football, it's okay. Do you play?" He lifted his hand. "I know you're not on the team. But there are other places to play."

"A pickup game now and then." Michael poured the drinks and disappeared into the living room.

Randi came out of the bedroom. "I'm sorry I was so curt earlier. You have been an enormous help, to both of us. And you're right. It might be the best thing for him." She poured herself a glass of tea. "But I don't know if I'm ready for my son to leave the house one morning and never come home to stay again." She set down the cup. "He'll be so far away." Her voice wobbled.

Troy put down the bowls and took her hands in his. "I'm sure my mother felt the same way." He willed her to understand.

"A mother holds on tight to the little guy who only exists in her mind." She swallowed. "But it's a smart decision. It won't be easy for me, but I'll try."

Michael came in and hugged his mom. Troy could only watch. Comforting a widow or encouraging a fellow soldier never felt like this.

This was love. Pure and simple.

Chapter 10

For the third weekend of the festival, Randi, Troy, and Michael drew the evening shift at the snow pavilion. Troy convinced them to join him for ice-skating on Saturday afternoon.

"I can't believe I'm doing this." Randi pulled rental skates over her feet. "These are even worse than roller skates. That tiny blade is supposed to hold all my weight?"

Michael laughed. "Have you ever watched ice hockey, Mom? Those guys put plenty of pressure on their skates. Remember the joke, I went to a fight and a hockey game broke out?"

That earned him a laugh. "So they skate and throw punches at the same time. I guess I can trust the blades to hold me up."

Troy skated across the ice in their direction. He had an athlete's physique, powerful muscles rippling beneath his sweater. "You made it!"

Few enough evenings were left before Michael's scheduled departure date. He took his last final on Tuesday. Randi felt sad that he wouldn't attend his graduation, but Michael didn't share her regrets. Excitement about his future crowded out sorrow. He didn't notice—he shouldn't notice—how her mood darkened as his brightened.

Mom planned an extra day off next week—unheard of before Christmas day—for a family trip to Disney World. Troy factored into a lot of their remaining time together. Randi tried to balance time alone with her son and time with the three of them.

She felt as confused as ever about Troy. He still hadn't mentioned any plans for staying in Christmas past the New Year. Neither had he mentioned Aranda H. for a while, seemingly content to spend as much time as possible with Randi and Michael.

This Saturday afternoon was one of those times.

"I can't believe you're doing this." Michael stepped onto the ice a few steps ahead of Randi, making a show of turning backward.

She grabbed hold of the rink fence and stood. Her ankles wobbled. "I don't like this." Panic colored her voice.

"You haven't come before?" Troy stopped by her side while Michael skated away. "I thought the ice rink was a staple of the festival."

"I've volunteered at the booth before. Does that count?" She tried to laugh it off.

Troy took her hands in his. "I'll show you how." He glided backward, as comfortable in skates as in his stocking feet.

She looked down, gliding her right foot forward and pushing with her left foot. Her legs spread apart, throwing her off balance. Troy hooked his arms under her shoulders and helped steady her on her feet. "Oops. Thanks for catching me."

"Any time." The warmth in his voice could melt the ice. He slid his hands down her arms until they were holding each other's hands again.

A hunched-over Michael sped by, creating a breeze that rippled Randi's sleeve. Her legs swayed in time to the music streaming over the loudspeaker, the Trans-Siberian Orchestra's rendition of "Carol of the Bells."

"I'm skating!" She glanced at her feet and her left leg wobbled.

"Whoa. Keep your eyes on me." Troy exerted pressure on her hands and picked up the pace a slight bit. "That's it. Glide, don't step. You've got it."

Michael whizzed past a second time and gave them a thumbs-up sign. Confidence surged through Randi, and she began moving in time with Troy, his legs matching hers stride for stride.

On the second trip around, Randi caught sight of Michael chatting with Maribel while she pulled on her skates. News of Michael's departure for the army had spread through high school and church since he had enlisted. As far as she knew, he had cut off contact with his questionable friends. Watching him with Maribel made her wonder "what if?"

What if? That was the question of the hour. What if she had told Troy she was Aranda H. right away? Troy had proved himself worthy of her trust over and over, but she didn't know how to tell him she was Aranda H. after so much time had passed.

Troy's fingers exerted a gentle pressure on her hands. He released first one, then two, then all of the fingers of her left hand. They skated that way for a few minutes before he dropped her second hand, and for a moment, she felt as alone as the man on the moon. Troy skated back toward her and took his place on her right, tucking his arm around her waist and entwining her hand with his.

The picture they formed was as classic Americana as a Currier & Ives engraving, except with four walls instead of evergreen trees framing the ice pond. A muff covering their joined hands couldn't have felt any more intimate. Could Troy forget about Aranda H. and fall in love with Randi Pearson?

She wanted to capture every moment they had together before he left, if he left. She decided to ask. It was a reasonable question, after all. "Have you decided what you are going to do once the Christmas rush is over and you're no longer needed at the post office?"

"That depends." Troy smiled.

Randi ground her teeth. Where was the definite yes or no answer she wanted, before she gave him any more of her heart?

"I'll be here through the end of the festival, since that's only an extra week past Christmas. After that, things are still up in the air."

Randi tamped down a disappointed sigh. Relax and enjoy the moment, she reminded herself. Next week, Michael would leave for basic training. Within two weeks, Troy would leave Christmas to pursue his post-army career. All she could do was enjoy today.

Randi looked up at Troy and stepped back into their Currier & Ives moment. Michael and Maribel skated by, Michael showing off a few special moves. She wanted the afternoon to stretch forever.

All too soon they had to leave for their evening at the snow pavilion. Troy headed for one of the food booths while Randi and Michael claimed a table behind the youth booth where they served the hot cocoa and roasted chestnuts.

Randi's legs quivered from the seldom-used muscles. Michael lounged in front of her, one foot on the bench. Business buzzed in front of the booth, creating a pocket of privacy between them.

"Mom?" Michael pierced her with hazel eyes that always

reminded her of his father.

Any sentence that started with that single word sent shivers up her arms. "Yes?"

"I know you haven't wanted to date much since Dad died."

Randi drew in her breath. "Your father was a special man."

"I just wanted you to know that. . .I wouldn't mind having Troy for a father." Michael removed his shoe from the bench. "Not that it's any of my business."

Randi blinked back the tears that glittered in her eyes. "When did you get so smart?"

"Since Troy came into our lives?" Michael flashed a cockeyed grin at her. "You don't have to worry about me anymore, Mom. I'll going to be all right."

"I always knew that. God loves you too much to let you go too far." She reached out a hand and gently touched his cheek. "I just lost sight of that fact every now and then. As well as the fact my little boy has become a man."

"Thank God for Troy."

"Thank God for what?"

Randi twisted from her seat on the bench and saw Troy approach, bearing hot dogs with all the fixings. "Thank God for the food. And for you braving the crowds." She scooted down the bench, but her legs protested at the effort. "I won't be able to walk for a week."

"Too bad, because I have plans with you before then." Troy winked.

❄

December 26. Where had the time gone? If Troy felt like the time between Michael's enlistment and departure had flown by, how much more so must it seem to Randi. He counted it a privilege that they invited him to join them on this difficult day, especially when Michael's grandmother said her good-byes early. She privately told Troy it was too painful to say good-bye to her grandson at the station. He waited with them, mother and son, for the recruiter who would drive him to basic training.

Troy held on to the handles of a shopping bag with Michael's going away/Christmas present inside. He hung back, allowing mother and son a few private moments. Michael already looked more mature, ready to defend freedom, family, honor, country. Randi stepped back and patted Michael's chest, looking up into her son's eyes, probably wondering when he had grown so tall. Michael grabbed her and pulled her close, the impulsive hug of the young boy he had once been.

Troy turned away, not wanting to embarrass the young man with his attention. Shuffling feet suggested the two had moved apart. Troy looked up in time to see them heading in his direction. As Michael approached, Troy stood to attention and saluted the young soldier. Somewhat self-consciously, Michael returned the salute, and then they both relaxed.

"I brought you this." Troy handed the shopping bag to Michael. He glanced at his duffel; Troy had helped him pare down what to bring with him.

"Don't worry. This won't take much room. I consider both of them essential to my kit."

"Go ahead and open your gifts." Tear tracks showed on Randi's face, but her voice remained steady.

Michael held the smaller gift next to his ear and shook it. Tearing off the wrapping revealed a plain white box. When he opened it, he found a standard compass.

"Until the army gets you one," Troy explained. "So you can always find your way back home. Think of it as your Jack Sparrow compass."

"The one that points to what you want most in the world," Randi whispered.

"Well, thanks." Michael dropped the wrapping paper into the bag, zipped the compass in one of the pockets of the duffle bag, and ran his fingers over the second present. "It's a book."

Troy just smiled.

Michael pulled the paper away to reveal a small volume bound in camouflage-patterned leather. Troy had a Bible just like it, almost pocket size, extra-thin pages in a book small enough to slip into his pocket. The ease of transporting it more than made up for the tiny print. "I guess this is supposed to point me to God."

"You got it."

"Thanks to both of you, I believe God is directing my steps again." Michael gestured with the Bible. "Thanks." He grasped Troy's hand in a firm shake. "Thanks for coming. I'm glad Mom doesn't have to be alone after I leave."

The recruiter pulled up in his car. Michael looked at Randi, neither one of them willing to repeat the earlier emotional exchange. "I'll write as soon as I can." Michael lifted the duffel bag and gave his mother a brief hug. "I love you, Mom."

"I love you, too. I'll be praying for you every day."

Michael took two steps backward before turning around and walking away. Troy put an arm around Randi's shoulders, offering silent support while Michael got in the recruiter's car and waved good-bye.

Randi held herself in until the car disappeared from view;

then a single sob escaped and she turned into Troy's arms. She clung to him without crying. The eyes she lifted to his were dry, free from tears. "Thank you, Troy. For everything."

She laid her head against his chest again then drew away. "Something is scratching my cheek." She reached for his pocket.

Troy covered her hand with his. "Allow me." Pulling out the offending item, he dangled a sprig of mistletoe over her head.

She stared at the symbolic flower and then at Troy before lifting her face to his. He brushed his lips with hers. "Merry Christmas, with love, Aranda H."

Her eyes flew open. "You know!"

He nodded. "I felt guilty when I began to fall for Randi Pearson when I came here to find Aranda. And then I learned you were the same person."

He brushed her lips again. "I know you feel like you've watched your family walk out the door today." He reached into his back pocket for the key ring he had hidden away earlier. Pressing it into Randi's hand, he said, "You are looking at the new director of the Boys and Girls Club here in Christmas."

"You're staying, here, in Christmas?"

"How can I not, when the woman I love has made her home here?" He dropped to one knee. "Aranda Rachel Hathaway Pearson, I came here to find a compassionate letter writer. Instead, I found so much more. Are you willing to risk a new family—by adding me to your family?"

The tears Randi had held back fell unheeded now. "Oh, Troy. Yes, yes, a thousand times, yes." Holding his hands, she lifted him to his feet and sealed their pledge with a kiss.

Award-winning author and speaker Darlene Franklin recently returned to cowboy country—Oklahoma. The move was prompted by her desire to be close to her son's family; her daughter Jolene has preceded her into glory.

Darlene loves music, needlework, reading, and reality TV. Talia, a Lynx point Siamese cat, proudly claims Darlene as her person.

A Blessed Angel Came

Kathleen E. Kovach

DEDICATION

To Jim, who gives me wings.

Chapter 1

Gabi Archer bagged the stuffed toy alligator. "That will be $16.57." She smiled at the man across the counter and felt the familiar warmth flood her face when he smiled back. Why did she have to be so shy?

Much more comfortable with children, she concentrated on the boy with him, probably around eight years old. "What a nice daddy you have. He brings you to Jungle Adventures Nature Park and buys you a toy."

The boy, a near carbon copy of the man standing next to him, scrunched his pug nose making the freckles dance. "How did you know my dad brought me here and bought me a toy?"

"I think she means me." The man shoved the boy playfully.

"But you aren't my dad." This proclamation was followed by a squinty eye as he scrutinized the adult.

Gabi hoped she hadn't started a family squabble. Perhaps this man was the boy's stepfather, or maybe his mother's fiancé hoping to get in good with the child.

The man laughed as he thumbed out dollar bills. "No, I'm not. And you should be thankful. I know a million ways to subdue a wild animal like you." He collected his change and accepted the bag from Gabi then handed it to the boy.

"Thanks, Uncle David. This was the best day ever!"

Ah, *uncle*.

Before they wandered out of the gift shop, the man glanced over his shoulder and waved. "Thanks!"

"Oh. Uh. . .thank you for coming in." Gabi always forgot to thank the customers as they left.

"Did you see the way he looked at you?" Naylene Burnett, her best friend ever since she moved to town five years ago, seemed to materialize at Gabi's elbow.

"What are you talking about?" Gabi squeezed past Naylene to straighten a rack of postcards that had been assaulted by a tourist.

Naylene stood behind the register. "He was totally checking you out."

Gabi looked around quickly to be sure no one was in the gift shop. Satisfied they were alone, she matched Naylene's volume. "He totally was not."

Naylene grinned as she leaned on the counter. "Totally."

A family of four entered the shop but that didn't stop the taunting. Naylene simply batted her eyelashes—the same color as her copper curls—every time Gabi glanced her way.

Naylene ceased her teasing as business picked up in the late afternoon. When the last customer left, she opened the register to count down the drawer and said, "Totally."

"First of all"—Gabi moved throughout the store straightening merchandise—"I'm twenty-nine and therefore too old to be playing these games with you. Second of all, you're crazy." Gabi circled her ear with her finger.

"Thanks." Naylene grinned. "I take that as a compliment."

A tall, handsome figure passed by the window and Gabi's heart did a little flip. She ran to watch Captain Rod swagger by as he talked to their supervisor, Harold Meyer, in his animated way. She pressed her cheek against the window and sighed.

"Oh great!" Naylene broke into her thoughts. "*You* can clean that smudge off the window." She joined Gabi and followed her gaze. "No," she stated with an emphatic downward motion of her hand. "No. . .no. . .no. I will not let you get hung up on Mr. Wonderful."

Gabi continued to watch until they were out of sight. "He is wonderful, isn't he?" She punctuated her remark with a large sigh.

"I was being sarcastic. He's a total sleaze."

"He is not."

"He totally is."

Gabi walked away from her friend to finish closing the store. "I won't get into this with you."

"Why do you like the bad boys?"

"I total—I don't."

Naylene proceeded to count on her fingers all of the crushes Gabi had shared with her since they met at church five years ago. It took all of one hand and part of the other. Of course, she had to use actors to make her point fully, but there were a couple of real-life men in her count.

"Captain Rod isn't a sleazeball or a bad boy. Where did you get that idea?"

"He's lied about being a real captain. He's never run expeditions in the Amazon. All he's ever done is pilot a boat around in a circle and give rides to tourists. I think you've fallen for the character he plays."

"How do you know?"

"Come on. If he really did all the things he said he did, why is he working here? What allure would a tourist attraction in bitsy Christmas, Florida, have on someone like that? He lies, and that makes him a sleazeball and a bad boy."

"If so, he sure looks good doing it." She caught Naylene's frown and spat out, "Totally!"

They soon locked up and walked through the break room to clock out. A notice pinned on the bulletin board caught Naylene's eye. "Ooh. . .we should totally do this.".

Gabi joined her, and as she read, she backed up, gauging her escape route. "I can't do that! I'd die!"

"Come on. They're just looking for people to dress in costume and represent Jungle Adventures at the Christmas festival. It'll be fun."

"It says, 'outgoing personality a plus.' They want us to greet people and get them to visit here." A couple of penciled-in signatures were already scrawled next to corresponding times.

Naylene shook her head and regarded Gabi with a sympathetic eye. "It's time for you to come out of your shell, girl. Your sister doesn't need you as much as she did after the accident. I got you this job to help reintroduce you to civilization."

"Jerica still needs me, but you're right, not as much as before." Gabi sat in a plastic patio chair, her shoulders slumped as she still felt the weight of the world. Fingering her *I Love To Write* keychain, she pressed her lips together. Had she been able to finish journalism in college, she wouldn't have found herself making minimum wage in a gift shop. "Jerica was so little when that drunk driver hit our car."

"But your mom moved you both here, and your aunt and uncle have been awesome in helping to raise her."

"She's thirteen and growing up so fast, despite her wheelchair and slow speech." Maybe it *was* time for Gabi to stretch her wings and fly.

But a costume character? Really?

Several people began to gather around the notice, some excited about the idea, and others wandering away in disinterest.

Harold entered the room and motioned toward the notice. "What do you think? Be a good way to advertise the park. I'm sending out representatives from the main attractions to give little presentations. For the rest of you, I'd like one or two people dressed as traditional Christmas characters to hand out flyers and coupons. All volunteers will be paid time and a half."

Captain Rod entered the room, and Gabi's heart accelerated to a million beats per minute. How could so much handsome live in one man? After they married, their children would have his dark, wavy hair and his chocolate brown eyes.

Naylene gave Gabi a sly look, obviously up to something. "Are you planning on working the Christmas fest, Rod?"

"I am. Harold has asked me to represent the Swamp Cruise."

"When are you scheduled?" Naylene dragged her finger down the page.

"Every weekday, six to eight."

Naylene grabbed the pencil dangling on a string next to the schedule and sketched in both her name and Gabi's—every weekday, six to eight.

Gabi looked for that escape route in earnest.

"Excellent!" Harold flung his arm around her shoulder,

pinning her in place. "Meet here an hour before and I'll have your costumes. The wife has access to some nice ones through her theater troupe."

Naylene hurried Gabi out to the parking lot before she could protest. When Gabi finally found her voice, it sounded thin and whiny. "I thought you didn't like Captain Rod."

"I don't, but I knew you couldn't resist working with him. There's more than one way to get you out of your comfort zone." Naylene blew her a kiss as she hopped into her car. "You'll thank me later."

Gabi watched Naylene spin out of the parking lot, still stunned at her friend's boldness. But then she smiled to herself as she slipped the key into her own car. Two hours of Captain Rod. That had to be worth every ounce of awkwardness she knew she'd feel.

Totally.

❄

David Preston greeted his sister as she entered her house. "Hey, sis. Need help with the groceries?"

"Sure." Connie shuffled the bags, looping the plastic handles off her fingers and onto his. "Where's Tyler? I could use his help."

"I'll do it. He's upstairs resting."

"Resting? Tornado Ty?" She raised an eyebrow.

"I wore him out pretty good today. We went to Jungle Adventures."

Connie laughed. "I'll bet he wore you out. How'd he talk you into that?"

"Aw, he's a good kid. Just needs an outlet."

David excused himself to bring in the remainder of the bags.

"Outlet." Connie continued the conversation when he came back in. "I've heard that from his teachers." She proceeded to put the groceries away. "You should be the one resting. You were out of the country for three months this time."

David opened a bag of pretzels and began munching. "Sweet assignment, too. I had a blast."

"Mm-hm. I'll bet you were in your element with all those bugs in the Amazon rain forest." She shuddered for effect.

"Photographed some. You wanna see?"

"No, thank you! I had my fill of bugs when we were little. I'll never get over your pet tarantula under my pillow."

"Upset your whole slumber party, didn't he?" David still got a kick out of that prank. He liked to think that Fred had fun, too; that is, after he skittered away from the screaming girls trying to flog him with their slippers.

A knock on the door drew their attention. Connie disappeared to answer it while David searched for more snacks in the remaining grocery bags. A moment later, Connie called from the living room.

"David, there's someone here to see you."

He shoved a chocolate chip cookie into his mouth. "Coming!"

When he entered the living room, he skidded to a stop. Flashbacks of that horrible night threw him back to when he was seventeen and this same policeman stood in his parents' doorway.

But this time, Officer Stanton was smiling. And he looked older. And he wore civilian clothes.

Officer Stanton held out his hand. "I heard you were in town so I thought I'd come by to say howdy." He paused. "You okay, son?"

David shook off the past and returned the handshake. "I am, sir, thanks to you."

A twinkle in the man's eyes could have been from joy at seeing his troubled teen project make good, or it could have been a tear. Maybe both. Before David knew it, huge paws pulled him into a bear hug and gently patted his back.

Connie asked both of them if they'd like to sit and chat awhile. "I'll bring out some refreshments," she said as she disappeared into the kitchen.

David's mentor took the sofa, dwarfing it with his well-over-six-foot frame. David sat in the matching armchair.

"So, staying out of trouble?"

"Define *trouble*." David chuckled. "I've been doing great ever since you introduced me to a camera, Officer Stanton."

"Hey, call me Rick. Been retired for some time now."

Connie brought in a plate of cookies and two cups of coffee. "I thought I'd serve these since they were already *opened*." She pointed a look at David. "And here's sugar and cream if either of you desire."

Both men thanked her as she left the room.

"I've heard how well you're doing," Rick said as he sipped the hot coffee, straight up.

David stirred in three teaspoons of sugar and a healthy drop of cream. "My life could have been so much different. You put me on a great career path."

"Hey, that old camera was just gathering dust on a shelf. You gave it a new purpose." He took another sip and set the cup on the coffee table. "I've followed your career. Even cut out some of your pictures from magazines and framed them. What a life you've already lived, and you're only. . .what?"

"Thirty-five, sir."

"Thirty-five. And you've already been around the world several times."

"I guess it did me good to get out of this town." He didn't elaborate that the reason for getting out of town was to escape the memories.

"It did, indeed. So, you're here for the holidays?"

David nodded. "I'm taking a couple months off before my next assignment. It's been years since I spent Thanksgiving and Christmas with my family."

Rick downed the rest of his coffee and stood. "Well, I just came by to welcome you back to Christmas. Hey! If you find yourself bored, I know the festival committee is looking for good photographers. It may be too simple for your talents, but I thought I'd pass it along anyway."

"I might do that. We could consider it a chance to finish that community service I never completed back in the midnineties."

Rick chuckled and shook his head. "You kept me hoppin', that's for sure. Glad to see you've matured. . .son."

With a wink, retired officer Rick Stanton walked out the door. The emphasis on *son* was not lost on David. That man had been more of a father to him than his own.

"That was nice of him." Connie leaned against the doorjamb to the kitchen, wiping her hands on a dish towel.

David rubbed the back of his neck, feeling the clamminess there. "Yeah. Great guy." He sank to the couch and she joined him.

"You okay?"

"It just brought back memories, that's all."

She squeezed his knee. "You're not that person anymore."

"I know. Colossians 1:13–14. 'For he has rescued us from the dominion of darkness and brought us into the kingdom of the Son he loves, in whom we have redemption, the forgiveness of sins.' Got that one tattooed on my brain."

"Well, never forget that. You have been redeemed, and no one can take that from you." She kissed his cheek and left to start dinner.

He *had* been redeemed, and yet his memories still haunted him. One family would never be the same. . .because of him.

Chapter 2

Gabi stood back while Naylene fawned all over the contents of the box Harold had brought into the break room.

"These are so cute!" Naylene held up two costumes, one of an elf and one of a snow fairy.

Gabi fingered the thin fabric.

Harold pointed to a large makeup kit. "The missus said to rosy up your cheeks. There's other stuff in there, too. You girls have fun with it."

Naylene immediately claimed the elf. "I love these big ears!" She slipped them on and looked into the full-length mirror Harold had brought from his house.

"They're so you," Gabi said, trying to sound as sarcastic as possible.

"And you can be the sweet little snow fairy." Naylene rummaged through the kit. "Ooh, there's spray glitter in here. We're going to be adorable!"

"First of all, I'm not that little." Gabi laid the white outfit aside. "And second, I'm not wearing this."

Both Harold and Naylene looked at her with surprise.

"Why not?" Naylene whined.

"It's too revealing."

"Seriously? Every inch of you will be covered up. It looks like a ballet dress with long arms and leggings." She held the pink tutu up to her face and implored with her eyes. "How can you resist this?"

"I like the tutu, but. . ."

Naylene crossed her arms and raised an eyebrow.

Gabi gulped. "My face will be exposed."

"Is that all?" Harold excused himself. When he returned, he brought with him a furry, antlered costume. "Would this work better for you? I left it in my car because I didn't think anyone would want to be in a full body costume in seventy-degree weather. But you two are signed up at night, so it shouldn't be too awful."

Gabi held up the reindeer, weighing the pros and cons of dying of heat stroke versus dying of embarrassment. "I like it."

"Well then"—Naylene whisked the tutu off the other costume—"at least wear it with this so people will know you're a girl."

They quickly changed in the Jungle Adventures locker room. The short drive to the festival site proved comical. People stared at Naylene and her ears behind the wheel of her tiny sports car. Gabi had left the reindeer head in the backseat because it wouldn't fit on her head in the close confines of the car. She cranked the air conditioner to frost then noticed Naylene's goose bumps.

"Okay," Naylene said as she turned into the festival parking area. "Tomorrow you can slip that costume on once we get here. It's not like you have to have a mirror."

Even though the festival had been open during the day, a steady stream of people surged onto the site. Gabi got out of the car and pulled on the reindeer head. "Ew! It smells like bad breath in here!"

"Yours or someone else's?"

Gabi folded her arms and glared at Naylene, only Naylene had no clue that's what she was doing. Good. If no one could see her facial expressions, they couldn't see the rest of her either.

Naylene grabbed Gabi's front hoof and led her to the site. "I have an uncle who used to work at Busch Gardens as a costume character. He said they always had spotters to help those in full costume since they couldn't see very well. I'll be your spotter."

Great. First Naylene told her what to do and now she was going to tell her where to go. How did her free time deteriorate so quickly? "While you're spotting, see if you can spot me a new best friend."

"What? You're muffled in there. My uncle also said the character never talks. You have to use your arms and body language to let people know what you're thinking."

Gabi stopped abruptly and slapped her fists to her hips.

"Don't use that kind of language with me, young lady." Naylene laughed and pulled Gabi further into the crowd until they were at their station.

A small stage had been set up with a grass roof and tiki torches on either side. Already present, Captain Rod regaled the gathering crowd of his Amazon adventures. She couldn't see much of him since two eyeholes shrunk her peripheral vision.

"Sheesh," Naylene spoke into Gabi's antler. "Isn't he supposed to be promoting the park?"

"He's probably just warming up the crowd."

"Hmm? Can't hear you."

Oh, this was going to be a long two hours.

They began passing out flyers, a difficult task for Gabi with her front hooves flopping. She had found a slit in the fabric where she could stick her fingers through. Naylene said it looked stupid, but she didn't care. It was better than just standing there.

Other than the heat and the smell, Gabi was actually beginning to enjoy herself. The crowd loved her. Children gave her hugs and Naylene suggested she do a pirouette to show her pleasure. Gabi had forgotten she wore the tutu. The crowd began calling her Dancer.

A strange thing soon happened. Gabi disappeared and Dancer took over. She found that she could be as crazy as she wanted to be—flirting with elderly men, stealing hats from little boys, she even blew Captain Rod a big kiss. Gabriella Archer would never have done that!

In their last fifteen minutes, Gabi spotted the man who had brought his nephew to Jungle Adventures the other day—the one Naylene had said was *totally* into her. He was taking pictures of the visitors in front of the large lit tree and a sign that said WEL-COME TO CHRISTMAS.

"Here," he said as he handed a slip of paper to the mother in one family. "You can pick up your picture before leaving, or you can go online and download it from here." He pointed to the paper.

Another family positioned themselves in front of a tree, but their child in a wheelchair began to fuss. The photographer knelt, making himself eye level with her. Good. He received a mark for manners. As he spoke, the child settled down, even giggling at one point. Another mark for connectivity. With her parents looking on misty-eyed, the photographer gave her a hug. A mark for compassion. Not many people would choose to touch a handicapped person.

As he set up for the shot, the child noticed Gabi and held her arms out. The simple gesture drew Gabi toward her as if she'd been lassoed. She stood next to the wheelchair holding the child's hand while the photographer took their picture, and afterward, he asked her if she'd like to stick around for more photo ops.

She curtsied then pointed to the Jungle Adventures stage.

"Oh, I see." He smiled from his eyes. Nice eyes. "You have other obligations."

She threw her right hoof up to her forehead, hoping for an "alas, I must go" attitude, and swept herself dramatically back to the stage where Naylene waited with a fistful of flyers.

For the rest of the evening, she noticed the photographer glancing her way, almost as if he were confused about something.

She was confused, too. The gentle smile he offered had created more emotion in her than Captain Rod ever had.

❄

Something about the reindeer in the pink tutu.

David's gaze wandered over to the Jungle Adventures festival booth. He recognized the one with the ears as one of the women working in the gift shop. Would that make the reindeer the other one who had sold Tyler his toy?

He thought back to that meeting. She was pretty, but in their brief time together, he felt perhaps she didn't realize it. Throughout his career, he'd taken photos of everybody from the homeless on the streets of New York to Aborigines in Australia. He'd learned to read people. Many of them had no idea they wore their life on their face.

And this one had been hurt. . .deeply.

The young woman from the photo booth came to bring him a memory card in exchange for the one in his camera. He liked the system. She would have his pictures downloaded in time for the festival-goers to retrieve them before going home. A portrait studio in Orlando sponsored the photo booth with intentions of donating a percentage of the proceeds to charity.

He finished out the night with promises to return the next evening. He'd forgotten how fun simple photography could be.

Before leaving the festival area, he stood near the tree taking in the sights and sounds. Christmas music played over a loud-speaker, and twinkling white lights adorned the bare limbs of the oak trees. Sweet, buttery aromas mixed with grilling meat, and happy voices of all ages created a pleasant white noise. Tiny bits of suds that looked like snow fell periodically, creating a magical effect. If it weren't for the balmy temperature and evening humidity, he could imagine himself at the Christkindlmarkt in Frankfurt, Germany.

As he watched couples heading for the mistletoe, loneliness descended upon him. With all his traveling, a relationship rated low on his list. But he felt the clock ticking. In five years, he'd be forty. And what did he have to show for it? A pocketful of awards but no house in which to display them. His sister graciously dedicated a room to his accomplishments in her home, but that wasn't the same as sharing with a significant other.

Shake it off.

No one would want to travel with him and live his crazy

lifestyle, and he wasn't ready to retire. If the Lord wanted him to have a wife, He'd have to be sure she had no roots and that she'd be willing to take off at a moment's notice.

And that was why he remained single.

At the end of his shift, he headed toward his car. Several people were leaving, but a pair of antlers caught his eye. The reindeer and elf had reached their small vehicle. The elf slid into the driver's seat, and the reindeer removed the head confirming his suspicions.

His heart warmed thinking of the woman inside the costume, and he wondered if Tyler was up to another visit to Jungle Adventures.

Chapter 3

Gabi thought about the photographer all weekend and during work on Monday. Before leaving that day, she shared her heart with Naylene. "So few people take the time to look beyond the wheelchair—to see the person inside."

"I know what that means to you, considering how much you love your sister."

"If I ever see him again, I'm going to tell him how much his tender act touched me."

Naylene lifted an eyebrow.

"Okay," Gabi said, raising her hands. "Who am I kidding? I'd never be able to approach him, much less discuss such an intimate thing."

A giggle erupted from Naylene. "Would you like to get to know him better?"

"No!" Gabi's heart thudded. Oh, why did she share this with her impetuous friend?

"I could arrange it."

"No, no, no. . ."

"It might take your mind off Bad Boy Rod."

Gabi's swirling emotions skidded to a halt. She hadn't thought of Captain Rod all day. Hadn't even watched for him out the window.

Naylene picked up the phone. "One call and I can have his name, address, and shoe size."

"Okay, I know you're good, but who do you know with that information?" Certainly, she was bluffing.

"My mom is on the festival committee. She knows everything."

And Naylene must have taken after her.

"Put the phone down. No hacking his personal information."

Naylene shrugged and placed the handset on the receiver. "Suit yourself. But if you change your mind—"

"I won't."

That evening Gabi went home and helped prepare dinner. Just as Auntie Bets pulled the roast from the oven, Jerica came wheeling into the kitchen in her motorized chair, a big grin on her face.

"I don't even need to ask where you've been," Gabi said as she reached for the bag of books on her lap. "What did you get this time?"

Mom followed, looking worn but happy. Joel 2:25 looked good on her. *"I will repay you for the years the locusts have eaten."* The locusts had ravaged her first marriage by taking her husband too soon and ruined the second when he'd blamed her for Jerica's condition.

"The question," Mom interjected, "is not 'what?' but 'how many?' I don't think the Alafaya Branch Library has a book in it she hasn't read."

Jerica helped spread the books onto the kitchen table with a wobbly hand while Gabi read the titles. "I see we have *Tuck Everlasting*, always a good choice. Here's *The Secret Garden* and *Little Women*." She glanced at the other three books on the table. "I wish I could read as fast as you."

Auntie Bets handed Gabi five plates and set silverware out for Jerica to place around the table. "Your uncle is going to think these books are good eatin' instead of good readin' if we don't get food on the table soon." She called into the belly of the house for Uncle Eric. "Soup's on!"

Jerica giggled.

"What's so funny, Jelly Bean?" Gabi placed the last plate and began setting glasses next to them.

"Eating. . .books."

Mom finished carving the roast just as Uncle Eric entered the kitchen. He tickled Jerica on his way to his chair, and she giggled again. Gabi's heart swelled with love for her little family.

While eating, she shared her thoughts about the photographer. "You should have seen him. He knelt down and engaged the little girl." She forked a small piece of meat. "It was beautiful. I thought about telling him how much I appreciated his sensitivity."

"Why. . .don't. . .you?" Jerica looked at her with the same intensity she'd been born with. Such intelligence behind those gray-blue eyes.

"Well, I may never see him again. Besides, it's not really my place. I mean, I didn't even know the child."

"True," Mom said, "but you do have experience with rude people."

Jerica nodded and snorted in agreement.

"Well, it doesn't matter now. Although Naylene said she could get his name and address from her mother who is on the festival committee." She laughed, thinking that was the funniest thing she'd heard that day. But no one else was laughing.

"You. . .could. . .send. . .a. . .thank-you. . .note."

Gabi's jaw dropped. "Oh no. I couldn't. Just out of the blue like that?"

Auntie Bets set her fork down, excitement dancing in her eyes. "Sure you can. And send it anonymously."

Anonymous. She could probably do that.

"I'll. . .write. . .a. . .poem."

Of course. This was Jerica's cause, too. More so than Gabi's. "That would be perfect, Jelly Bean. You could word it much better than I ever could."

She became excited at the prospect of thanking this man, and she prayed he'd understand her good intentions.

When she finished dinner, she phoned Naylene.

❄

David loved his photography job at the Christmas festival. He'd been at it a week and had brought his camera to snap pics of the people coming and going, the displays, the volunteers. He especially loved catching the tutu-clad reindeer in her zany poses.

However, he had only committed to work nights, and he found his days boring. Tyler was back in school, and his sister and brother-in-law worked.

Friday morning, he decided to call the folks at Jungle Adventures to ask permission to take pictures there for a magazine article. Harold Meyer quickly agreed to give him free rein.

Before David left the house, the mail had come. Since his parents lived overseas—his dad a civilian contractor for the military— he used his sister's address as his own. Then, she would forward his mail to him whenever he found himself in one place long enough. Among the house bills, ads, and usual pile of unwanted mail, he found one addressed to him. The penmanship looked feminine.

"My first Christmas card of the season?" All mail coming to the house from their post office had the Christmas, Florida, postmark, but getting a Christmas card stamped with those words just made the season more special.

He slipped his thumb under the seal, wondering who it was from. It wasn't a holiday card, but rather a thank-you card. Curiosity made him flip to the inside and pull out the folded stationery without reading the sentiment.

A poem was scrawled in the same handwriting:

Your good deed did not go unnoticed;
Your Samaritan act was caught.
I want you to know you were witnessed
Acting as you ought.

It went on to explain how this person had seen him interacting with a child in a wheelchair at the Christmas festival.

"Hmm." He flipped the card open to see who had sent it, but it simply said, *From an interested bystander*. "That's cool." He had no clue who might have sent it. There were so many people there. But he did remember the little girl and how his heart went out to her. He saw all children differently since that day long ago, but those in wheelchairs particularly tugged at his emotions.

Setting the letter aside, he grabbed his camera and headed out, excited at the prospect of seeing more of the girl in the gift shop.

When he got there, the place was buzzing with tourists. Handing out flyers at the festival must have been working for them. Several people browsed the gift shop, but he managed to snap everything from alligator heads to the shy woman behind the counter.

If he hadn't seen for himself that this person was also Dancer the Reindeer, he wouldn't have believed it. She rang items up without making eye contact with any of the customers. But if a child were near, she talked to them directly in soft, loving tones.

At one point, he had her focused in his lens when she looked up and caught him. Her brown doe-eyes surprised him as much as he surprised her. He quickly lowered his camera and turned to finger T-shirts on a rack.

Soon, there were only two customers in the store, so he decided to introduce himself and explain why he was there.

Holding his hand out over the counter, he said, "Hi, I'm David Preston. Harold Meyer gave me permission to wander the grounds and take pictures. I plan to submit them to a travel magazine."

The woman waited through his entire introduction before raising her hand to grasp his. Although maybe *grasp* was too energetic a word. Their fingers barely touched before she pulled away. Her cheeks turned a pretty rose color that quickly spread down her neck and up into her strawberry-blond hairline.

Another hand thrust its way into his, and he turned to see the other cashier, shorter and pushier than Dancer. "Hey, I'm Naylene Burnett, and this is Gabriella Archer."

David released the strong grip. "Nice to meet you." He looked back at Dancer, tilting his head to capture her gaze. "Gabriella. Nice name."

A soft breath escaped her lips as she said something he couldn't make out.

"Excuse me?" he asked.

"Gabi." She twisted a piece of her hair around her finger. "That's what people call me."

"People call me Naylene." The small one, who surprisingly still looked like an elf without the ears and makeup, grinned up at him. "Named for my gramma. They said I had her cheeks, although I never saw hers without wrinkles. Maybe I was a wrinkly baby." Dancer, or rather, Gabi, nudged her with her elbow while still avoiding eye contact with him.

"It's nice to meet both of you."

Customers began to fill the small gift shop, so David excused himself so he could do his job. As he walked out, he glanced over his shoulder and waved good-bye to the two women. The elfish one offered a huge smile and waved back, but Gabi quickly looked away and fanned herself with a postcard.

As he walked around the park, he could only think of Gabi Archer. That name didn't suit her. She wasn't gabby at all but too shy for her own good. However, if Dancer could talk, the reindeer probably would live up to that name.

Gabi needed a confidence boost, someone confirming her beauty, inside and out.

He checked his watch. About time for him to work the festival, but first he'd stop and pick up a card.

Chapter 4

See what I mean, Jelly Bean? It's beautiful!" Gabi strolled beside Jerica's chair as they entered the festival site. She watched Jerica's face glow with joy as she passed under the strands of Christmas lights forming a tunnel into a winter wonderland.

Gabi chose Saturday night to introduce her sister to the festival since she wasn't working it. She almost hoped that whoever had sent that beautiful card would show himself. Her heart warmed thinking of the pretty Christmas card, an angel on the front declaring the good news to the shepherds. The signature inside read, *From an admirer*. Had it been Captain Rod?

She wasn't as thrilled as she should be over the prospect. Something had changed. Listening to him night after night may have cured her from thinking him so adventurous. The kicker, though, was how his stories changed, as if he was editing as he went. Naylene swore he was making it all up, and now Gabi wondered.

But he was still a handsome man. And the way women, young and old, gave him way too much attention confirmed it.

She'd have to decide how she would react if it was Captain Rod who had sent the card. Should she bat her lashes and thank him coquettishly? Should she reciprocate and tell him how she admired him, too? But did she?

Now she almost hoped he hadn't sent it. But if not him, who?

The festival looked different when looking at it without the reindeer peepholes. She'd never seen it look nicer in all the years they'd put it on. This year a refrigerated tent had been set up, and a snow machine cranked out tons of flakes for playing in. Southern children romped in the white stuff as if they had done it all their lives. Once they entered, Gabi scooped some and placed it in Jerica's hands.

"It's. . .cold."

"Of course, silly. It's ice."

Gabi felt something hit her shoulder and shivered at the cold wetness inside her collar. She turned to Jerica, wondering if the child had learned to throw a snowball from the ruffian boys inside the tent. But she was still holding hers, shifting it back and forth between her hands, assumedly to keep them from freezing.

A chuckle from behind made her look over her shoulder, where she saw David standing next to his nephew, much too innocent for his own good.

She shook her jacket and wiped the ice from her ear. "Are you the perpetrators?" She smiled to let them know she took it in stride.

David pointed at the boy. "He dared me."

The boy's jaw dropped. "Did not!"

The pair approached, and when they were near, a small bit of wet ice flew past Gabi and landed a foot from David's shoe. They both turned to Jerica who broke into full-blown laughter. While David was distracted with Jerica, Gabi reached down and hefted two handfuls of snow into his face.

The amused nephew now joined Jerica, and they both doubled over in a fit of giggles.

"Oh, game on!" David shoveled more snow into his hands and began chucking snowballs at Gabi and Jerica, underhanded so as not to hurt them.

Gabi retaliated but quickly lost the battle because she had to make snowballs not only for herself, but for Jerica, as well. Even so, the two fought well and with valor—and ended up looking like two snow women.

"I surrender," Gabi said as she brushed herself off. Jerica, still giggling, emptied her lap of a couple of gallons of snow.

Winded, David bent over to rest his palms on his knees. "Sorry for the instigating snowball. I just couldn't resist."

"That's okay." She glanced at Jerica. "I haven't seen her that excited in years. It was worth it."

She introduced David to her sister, and he knelt to look Jerica in the eyes just as he had done the other night. He even warmed her hands, red from holding the snow.

"Pleased to meet you, Jerica." He pointed to the boy with him. "And this tough guy is my nephew, Tyler."

They wandered off together through the rest of the festival, as if they had all come together. And Gabi didn't mind. At all.

David shook his head. "Man, that brought back fond memories."

"Oh? Were you raised where there's snow?"

"No, I grew up here, but I've traveled a little bit. You?"

She shook her head. "Never left the state of Florida. Born and raised in Pensacola, but we've lived here with my aunt and uncle since 2007. My mom moved us so she'd have help with Jerica."

She stopped behind Jerica who had honed in on a hot chocolate stand. After buying cups of cocoa and bags of popcorn, they sat under a tent where tables and chairs had been set up. Gabi and David sat on the bench facing away from the table so they could continue to people watch, and the children pulled themselves up to the table so their cocoa wouldn't spill. Tyler seemed to hit it off nicely with Jerica, which pleased Gabi.

"Why are you in a wheelchair?" Tyler asked. It sounded like the boy truly cared.

Jerica pointed to her head. "Brain. . .trauma."

Before she could explain to the eight-year-old what that meant, David intervened. "Tyler," he said, "maybe Jerica doesn't want to talk about it."

Gabi placed her hand on David's arm. "It's okay. We've never shied away from the subject." She glanced at Jerica, who nodded back. With her silent confirmation, Gabi explained. "My mother was driving home from a friend's house. She stopped at the grocery store, and while she was in there, it began to storm. It was dark by then, but she didn't have far to go. Only a few blocks from our house, a drunk driver skidded out of control at a stoplight and slammed into her car. Jerica was only three and in her car seat in the back, but the impact caused the groceries to fly out of the bag and a large can of soup hit her head. It was a freak injury, but not a freak accident." She became agitated as she told the rest of the story. "The driver stumbled out of his car and tried to run, but bystanders grabbed him and kept him there until the police arrived. Seems he was a sailor on leave and celebrated a bit too much."

David went completely pale. "I'm so sorry." He reached for

Jerica's hand. Was he shaking? "I'm so, so very sorry."

Gabi continued. "He was court-martialed. Seems it wasn't his first offense. People need to stay off the roads when they've been drinking. Why don't they get it?"

David drew in a deep breath, as if composing himself. What a sensitive guy. Finally, he cleared his throat. "Have you ever told your story? I mean, to a group of people who could make a difference?"

"A group?" It was Gabi's turn to blanch. She felt the blood bottom out at her toes. "Oh, I could never stand up in front of a group of people."

"Not even to tell your sister's story?"

Gabi looked at Jerica, who had those intense eyes trained on her. "I. . .would. . .do. . .it. . .Gabi."

Of course she would. If she were well and whole, she would probably be an actress or a dancer. Maybe an athlete or a myriad of other things that people with working legs and tongues could do. Jerica was amazing. And Gabi wished, not for the first time, that she had been the one in that car to spare her sister this life. A life not of her choosing, thrust upon her in a thoughtless manner.

"We'll talk about it," she finally said.

❇

David stood to throw away their cups and to escape his own thoughts, though the latter didn't work. But as usual, he managed to tamp down his memories as the group continued through the festival.

They oohed over the donated trees that local companies had

decorated to sell for charity. They aahed over a skating rink and wondered aloud how they got the ice to freeze.

"Want to give it a try?" David motioned to the skate rental booth.

"I've never skated in my life." Gabi placed her hand to her chest, perhaps to keep her heart from leaping out at his suggestion.

"Neither have I." David laughed as he pulled Gabi to the booth.

Tyler danced around them sing-songing, "We're going skating. We're going skating." But then he stopped suddenly. "What about Jerica?"

David winked at Jerica and said, "You game?"

She nodded, a huge grin on her face.

Before long, three of them had on skates and were using Jerica's chair to keep themselves upright as they pushed her along the ice. She raised her arms and squealed. A few times she ended up whirling in circles while the others picked themselves up and staggered to catch up to her.

An hour later, an announcement came over the loudspeakers, interrupting the Christmas music that had been playing. "Hope y'all are enjoying the Christmas festival, but we'll be closing in ten minutes. Tell your family and friends to come on out."

"Aw." Gabi made her way to a bench to remove her skates. "This was too much fun. I don't want it to end."

David plopped down next to her. "It doesn't have to. When are you free again?"

She turned a startled gaze toward him then looked away.

Shy Gabi was back.

She lifted a shoulder. "I'm working all next week, but I'm off next Saturday."

Tyler, who had taken off his skates and was walking around in his socks, said, "We're going to Jungle Adventures next week, aren't we, Uncle David?"

"Again?" Gabi laughed.

"Yeah," David said. "We didn't get to hold an alligator last time because it got too late, so I promised him another trip there."

"Jerica has held an alligator, haven't you, Jelly Bean?"

Jerica grinned from ear to ear, reminding David of Lucy putting one over on Charlie Brown. "And. . .I'm. . .a. . .girl."

"Okay, that does it." Tyler stomped his stocking foot. "I gotta do it, Uncle David, I just gotta."

"Simmer down, Tornado Ty. A promise is a promise." He looked at Gabi. "I know you work there, so this might not appeal to you, but you're welcome to come with us. Tyler and Jerica seemed to hit it off. It might be fun for them."

She glanced at her sister, love radiating from her gaze. David almost felt guilty for using the children. Almost.

"Okay. Jerica loves the Wildlife Show."

"Wahoo!" Tyler whooped.

"Yay," Jerica said with a weak fist pump.

Gabi shrugged, a shy smile on her face. "I'll see you Saturday."

Chapter 5

The week flew by for Gabi. She looked forward to playing Dancer the Reindeer every evening. Dancer, to her surprise, was mischievous and often played tricks on David while he took pictures of the festival-goers. She stood behind him, holding her hoof above his head trying to make rabbit ears, which made his subjects laugh. He must have shot some hilarious photos.

She thought with her newfound boldness, she would be okay. But when David showed up at Jungle Adventures on Saturday with Tyler, she wished Dancer would come out to play. Alas, only dull old Gabi Archer joined them, following the real star of the show. Jerica motored through the crowds showing them her favorite parts of the park. The first stop was the black bears playing in their pond.

"Can I feed them, Uncle David?" Tyler asked.

"Sure, that's why I bought the bear chow when we came in." David handed Tyler and Jerica the treats. As they slid them down the chute, David said, "Now that's the way to eat. Just open your mouth and someone from above provides it."

Gabi took her turn at the chute. "Sounds like a religious commentary."

He nodded. "So it does. What's your stand on the Santa-Claus-in-the-sky theory?"

She stepped back to let the children finish feeding the bears. "I believe in relationship. Right after the accident, I couldn't understand why a loving God would hurt an innocent child. But through counseling and a great support group at church, I now see that He hurt right along with us at the world's injustice. We drew near to Him for comfort, and I know Him in ways I never would have if it had not been for the accident."

A shadow darkened David's face for just a moment. "I agree. Sometimes it takes a tragedy to wake us up and see how loving and. . .and forgiving He is."

She did not miss how he had stumbled on the word *forgiving*. David seemed so perfect. But was there something in his past for which he needed forgiveness?

They continued on until Jerica started to pass by the Jungle Swamp Cruise.

"Hey," Tyler called out to her. "Wanna go on the boat?"

Gabi placed her arm on his shoulder. "The cruise isn't handicap accessible, Tyler."

He screwed up his face. "What's that mean?"

David knelt in front of the boy. "It means that wheelchairs aren't allowed. It's probably not safe for people with special needs."

Tyler's countenance fell. Gabi thought he was upset about not getting to go, but he walked over to Jerica and said, "You mean, you've never been on the cruise?"

"Sometimes." Jerica looked down at her hands in her lap.

Gabi touched Jerica's head and let a chestnut strand slip through her fingers. "Jerica loves riding on the boat but hasn't since she's grown so tall. Uncle Eric has taken her before, but he doesn't visit the park very often, and she's gotten too big for me to lift."

David pulled Gabi aside so the children couldn't hear. "Could I carry her onto the boat?"

Who were this man and little boy? Swallowing the lump in her throat, she answered, "She would need support once you're seated."

"Do I have your permission?" He looked like a boy asking for a puppy.

She nodded, excited for Jerica.

After David explained to Jerica what he wanted to do, she heartily agreed with squeals and hand clapping. He gently scooped her out of her chair and made it onto the boat, where he set her down and then supported her with his arms and chest. After Captain Rod introduced himself, explained the rules, and told one of his stories, they pulled away from the dock. Jerica couldn't have grinned bigger without hooking the corners of her mouth over her ears.

Gabi touched David's arm and whispered, "Thank you."

"No problem," he whispered back.

Gabi realized at that moment how close their heads, and mouths, were to each other and that he didn't seem eager to pull back. So she did, but she regretted it.

Captain Rod flirted with a woman sitting near the captain's chair. This never fazed Gabi, especially now with David so near.

"Why is the water so green?" The woman had a distinctive Georgian accent.

"The water is this color because of the duckweed, or *Lemna minor*," he said as the boat sliced through it. "It's a small herb that grows in freshwater and serves as food for the inhabitants here. Like this big fella on your right."

Two eyes peered out from the duckweed, revealing a large alligator. The woman let out a squeal, meant more for Captain Rod than for herself.

They all enjoyed the twenty-minute ride, although Gabi had already become bored with Captain Rod's stories. They were the same ones he told at the Christmas festival, further embellished. She still enjoyed looking at him, however. Now, if he would only shut up.

The boat came back to the west landing and docked with ease. They waited until all the others passengers disembarked. Then David lifted Jerica and left the boat, followed by Tyler and Gabi. While David helped Jerica to settle back into the chair, Gabi overheard a remark by one of the women standing in line waiting for the next trip.

"I thought this ride wasn't handicap accessible. We have to wait while they break the rules."

Heat seared Gabi's cheeks. She looked at Captain Rod, whom she was sure would defend their actions. But he said nothing.

Something snapped inside of Gabi. She was tired of rude people, and she'd been silent for too long. She marched up to the offending woman, who stood near the back of the line. "For your information, wheelchairs aren't allowed because the boat isn't made for them. However, my sister has every right to enjoy the ride. Thanks to my friend, she was able to today, and she deserves an apology for your tactless remark."

The man standing near the woman took her elbow and guided her past Gabi toward the boat. "Back off, lady."

As they boarded the boat, Gabi called out, "It's because of attitudes like yours that some deserving people with special needs feel less than human." She felt someone's hand on her arm. "Get a clue, people! No, get a heart!"

"Gabi." She turned and saw the hand on her arm belonged to David. Flames leaped from her burning cheeks.

But it was worse than she thought. Her boss, Harold, stood on the walk with his mouth open. "Gabi, may I have a word with you?"

Gabi looked back at the boat pulling away from the dock, and she heard Captain Rod's voice drone on as if nothing had happened.

❄

David wanted to applaud Gabi. He hadn't known her very long, but he knew this was some sort of breakthrough for her. It was as if a dam had broken and everything she ever wanted to say just spilled out into a pile at the offender's feet. He prayed she would learn to harness her message so it would draw people in, not push them away.

Gabi shuffled toward Harold, her head hung low. "I'm sorry, Mr. Meyer. I don't know what—"

"I don't care that you're not on the clock right now." He kept his voice low, but his reprimand was loud and clear. "You never treat a paying customer that way."

David stepped in. "May I say something on Miss Archer's behalf?"

Gabi shook her head. "David, you don't have to—"

"The woman made a rude remark," he continued. "Miss

Archer was only defending her sister. I'm sure you would have done the same in her circumstance."

"Yes. Well. . ." Harold, who seemed a fair man, glanced at Jerica who sat out of earshot with Tyler. "I can understand how much you love your sister. And I don't know how you handle this sort of thing outside of the park, but I'd like you to refrain from upsetting the guests. There are better ways to speak to difficult people."

"Yes, sir. I've never done anything like that in my life." She swallowed visibly. "Am I fired?"

Harold's gaze grew tender. "No. But please, learn how to control your anger."

He wandered off, and David chuckled. "You? With an anger management problem?"

Gabi laughed with him, no doubt relieved the incident was over. "I guess it's got to start sometime."

They joined Jerica and Tyler, and the four continued walking.

"You. . .in. . .trouble. . .Gabi?"

"Oh! Not at all, Jelly Bean. Mr. Meyer understood. But you do realize I went about it the wrong way. I shouldn't have yelled at that woman."

A huge smile spread over Jerica's face. "I. . .thought. . .it . . .was. . .great!"

"Me, too!" This came from Tyler. "I thought you were going to punch her!"

"Oh!" Gabi blinked her eyes in surprise. "I think I'm sending the wrong signals today."

To change the subject, Gabi suggested they hold the baby alligator before it got too late. This worked, as the children made no mention of the potential fight the rest of the day but rather argued about who looked more frightened holding the alligator.

By the end of the afternoon, the adults dragged to the parking lot while the children raced. Jerica had a slight advantage on Tyler since she had four wheels and he only had two legs.

"Be careful, Jerica!" Gabi called out. "You're not a NASCAR driver."

"Yet!" Jerica laughed as she slowed to let Tyler catch up.

Tyler began to step heel to toe, walking the length of the building. Children loved "Swampy," the long building that looked like an alligator where admissions and the gift shop were located. Tyler counted as he stepped, apparently measuring Swampy with his footsteps, from the alligator's open mouth full of teeth to the tip of his tail.

Gabi shook her head. "At least they have to go slow for that."

She stopped at her car and looked at David "Thank you for today. I've never seen Jerica so happy. And I'm sure she'll talk about the river ride in her sleep tonight."

"It was my pleasure. You have a very special young lady there."

Gabi's eyes misted. "And to think we nearly lost her."

David's heart sank to his shoes.

Gabi continued, oblivious to what her words were doing to David. "I sometimes dream of what she would look like if the accident had never happened. What would be her goals? What would she want to do when she grew up?" She leaned against her car and looked down at her folded hands. "It's silly, I know. But that drunk driver took so much away from us."

Lifting her chin with his finger, David looked into her eyes. "But God has redeemed so much. She may not be what she would have been, but then again, if the accident hadn't happened, she wouldn't be the person she is now."

Gabi's brows drew together as she gazed into his eyes. "What's your story, David? Every time we talk about Jerica, it's as if you're in pain, too. Yet you hardly know her."

He broke contact and fumbled with his car keys. "It's getting late. Tyler's folks are going to get used to him being gone, and they'll never let him back in the house."

He called to Tyler, who grumbled, "Aw, we were halfway there."

"Swampy will still be there next time. Remember where you were, and you can continue counting footsteps. But for the record, he's two hundred feet long."

"Aw, you ruined it! Now I don't have ta figure it out."

"Sorry." David opened the door. "Get in the car, you hooligan."

Tyler wrinkled his nose, but complied. "Who-lee-what?"

"Never mind." As David closed the door, he called over to Gabi, who had parked several spaces from him. "You need help?" But Jerica was already in the car, her wheelchair secured to the back.

Gabi waved. "We got it. See you Monday!" She seemed to realize what she'd just said. "I mean, see you. . .sometime." Then she slipped into her car and drove away.

David chuckled as he pulled himself behind the wheel of his own car. Apparently, he wasn't supposed to know that Gabi was Dancer the Reindeer. Fine, he'd play along. She had her secret, and he had his.

How was he supposed to tell her that he was no better than the person who hurt Jerica?

Chapter 6

Monday afternoon, Gabi and Naylene were closing the shop when Captain Rod swaggered by the window. Gabi barely took notice, but Naylene ran over to peer at him through the panes of glass.

"What are you doing?" Gabi said as she straightened the postcard rack for at least the tenth time that day.

"I was just wondering why you're not racing over here. I miss our routine."

Gabi shrugged a shoulder. "I see enough of him at the festival."

Naylene's eyes went wide. "You are so totally not into him anymore."

"I didn't say that." Gabi grabbed a broom, creating a plume of dust until she resembled Charlie Brown's friend, Pigpen.

"You don't have to. I've noticed how your big reindeer head is always pointed at the photographer."

Gabi felt a blush spread up her cheeks.

Naylene giggled and pointed at her. "You totally like David Preston!"

"What are you? Thirteen? Are you going to start singing that stupid song about us being up in a tree?"

Naylene opened the register to count down the drawer. Under her breath, she murmured, "K-i-s-s-i-n-g."

"Stop it." Gabi tried to be stern, but a smile lingered just behind her frown. As much as she would love to be mad at her friend, the thought of k-i-s-s-i-n-g David, in a tree or any location, appealed to her.

She thought back to the day before, when she'd spent the whole day with him and Tyler. They were like a family. She shook her head. David had told her he traveled. She'd never be able to go with him. Jerica may not need her as much as before, but she didn't feel she could leave her permanently.

They clocked out and headed to the festival. On the way there, Naylene seemed deep in thought. Gabi enjoyed the silence, so rather than engage conversation, she ruminated on the past few days and her new friendship with David. . .and Tyler, of course.

Christmas was a week away. David mentioned he was only in town to be with his family for the holidays. How could he afford to take two months off work? She still wasn't sure exactly what he did. He'd just told her he was a freelance photographer, traveling here and there to make a buck.

When they got to the festival, Gabi pulled on her costume. Naylene seemed distracted as she looked toward the Jungle Adventures stage. Before Gabi put on the head, she asked, "Are you okay?"

"Sure. Why do you ask?"

"No reason. You just seem preoccupied."

"Just ready to go play an elf, I guess. Hurry up."

Before Gabi managed to put on her costume, Naylene had

disappeared into the crowd, leaving Gabi to walk by herself. It took her fifteen minutes longer because of the children who wanted to hug her and the parents who saw that as a photo op.

By the time she made it, Naylene had the flyers in hand, but she wasn't passing them out. She was talking to Captain Rod. Probably giving him an earful of why she thought he was a phony.

Then again, she didn't look to be in reprimand mode. In fact, she looked a little flirty. Gabi grabbed her large reindeer cheeks.

Naylene was flirting with Gabi's Captain Rod!

For much of the evening, Gabi and Naylene competed for attention from Captain Rod. Naylene won, of course, because she could talk. She interacted with him as he told his stories, and she even threw in some whoppers of her own.

Gabi pulled her aside and spoke loud enough to penetrate the fur. "Since when did you run an exhibition to the Antarctic?"

"Hey, I'm an elf; it's plausible. I'm just playing a role, Gabi. Lighten up."

"Well, while you're acting, you might do some research. Your expedition happened at the opposite end of the globe. The North Pole is up." She pointed a hoof upward. "The Antarctic is where the South Pole is." She pointed down.

"Whatever. It's not like anybody knows that."

Gabi stomped her hoofed foot. "Everybody knows that!"

"Why don't you go play with your photographer friend? Captain Rod and I have this."

Gabi twisted to see David watching them. Great. What must he think of a reindeer fighting with an elf?

"Fine. I can give out flyers just as well from there."

"Fine."

Occasionally, through Captain Rod's presentations, various trainers would bring over animals. Sometimes it was a small alligator, sometimes a snake or a bird. This night it was Oswald's turn. Gabi always loved the big, docile orangutan. At Jungle Adventures, he loved showing off for tourists, swinging on his ropes and puckering up for the ladies in the crowd. One of his shticks was chasing the trainer, tripping him up, and then giving him a big kiss on the mouth.

Captain Rod had stepped off the stage, probably to give them room. But then Gabi noticed him standing behind Naylene, and not in an "I want to be close to you because I like you" way. He kept his eye on Oswald while trying to make himself small behind Naylene—impossible since she must have been a foot shorter—and he was chewing his thumbnail.

Oswald performed to perfection, and the growing crowd loved it. When the pair finished, the trainer began leading Oswald off the stage. Captain Rod hopped back on, his boldness seeming to return.

But he must have unwittingly waved his arm in a signal known only to Oswald, who lumbered toward him. If he had stood still, it probably would have been fine, but instead, he shrieked like a girl and ran the other way. This was Oswald's cue to chase him as he had the trainer.

The crowd howled with laughter thinking it was part of the show, but the look of terror on Captain Rod's face said otherwise. Gabi got a good look at that terror as he ran straight toward her. He grabbed her shoulders and thrust her between him and Oswald. Apparently, he thought the reindeer costume would be a deterrent. With nothing but air between Gabi and Oswald, she began to feel some of that terror. The trainer swam through the crowd, calling to Oswald, but the orangutan couldn't hear him for all the laughter.

Before the big lug could make it to her, a body lunged between them.

David!

He stood with his head low and his shoulders down in a submissive stance. Oswald slowed down and came to a stop next to him, but David never made eye contact. By the time the trainer had caught up, Oswald sat next to David with his huge paw in David's hand.

After the trainer led Oswald away, David faced Gabi and rubbed her arms. Peering into the eyeholes, he asked, "Are you okay?"

Gabi managed to squeak yes. Then she heard Captain Rod behind her. "I was just about to do that, but you got there first."

David gently moved Gabi from between them. "You ran behind this woman, potentially putting her in harm's way."

The crowd booed as they slowly realized none of it was an act. The two men stared each other down. No longer submissive, David rose to his full height. "Apologize."

"I didn't do anything wrong. I was just getting out of the monkey's way."

Rod marched away toward Naylene, who folded her arms and glared at him then said something as he passed. He said something back then noticing Oswald and his trainer standing on the stage, he purposefully walked past them. Was that to prove his courage? Or did he see that the orangutan was fully under the trainer's control?

Oswald apparently wanted to make amends. He reached out and grabbed Rod, planting a wet one on his mouth. Rod shrieked again and, while storming off the grounds, he wiped furiously at his face with his sleeves.

Howling laughter followed, but Gabi felt sorry for him. He proved himself a fraud after all his big talk. He was no more a big safari hunter than she was.

With the danger over, if one could call it that, the crowd began to disperse. Some followed Oswald out of the festival, and others questioned David on how he knew what to do.

"I'm a travel photographer," he said. "I often film animals in the wild. What I just did is more for gorillas, but I figured it would work." When asked why he stood instead of crouched like someone had seen on television, he said, "I was taught that if you crouch, it makes you too vulnerable. Another thing I learned was never to run. They tend to want to chase you." This elicited some laughter from the crowd. "Fortunately, Oswald was just playing, but in the wild it could have been a much different story."

The question-and-answer period continued for several more minutes, giving Gabi new insight into her friend, David. He had photographs in prominent works, such as *National Geographic*. He was a world traveler, covering exotic locations that few were comfortable with in their itinerary. And he was humble, which she knew, but in light of his accomplishments, it made him even sweeter than she'd imagined.

Finally, the lingering few left, and it was time for Gabi and Naylene to do the same.

On the way home, Naylene gripped the steering wheel and started to say something then must have decided not to. The false starts fizzled a couple of times until she finally spoke. "I'm sorry."

"For what?" Gabi had the window down, attempting to dry out her sweat-soaked shirt.

"For pushing you away back there."

"No. I'm sorry," Gabi said. "You were right about me not having feelings for Rod anymore. But I was jealous that he noticed you when he never even gave me the time of day."

"Well, you don't have to worry about that anymore." Naylene turned down St. Nicholas Avenue where Gabi lived. "Just before he left, I may have said something."

"May have?"

"Okay. I called him a jerk. How dare he hide behind you? And then do you know what he said?" Naylene pulled into Gabi's driveway. "He said I'd just missed my chance with him."

"Really? After his cowardice he still had some bravado left?"

"Well, until the monkey kissed him and sucked the rest of his bravado through his face."

The two giggled until the tears ran. Gabi finally opened her car door. "Oh, Naylene. I love you, you crazy nut."

"Backatcha, girl. Let's promise to never let a man come between us again."

"Pinky swear. And speaking of that, what changed your mind about him?"

"I don't know. I guess I started to see your handsome captain after spending so much time with him at the festival. Then when I realized your feelings were fading, I thought I'd go for it. That won't happen with David, though."

Gabi stood and closed the door. She poked her head through the window. "Why do you say that?"

"Because he's clearly yours. And if you haven't noticed, you're his."

Gabi couldn't respond to that. She was too busy relishing the warmth in her chest thinking about Naylene's confirmation.

As Naylene drove down the street to her own house, Gabi hugged herself. It felt good when David rescued her, even if he didn't know she was Dancer. Maybe tomorrow she'd send him a "Thank you for saving my life from a monkey" card. But she wouldn't reveal her identity. She was having too much fun falling in love with the help of a reindeer in a tutu.

Chapter 7

"Gabi, I have a favor to ask." Harold entered the gift shop with—oh stop her heart—David.

Naylene winked at her then turned to busy herself while humming k-i-s-s-i-n-g.

"David wants to take some more pictures of the park this morning," Harold said. "Since it's slow right now, would you mind taking him around? I have a meeting in a few minutes."

David smiled. "I need special access. Mr. Meyer said I'd need an employee for that. He remembered seeing us here on your day off, so he suggested you."

Gabi fussed with her hair a moment, wishing she'd taken more care with it that morning. "I'd be happy to accompany you." She led the way out into the sunshine. "You'd never know Christmas was next week, would you?" She cupped her hand above her eyes to shade them.

David laughed. "Funny, even born and bred Southerners seem to expect it to get cold for Christmas."

"I think it's all the holiday movies pumping themselves into our culture."

"My favorite is *How the Grinch Stole Christmas*. What a great movie about redemption. Second to that is *It's a Wonderful Life*. I like that it shows God taking an active role to help such a messed-up individual." David removed the lens cap from his camera and fiddled in the case he carried over his shoulder. "What's yours?"

"I like *Rudolph the Red-Nosed Reindeer*. Something appeals to me about misfits making good."

They stopped at the bird exhibit, where a peacock showed off for a small crowd. His blue and green plumage spread out like a fan, and he strutted in a three-hundred-and-sixty degree circle so everyone could take in his full beauty.

Much like Captain Rod.

Gabi giggled at the thought.

David raised his eyebrow. "What's funny?"

"Oh, just thinking about Rod last night. You de-feathered him pretty good."

"No, he did that all by himself." David squatted near the bird and began clicking away. "A pretense can only go so far. 'Truthful lips endure forever, but a lying tongue lasts only a moment.' Proverbs 12:19."

"Wow. I'm impressed." She leaned against a fence and folded her arms.

"Don't be. There was a reason I had to memorize that as a kid."

"Wild one, were you?"

"I was a boy, wasn't I? Aren't we all wild?" A vein jumped in his temple while he stood and focused his lens on a macaw. "The trick to photographing birds is to get them to smile at the camera."

Gabi giggled, but she studied David as he took pictures. He

had effectively changed the subject, as he had the other day when she'd asked what his story was. It seemed his past was a closed book.

"Hey." He removed a lens from his camera. "I'd like to talk to the animal wrangler, the one who actually gets in the water with the alligators."

"Safari Todd." Gabi checked her watch. "He should be doing a show right now, but we can catch him when he's through."

They spent the next few hours wandering the park, taking pictures and Gabi convincing employees that David was a professional and knew his way around a jungle. As a result, he got some great up-close shots of alligators, Florida panthers, and wolves.

"So," Gabi asked as they headed back toward his car, "do you write the articles that go with your photos?"

"Usually a reporter is commissioned to write the article and I'm commissioned to take the pictures. I'm not much of a writer, but I take copious notes."

"Interesting." What would it be like to write for a prestigious magazine?

As David put away his camera in the trunk of his car, he glanced Gabi's way. "I'm working at the festival tonight, but I'll get off around eight o'clock. Would you like to meet me there? Maybe walk around without the kids?"

Gabi gulped. A date? How would she handle herself without Jerica as a buffer? But then she realized she'd been doing it all day. Why couldn't she go on a date with David?

"Sure, why not?"

"Great," he said as he shut the trunk. After sliding into his car, he rolled down the window. "See you tonight then."

"I'll be there."

As he drove away, panic struck her. "Oh, no! I *will* be there! As Dancer!" Whenever she wore that costume, she had to go home and shower. She reeked, and the head did a serious number on her hair.

"Naylene!" Gabi flew into the gift shop then skidded to a stop until a woman finished paying for her purchases.

When she left, Gabi grabbed Naylene and shook her. "I have a date with David!"

"Wonderful!"

"No, not wonderful. It's tonight at the festival."

"When you're working?"

"No, right afterward. But he still doesn't know I'm Dancer."

"Then slip out to the car and take off the costume."

"I can't change there for our date. I always look a mess after working in that costume."

Naylene snapped her fingers. "You don't need to be there tonight. I can handle the flyers."

"No, then he'd know I'm Dancer. It would be too coincidental."

"Let me think." Naylene tapped her lip. "What about getting a substitute to play Dancer tonight?"

Gabi pulled her into a tight hug. "Yes! Thank you." She released Naylene as if she were a rag doll. "But who? Who would agree at this late date?"

"Leave it to me. I'll find someone."

"Thank you, thank you, thank you!"

"Just spend the extra two hours getting pretty. You deserve this."

Gabi stepped back. "I do?"

"Think of all the times you turned down dates or refused a relationship because of your sister. It's time for you, Gabi."

Yes. Time for Gabi. She was going to enjoy herself, for the first time in a decade.

❄

David looked at his watch. His shift was about up. He'd been watching Dancer, who was obviously not Gabi. This person stood stiffly and barely interacted with the people. Whoever this was did not respond to the children and seemed uncomfortable with their hugs. And this person never danced. Not even a toe tap.

But none of that bothered David because he figured that Gabi had taken the evening off so she could prepare for their date.

What did bother David was Rod. The man glared at him all evening. It surprised David that he showed up at all after his humiliating experience last night. And he apparently blamed David.

By seven forty-five, Gabi entered the festival grounds. She looked beautiful with her red-blond hair in soft waves, jeans that showed off her legs, and a camel suede jacket that fit her curves nicely.

She waved but stood near the elf until David's last customer left. He joined her. "You look very nice." And she smelled amazing. He took her hand and led her away. She thanked him with a pleasant smile gracing her lips.

They walked past the snow pavilion. Gabi pointed at it. "What, you're not going to challenge me to a snowball fight?"

"You want me to?"

"No!" She grabbed on to his elbow. "Not tonight."

He got the message. No more acting like children. This night was for the adults.

They wandered through the vendors, listened to Christmas music, and marveled at the falling snow. Gabi held her hand out to catch the "flakes." The manufactured stuff fell every so often, delighting the festival-goers.

"See?" She flung her arms wide. "We are transported back to Bedford Falls, and we are no longer in the South."

"You're right. Christmas movies have influenced us."

He jumped onto a container holding a lamppost. "You want the moon, Gabi? I'll lasso it for it you."

Gabi giggled. "If you expect me to sing the song about misfit toys, you're mistaken."

David hopped down and reached for her hand. "Nah, but I am serious about the moon." With a tiny tug, he pulled her into his arms. His gaze lingered on her face for a moment, and then his lips touched hers. He intended to give her a short, sweet kiss, but when she leaned into him, he knew she had given permission for something deeper.

When they parted, she glanced around, a blush coloring her cheeks. But he wasn't about to apologize for kissing her in public. Gabi deserved to be kissed—and often.

A small grin played on her lips.

"What?" he asked. "I didn't think my kiss was that goofy."

She pushed at him playfully. "No. I was just thinking of my sister. She predicted we'd have our first kiss tonight."

"Jerica is a special little girl."

"Not so little. She's a teenager now." A frown replaced the

smile. "I wonder if she will ever experience a first kiss."

David didn't trust himself to respond to that. Gabi deserved to know the truth about him, how he could easily identify with the tragedy. But right after a first kiss was not the time to tell her.

Chapter 8

Naylene ran to Gabi as she entered the gift shop the next day. "Well? What happened? Did he kiss you?"

Gabi laughed, something she realized came easier ever since she'd met David. "Whoa! That's not what last night was all about."

"That's what last night was totally about. Come on. I want details."

"We had a very nice talk."

A smile blossomed on Naylene's face. "Oh, he totally kissed you."

Gabi nodded, and then she found herself in a vigorous hug with Naylene.

Captain Rod stopped outside the window at that moment while chatting with Jason, the other boat captain. Both women burst out laughing.

"I don't know what I ever saw in him," Gabi said.

"Me either. It's like our signs say: 'Pretty to look at, nice to hold, but, man, those stories sure got old.'"

"Our signs don't say that."

"I improvised."

In the short amount of time when they weren't chattering, Gabi thought she'd heard Rod say David's name. She stood near the window.

"Ooh," Naylene said, oblivious to Gabi's eavesdropping. "Here's another one: 'Pretty to look at, Rod's not so bold—l'"

"Shh." Gabi waved at Naylene to be quiet.

"Yeah," Rod was saying, "that Preston guy is lucky this whole town doesn't turn on him and run him out."

What big story was he telling this time? And why did he involve David in his tale?

"I heard he was a real rebel when he was a kid," Rod continued. "No home or business was safe with him around. And now he acts all high and mighty, like he's better than us."

More of Rod's lies. Their voices faded as they moved away from the window, but Gabi heard the other man say, "That's not all. Everyone knew the kid couldn't stay sober. I heard he was drunk and caused an accident one night."

"Yeah. I heard that, too. . ."

Gabi felt all the blood drain from her face.

Naylene must have heard it, too, because her eyes registered as much surprise as Gabi felt. She shook her head. "No, Gabi. They're wrong. It's just Rod shooting off his big mouth again."

Had Gabi's chest just imploded? She willed air to fill her lungs. "But it wasn't just Rod. Jason is the one who mentioned an accident."

"Well, he got his facts wrong then."

"Maybe not." Gabi leaned on the counter. Her knees wobbled as realization dawned. "I've tried to get David to talk about his past, but he changes the subject every time." Roiling acid crept into her throat. "Oh, Naylene. What if he really did hurt somebody? Why wouldn't he tell me?"

"How could he tell you? He's gotten close enough to know how passionate you are about the subject."

Gabi heard Naylene but wasn't ready to listen. "He even tried to convince me to tell Jerica's story."

"Maybe he's working up the courage to tell you."

"Courage?" Gabi glared at Naylene. "The all-perfect David is a coward. He should have told me before he kissed me."

"Or maybe he was hoping to show you who he really is now before shocking you with who he was in the past. If he'd opened with that, you wouldn't have given him the time of day."

Gabi considered this. "People change, don't they?"

"All the time."

"I'll talk to him tonight; he's coming over after the festival. The David I know is thoughtful, loving. He cares for his nephew, and he's made a friend in Jerica. Something doesn't add up."

She managed to make it through the rest of the day, focusing on the kiss and the beautiful evening they had together. She remembered his thoughtfulness to include Jerica in the ice-skating and his gentleness with her during the boat ride.

But was he only trying to be extra nice because of his guilt?

❄

David had looked forward to seeing Gabi again, as Dancer and as herself later that night. But as he watched Dancer, he wondered if Gabi had decided to stay home again. This Dancer wasn't as dull as the one from the previous night but certainly not as animated as Gabi. She never came over to tease him, and her dancing seemed stiff, like she was forcing herself to have a good time.

Once in a while, he'd catch the reindeer and the elf watching him, but then they'd quickly turn away.

If it was Gabi in the suit, something was wrong. He searched his memory for anything he may have said to offend her, but all he came up with was the great time they'd had last night.

And the kiss. She was into that kiss.

Rick Stanton entered the festival grounds. The tall ex-police officer still prompted an instinct in David to run, but he held his ground and reminded himself he was no longer the boy who couldn't stay out of trouble.

"I see you took me seriously," Rick said as he got closer.

"Yes, sir. This gig has been fun."

"Best community service you ever performed?"

David remembered joking about this with Rick when he'd visited him at his sister's house recently. "Or at least a close second. Nothing could beat garbage detail during the festival of '93." He snickered at his own sarcasm.

"The vendors appreciated your service that day. Felt it was sweet revenge. You had them jumping the year before."

"Hey, not entirely my fault. A friend dared me to shoplift one item from each booth."

Rick's eyebrow arced, and David felt like that sixteen-year-old delinquent again. But then Rick laughed, a hearty sound that warmed David's heart.

"Well," Rick patted David on the shoulder. "Looks like you've got some customers."

A family with three teenage daughters positioned themselves in front of the tree with the help of the assistant.

Rick walked away but said over his shoulder, "Maybe this is one community service you'll finish."

David shook his head. He hoped if anyone had heard Rick, they would know he was kidding.

The line began to grow, keeping David busy for a half hour. When he turned to see how Dancer was doing, she was nowhere in sight. Naylene was gone, too.

Strange, they rarely left their post together.

Maybe Gabi was just nervous about seeing him that evening and Naylene left with her to help her get ready. It wasn't like they were going on a big date, but it would be the first time they'd seen each other after their kiss.

Even David began to feel nervous. Only, his nervousness didn't center on how he looked but rather on what he needed to tell Gabi before their relationship deepened any further.

In a few short hours, he would know whether he had a shot at a future with Gabi.

Chapter 9

I can't believe this." Gabi combed through her freshly shampooed, wet hair, staring at her pale face in her vanity dresser mirror. She and Naylene had slipped into her bedroom before Jerica could see them. She didn't want to explain why they were home early.

Naylene sat on her bed, still in elf costume, but thank goodness she had taken off the ears. "Me either, but I know what I heard."

"Community service?"

"Yep. There was Officer Stanton telling him he'd better finish his community service."

"Isn't he retired?"

"Yeah, but I'm sure he still has friends on the force."

"It doesn't make any sense. David hasn't been here long enough to get into trouble and certainly not long enough for a court hearing and sentence."

Nausea roiled in Gabi's stomach. "Do you think it has anything to do with the accident he caused?"

"I don't know." Naylene fell silent. Very uncharacteristic of her.

The doorbell rang and both of them jumped.

"It's him." Gabi grabbed a hair tie and pulled her moist hair into a bun.

Naylene hopped off the bed and reached for the bedroom doorknob. "You want me to get rid of him?"

"No. I have to talk with him. Clear the air."

As they walked down the hall toward the living room, Jerica's voice greeted David. Gabi swallowed the regret in her throat. How would this new revelation affect her little sister?

"I brought you something from the festival." David handed Jerica a small square box with a red ribbon tied around it.

"What. . .is. . .it?" She rolled the box in her hands.

"Let me help you open it." He untied the ribbon, leaving the actual opening of the box to Jerica.

Her eyes grew large as she unveiled her surprise. "A. . .snow . . .globe!"

"Look." David seemed as excited as Jerica, and Gabi wanted to erase everything she'd heard about him and start over. David shook the globe. "See the penguins ice-skating in there? I thought it would be a nice memory of our first *date* together."

"Oh. . .David! I. . .love. . .it!"

She threw her arms around his neck, and David returned the hug.

He stood and noticed Gabi. Slipping his hands into his pockets, he rocked on his heels. "I couldn't wait until Christmas."

Could the man make this any harder?

He seemed to take in her appearance, and his face fell. "I *was* supposed to come tonight, wasn't I?"

Gabi took great care in not caring about her appearance when she arrived home from the festival that evening. She'd thrown on gray sweatpants with her faded Florida Gators long-sleeved T-shirt.

"This is what I look like every night. We all have our little secrets, don't we?"

He blanched slightly. "I'm sorry—I didn't mean—you look great."

"Liar."

She hoped it didn't come out as mean as it sounded, but when Naylene sprinted to the door and opened it, saying, "Okay, kids, let's take this outside," Gabi began to regret her attitude, especially in front of Jerica.

With a deep breath, she placed a smile on her face. "Thank you, David, for being so thoughtful. I'm sure Jerica will cherish her gift for years to come." She turned to Jerica. "We're just going out to the porch to talk. Okay?"

Jerica smiled and nodded then wheeled away with the snow globe in her lap.

Before Gabi could say anything, Naylene stood just inches from David, her arms folded and a defiant look on her face. Clearly, she thought she was going to be a part of the showdown.

"Um, Naylene." Gabi pressed her friend's elbow and led her off the porch. "I'll see you tomorrow. Thanks for, um, coming over on such short notice. You're a great friend."

Naylene backed away, understanding dawning in her features. "Okay, but call me later."

"I will."

As Naylene drove away, Gabi turned to David. Even in the dark, she could see how confused he looked. "Please"—she indicated one of the two wooden porch chairs—"have a seat."

"I think I'd rather stand."

"Okay, suit yourself."

"Are you breaking up with me before we even become a couple?"

She leaned against the porch rail. "It depends."

"What did I do?"

Might as well launch right in. "It's what you didn't do. Why didn't you tell me you had been an alcoholic and caused an accident?"

❋

An expletive nearly slipped from his lips. How did she find out? He didn't want her to learn through gossip.

He drew his hands in front of him, trying to push the accusation away. "I was going to tell you tonight."

She pressed her collarbone and gasped her next breath. "Then it's true?"

"Gabi, I—"

"No, let me get this straight. You had this in your past, and you didn't think of telling me before now?"

"I'm not that man—"

"You lied to me. You lied to Jerica."

"Now, wait a minute." He took a step forward, and Gabi lifted her chin. "I didn't lie. It just never came up in the conversation."

"Oh, how about when we discussed Jerica's accident? It might have been good for you to slip it in then, don't you think?"

"No, I don't think. That was a tender moment, hardly the time to bring something like that up. If I had, you'd probably never have wanted to see me again."

"Well, guess what?"

The hard look in her eyes nearly destroyed David. It was exactly as he had feared. But if he'd been the one to tell her, he could have eased her into it. Softened the blow. With him on the defensive, how could he soothe her wound?

He took a step off the porch then turned. "How did you find out?"

Her mouth clasped shut, as if she were reluctant to tell him. Finally she blurted out, "Captain Rod."

"Are you serious?"

"And another man. They were talking about it just outside the gift shop. But then Naylene heard you talking to Officer Stanton at the festival."

Officer Stanton? Oh. He closed his eyes, embarrassed at what was coming next.

"She was passing by and heard him mention that you were finishing your community service. So, I assume you're not the man I thought you were."

With a mirthless chuckle, he attempted to explain. "When I was a teen, I had a drinking problem. I was bored and had way too much time on my hands. I kept the police on their toes. Mostly light stuff, pranks, small misdemeanors. As punishment, I ended up doing everything from dog walking to mowing the cemetery. Once, I skipped out on finishing a sentence. I was put in jail for three days to make up for it." Only the sound of frogs croaking in the darkness met his ears. "Officer Stanton was joking."

Gabi stood on the porch glaring down at him. He knew he wasn't defending himself very well, but at least he was able to tell her everything he had meant to.

She hadn't booted him off the property yet, so he continued. "Officer Stanton and I became close during those years. He's a great guy and saw potential in me that no one else, not even my parents, could see. He gave me his camera, realizing that I needed a creative outlet. It was my ticket out of here and out of the destruction I had been building for years."

"What about the accident?" Her voice lay flat, like a panther stalking its prey.

"I was seventeen. It wasn't the first time I drove drunk, but it was the last time. I was out joyriding with friends. We scored a couple of bottles of Jack Daniels. I honestly didn't think I was drunk; I just thought I was buzzed. We were coming home from a party in Wedgefield and were driving pretty fast along Colonial when we came on another car going the same direction. We—I passed it, but misjudged how close, and I ran the car off the road. It was dark, and it was—"

"Raining." She closed her eyes while finishing his sentence.

"Yes."

Gabi folded in two as she grabbed her stomach. She reached for the chair and slid into it. "Just like the night of Jerica's accident."

The two were silent for a moment. Finally, she asked, "Was there anybody hurt?"

Oh, man. She didn't know that part. It was his turn to crumple to the porch step. "An unborn baby. The driver was a young pregnant woman. She was alone." He threw his arms over his head.

An unearthly wailing sound came from Gabi's throat.

"I was just a kid, Gabi. A stupid little rebel." His voice cracked.

When he could trust it again, he looked at her. "But after I did my time for that one, I made sure neither I nor any of my friends drove drunk when I was with them. I'd like to say I straightened myself out after that, but the accident only made things worse. My parents were ready to kick me out of the house. If it hadn't been for Officer Stanton. . . ." He let his voice trail off, sensing that Gabi didn't really care about him at this point.

He stood, but she wouldn't look at him. "That's it. No more surprises from me. I promised my sister I'd be here until New Year's, and then I'll be gone. Nothing but a bad memory for you."

He left Gabi in a fetal position on the front porch.

Chapter 10

Gabi drove past the festival site on her way to work. Clouds hung low, and the forecast was bleak.

The gloom in the sky matched her heart. David's revelation last night felt like he had rained on her parade, and judging from her soggy pillow that morning, it had extended into her dreams.

Normally, she and Naylene took turns carpooling to work, but today she needed to be alone before subjecting herself to Naylene's constant chatter. She pulled into the Jungle Adventures parking lot, turned off the ignition, and sat in the silence for a moment longer.

"Lord," she prayed, "why did You let me give my heart to this man? David could have easily been the one to cause Jerica's accident. I know he said he changed, but do alcoholics ever truly heal?" The court report had said that the man who hit Jerica had several DUI's. And she knew from friends with alcoholics in their families that it was easy for them to fall off the wagon. "I can't risk it. I know You can do anything, but I can't subject Jerica to the potential heartbreak."

Once she composed herself, she left her car and entered the

building just as sheets of rain began to fall.

Naylene stood looking out the window with her arms folded. "Going to be a long day. I doubt anyone will come out in this." When she turned to look at Gabi, she must have seen her anguish, and she ran to her. "I'm so sorry about David," she whispered with a hug.

Gabi wiped her cheeks. "Thanks for talking me down last night after he left. I was a mess."

"I doubt that we both have to be here today. You want to ask Harold if you can go home?"

"No, I'd rather keep myself busy here."

With only a handful of brave tourists visiting the park, Gabi spent the rest of the day deep cleaning the shop.

Rain still fell by the tub full, so by closing, Naylene called her mother to see if the festival was open.

After a brief chat, she hung up. "Nope. They're predicting more rain this evening. But looks like it'll dry out tomorrow and be nice the next five days through Christmas."

Gabi, grateful not to have to pretend to be perky in her Dancer costume, went home and mustered up the courage to talk to Jerica. Gabi had slipped into her room last night after talking to David and left before Jerica awoke. She hadn't told her about him yet.

After dinner, she sought Jerica out. Finding her in her bedroom, Gabi knocked lightly. "May I come in?"

"Sure." Jerica sat in her chair, parked under her reading lamp in the corner. She set her book aside and gave Gabi a wary look. "You. . .okay. . .Gabi?"

"Yeah." The snow globe sat on Jerica's bedside table. She

probably went to sleep looking at it last night. "Actually, no." Gabi sat on the end of the bed.

"You. . .were. . .quiet. . .at. . .dinner."

"I know."

"Is. . .it. . .David?"

Gabi's jaw dropped. "How did you know?"

"You. . .weren't. . .happy. . .to. . .see. . .him. . .last. . .night."

"No, I wasn't." She looked down at her hands. "I found out something about him. Something that will change our relationship with him." She paused, searching for the right words. "A few years ago, he drove a car while drunk and hurt someone."

"How. . .many. . .years?"

"What does it matter? He never told us about it. That's why I'm angry with him."

"Does. . .he. . .still. . .drink?"

"I don't think so." She thought about all the conversations she'd had with him. "No. He doesn't."

"David. . .is. . .good."

"I know but—"

"He. . .would. . .never. . .hurt. . .us."

"He should have told us."

"But. . .*that*. . .would. . .have. . .hurt. . .us."

Gabi looked at her little sister, growing up before her eyes. "So, you're saying that maybe he didn't know how to tell us for fear of causing pain?"

Jerica gave her a "Well, duh!" look.

"He did say he was going to tell me last night, but I accused him before he had a chance." Gabi groaned. It was because he didn't want to hurt them that he had delayed revealing his past.

"Are you okay knowing David did this?"

"Has. . .God. . .forgiven. . .him?"

Ouch. Another good one. "I'm sure He has."

"Then. . .maybe. . .we. . .should. . .too."

Gabi kissed Jerica's head. "You're right." She kissed her head again. "And you're smart." She kissed her head again, and Jerica giggled. "And you're growing up way too fast."

She left the room and went to her own. Her cell phone lay on the dresser, and she snatched it up. She and David had exchanged phone numbers the night of the kiss.

The kiss.

Such a simple and sweet gesture, but in that moment she had silently pledged to trust David. And she had let him down.

"Lord, please forgive me for refusing to listen. For using my own pain to cause pain in someone else. Help me to channel my feelings in a productive way."

Palming her phone, she scrolled to his number. After three rings, it went to his voice mail. She left a message for him to call her but wondered where he might be. Surely he always had his phone with him.

Or was he ignoring her?

She shook off that thought and prayed he'd call back before she went to bed.

❄

The next morning, Gabi awoke and there still was no phone call from David. She thought of calling him again but decided against it. She didn't want to appear pushy.

Throughout her day at work, she had trouble concentrating.

Why hadn't he called her back? Well, he couldn't ignore her later, when they were both at the festival. Of course, she'd have to reveal herself as Dancer, but that was okay. They'd had enough secrets for one relationship.

When Gabi and Naylene arrived at the festival that evening, much of it was still soggy. But thanks to straw pathways and volunteers with towels, the place was open for business. She donned her reindeer costume, thankful her festival job was almost over. Naylene had signed them up until December 21 because she was going out of town the week of Christmas.

David wasn't at his post. Another photographer was there, chatting with festival folk and shooting away. Gabi tapped Naylene on the shoulder and pointed to the photographer.

"Where's David?" Naylene asked, as if Gabi had the answer.

Gabi shrugged.

"You want me to go find out?"

"Yes," Gabi yelled in her costume head.

She watched Naylene as she talked to the photographer then had to will her heart back down her throat when she saw Naylene gasp and cover her mouth with her hands.

Naylene ran back to her. "He's been in an accident."

Gabi ripped off the reindeer head, not concerned at all that it ruined the effect. "What? How?"

"I don't know. All this guy could tell me was that it happened last night and drinking was involved."

Nausea swept through Gabi. "And it was raining. Oh Naylene, how could he?"

People were beginning to stare, so Naylene pulled Gabi behind the Jungle Adventures booth. "Maybe he fell off the wagon after your talk."

"So, it's my fault." Gabi marched toward Naylene's car.

"Where are you going?"

"To get to the bottom of this. If you don't want to go, then give me your keys."

"Oh, I'm going." She sprinted to catch up. "I may have a few things to say to him if he's in any shape to hear it."

Gabi shrugged out of the reindeer costume and threw it, along with the head, in the backseat while Naylene hopped in and gunned the engine.

They drove to Titusville, where the nearest hospital was. Once inside, Gabi started to search out the information desk, but on the way, she saw Tyler walking toward the door with a woman.

"Tyler?" she called out to the boy before they disappeared out the door.

"Gabi!" He ran to her and hugged her waist. "Where's Jerica?"

"She's not with me right now." She wanted to ask him about David but was afraid the news might be too bleak for an eight-year-old to share.

The woman joined them. "Hey, Ty. Who is this?" She was the female version of David, including his expressive green eyes.

Gabi held out her hand. "I'm Gabi Archer, and this is Naylene Burnett." Naylene still had on the elf ears.

"Ah. David's Gabi. I'm his sister, Connie Baxter." Her genuine smile put Gabi at ease. "Are you here to see David?"

"I'm here to find out what happened. Is he okay?"

"Let's talk over there." Connie led the way to a small group of chairs near a Christmas tree tastefully decorated with tongue depressors. "They're releasing him today. They kept him overnight because he had a nasty bump on his head, and they feared a concussion." She glanced at her watch. "And with the hospital on half staff for the holidays, it took them all day to release him. My husband is in there helping him get ready."

Gabi shook her head. "Why is it they always walk away?"

"Excuse me?" Connie tipped her head to the side and frowned.

"Oh, don't get me wrong. I'm happy he's not hurt—"

"I wouldn't call a near concussion, jammed knee, and dislocated shoulder 'not hurt.'"

"You're right." Gabi tried to will herself not to say what she was really thinking. That David shouldn't have been in the car after drinking in the first place. She'd reserve that for him. "I'm sorry. Can you tell me what happened?"

Connie's phone trilled, and she looked at the incoming text. "This is my husband. David's on his way out, and he wants me to have the car ready. I'm sure he can fill you in."

She left with Tyler, who was now wearing Naylene's elf ears. Apparently, she was keeping the boy entertained while they talked, and she now followed them out.

A man whom Gabi assumed was David's brother-in-law came into the lobby pushing him in a wheelchair, his left leg propped up and his right arm in a sling. He also held a crutch, and Gabi assumed hospital policy forbade him to walk until he was safely in a vehicle.

David saw her and his face lit up. "Gabi!"

When she didn't run to him or exclaim over his injuries, his face fell. She remained stoic, her arms folded.

"Your ride will be here soon," his brother-in-law said after looking at a text on his phone.

David looked at Gabi warily but said, "Tell her to wait a

minute." Then he spoke to Gabi. "Are you still angry with me?"

"What do you think?" She spit it out and was surprised at the tone in her own voice.

He frowned. "Look, I apologized for not telling you about my past. I don't know what more I can do. Why are you here?"

"I wanted to look you in the eye and tell you how disappointed I am in you."

"Whoa, lady," David's brother-in-law said. "Aren't you being a little harsh?"

David held up the crutch and handed it to him. "Easy, Shawn. Why don't you go watch for Connie?"

Shawn left but looked back before disappearing out the door.

"Now," David leaned forward and winced. "What's this about? I get the feeling we're not talking about my past anymore."

Gabi's instincts were to reach out to him, let him know that she hurt because he hurt. But she steeled herself. "How could you start drinking again?"

"What? I haven't started drinking."

"The photographer who substituted for you said you were in an accident and it was drinking related."

David nodded his head, exaggerating the motion. "Okay. It was drinking related. You heard me say it, now you can leave." He tried to back up the wheelchair but went in a half circle due to using only one hand.

"Wait. Won't you tell me what happened?" Gabi pressed her hand to her heart. "Did I cause you to stumble?"

He spat out an ugly laugh. "You? You think you're that important that I would throw away fourteen years of sobriety because we had a fight?"

"Well, what then?" Her voice had shrunk a notch. This was not going the way she'd planned in her head.

"Listen, Gabi." His voice dropped to just above a whisper. "I know you have issues with drinking and driving. And I'm happy you're finally beginning to show your feelings. But I thought we had something special. If you jump to conclusions every time something like this happens, then maybe we're not meant to be."

He finally wheeled to where he was facing the door and tried to move toward it, but the chair still only responded to the one wheel, and he came back full circle to her. He sat back and sighed. "Would you mind pushing me outside?"

"What do you mean jumping to conclusions? Were you drinking last night, or weren't you?"

"No, I was not. I'm the victim. The other guy got the DUI."

"Oh."

"Yeah. *Oh.*" He rubbed his temple. "Listen. I'm sorry for the way I just reacted, but I have worked so hard to get that monkey off my back. I am not the same guy I was when I lived here. I have since quit drinking, paid restitution, and made amends to everyone I hurt along the way."

❄

David's heart pounded as Gabi retreated into the back of her chair. Her cheeks had flamed red while accusing him but now they went ashen. She squeezed her eyes shut. "I'm so sorry." She took a moment, apparently composing herself. After a deep breath, she opened her eyes and looked at him. He saw tangible regret in their depths. "I've abused this newfound boldness. I can't explain my actions other than to say all of this has built up over the years.

You're the unfortunate soul who happened to be in front of me when it blew."

David understood, all too well. "I kinda dumped on you, too." He reached for her hands. "You know, I've been running from my bad-boy stigma for a while now. I threw myself into my career, and the only thing lacking has been someone to share it with. You were the first person, and I was hoping the only person, I would ever consider sharing my past, present, and future with." He wiggled her hands to emphasize his words. "But I don't need someone suspicious of me. I need someone supportive, trusting, dependable."

"I can be those things." Her words were so soft, he thought shy Gabi had returned.

But then she stood, placing her hands on the arms of his chair, and gazed directly into his eyes. "From now on, I can be supportive." She pecked his lips gently. "Trusting." Another peck. "Dependable." A deeper kiss that he could not reject if his life depended upon it.

"Have you two made up?" Naylene stood close, wearing those silly ears.

"I think so," Gabi said. She looked at David, while still inches away from his face. "We good?"

"Oh, we are very good." He wrapped his arm around her waist and pulled her to his lap. "And getting better."

Chapter 11

Is. . .David. . .coming. . .over. . .today?" Jerica sat at the table cutting cookies out of the dough Gabi had just rolled out for her.

"He is." Gabi stood at the stove stirring fudge. She loved their tradition of baking on Christmas Eve. Just her and Jerica. What had started out as therapy years ago for Jerica's motor skills had turned into their special present to the family. "We're all going to church tonight, his family and ours."

"Yay."

"You like David, don't you, Jelly Bean?"

Jerica nodded. She had lost her heart to David as much as Gabi. "I. . .like. . .Ty. . .too." She struggled with a cookie dough bell as she laid it on the sheet. It stretched until it looked more like a misshaped candy cane than a bell. This didn't faze her as she moved on to the next one. "Will. . .he. . .be. . .my. . .cousin?"

"Who?"

"Ty. When. . .you. . .and. . .David. . .get. . .married."

"Whoa. He didn't officially propose. We just met, you know." Jerica shrugged, as if this were only a minor technicality.

"Besides, I don't know if I could ever leave you."

242

They worked in silence for a moment, and then Jerica pointed a look at Gabi. "Why. . .didn't. . .you. . .trust. . .God?"

"What?" Gabi swung away from the stove, and a dollop of fudge dripped to the floor.

"He. . .changed. . .David."

"So, you're asking why I didn't trust that He'd changed David?"

Jerica nodded.

Gabi placed the spoon down and pulled a chair up to Jerica. "It's more complicated than that, Jelly Bean."

"Why?"

"Well, because people have a mind of their own. God may have changed him on the inside, but it was up to David to allow that change on the outside."

"Why. . .don't. . .you. . .trust. . .God. . .with. . .yourself?"

"What are you talking about?" Sometimes Jerica had trouble forming thoughts in her head. This was undoubtedly one of those times.

"I'm. . .okay. Now. . .it's. . .your. . .turn. . .to. . .be. . .okay."

Then again, maybe not. "Are you telling me it's time to join the human race?"

"You. . .have. . .a. . .mind. . .of. . .your. . .own." She placed a doughy hand on Gabi's arm. "Trust. . .God."

The two hugged—a long, sisterly hug, but also in some respects a good-bye hug. Jerica had just told Gabi in her own way that it was time to leave the nest.

That evening, the two families worshipped together. Gabi had already apologized to Connie for her rudeness when she thought David had been drinking. Connie graciously accepted. And now they were all singing "Silent Night" together and lighting each other's candles.

Gabi followed David's family home. He still wasn't able to drive, but he wanted to be alone with her for a little longer. They sat on his sister's porch talking into the night, and a bittersweet feeling came over Gabi as she realized he would soon be leaving.

She remembered Jerica telling her that it was her turn to be okay. To trust God.

"David." She snuggled into his side as they sat on the porch swing, immobile because David's leg was propped on a pillow in an Adirondack chair. Still, it was romantic.

"Hmm?" He nuzzled her hair.

"I think I'm ready to tell Jerica's story."

He pulled away so he could look at her. "Really? In front of people?"

"Even worse. I'd like to write a book and use it as a speaking platform."

"Wonderful. You'll be great." He settled back in.

"And I want to put your story in there, too."

This made him sit up straight. He started to say something, but apparently, the words wouldn't come.

Gabi continued. "I want to tell it from both perspectives. You have a very powerful story of redemption. Hers is of forgiveness. I've already started an outline." To continue to make her point, she added, "It would be healing for all of us."

❄

Now the shoe was on the other foot. David gazed at the woman by his side, remembering how shy she was when he first met her at the gift shop. So much had happened between then and now.

He had wanted her to tell Jerica's story, but he wasn't sure about his. He'd worked so hard at burying it—could he allow it to resurface now?

"Say something." She gazed at him, worry drawing her brows together.

"You know, when I first met you, I wondered about your name. You weren't at all gabby, but so sweet and shy. But now I think you're more like the angel Gabriel who had an important message to tell the world."

"I do have a message, and I've been testing it out, but I haven't been relating it very well. I want people to understand that God can help change the addict who wants out. He can help the victim to forgive. He's a God of justice and mercy. His laws are firm, but His grace is sufficient. I don't want to be just another angry person seeking retribution. I want to let people know that there is an escape from their prison, and God is the door."

"Oh, that's good. Did you write it down?"

Gabi snuggled again into his chest. "It's in my outline."

"You know, I've seen both sides of the coin, as an offender and as a victim. When that guy hit me the other night, a strange thing happened."

"What?" Her concerned gaze helped him form the words he'd not been able to articulate until now.

"In an accident, some people see their lives flash before their eyes. But I saw the life I had taken. The child who never had the chance to meet his parents. The child who never learned to walk or to play. Who never went to school. It felt like an odd court sentence, to feel what that family must have felt at the moment of impact." He rubbed his neck. "That was more effective than any jail time or community service. If you can write that experience, then I would be honored for you to tell my story."

"Really?" She gazed up at him.

"If it changes just one life, it would be worth it." He kissed her head. "So, proclaim your message, Angel Gabriella. Give people hope."

Chapter 12

After Christmas, Gabi had her first opportunity to unfurl her angel wings. She learned of a Victim Impact Panel given by Mothers Against Drunk Driving in Orlando, strategically scheduled before New Year's Eve to make their point not to drink and drive that night.

Located in a church, the program gave victims and their families a chance to share their stories with DUI offenders—without confrontation.

David offered to go with her, and she knew what a sacrifice that was. How could he sit there and listen to the pain-filled speeches when he could easily be on the side of the offenders? Yet recently, he also knew what it was like to be a victim.

When it was her turn, she wiped her sweaty palms on her skirt. Jerica reached over to squeeze her shoulder, lending much-needed moral support. She took a deep breath and searched out David who smiled at her from the back of the room.

She spoke as she had to David on the porch swing a few nights prior. In fact, she looked right at him, pretending they were alone again. After she was through, there was barely a dry eye in the house. She prayed that God's message came through, not just hers.

A few days later on New Year's Eve, Gabi sat with David in the wicker love seat, aptly named as she snuggled under his arm breathing in the scent from his black leather jacket. His cane leaned on the railing, and the sling propping his arm was gone, although Gabi thought that a little premature.

Because she had worked so hard at the Christmas festival, Harold had given her the holidays off plus a bonus. Naylene, of course, had already taken time off for a vacation, but she had received a nice bonus, also.

Gabi lifted her face to the sunshine, letting it soak into her skin. The breeze nipped a little, but the warm rays helped Gabi to imagine the coming of spring.

But did she want time to pass quickly? She sighed.

"What is it, Gabi?" David nuzzled her hair.

"Just hold me and never let me go."

"No problem." He lifted her chin with his finger and kissed her.

Someone cleared their throat, startling the couple. "I'm sorry," the mailman said. "Letters for you, Miss Gabi."

She stood, regretting the cool air that invaded her warm side now that David was no longer protecting it.

"Thanks, Dwight." She reached for the mail.

The older man tipped his hat at David. "Nice day for sittin' on the porch." His eyes twinkled as he turned. "Happy New Year, y'all."

Gabi grinned at David, happy to see his cheeks blush. She, herself, must have looked like a cranberry.

She joined him again and wiggled her way back to her spot.

With the envelopes in her hands, she started riffling through them. "Three late Christmas cards, a bill, and. . .what's this?" She lifted a card and set the others aside. "A card from you?"

He shrugged and she planted a kiss on his chin. "You're so sweet."

Gabi brushed her finger over his name then over the Christmas, Florida, postmark. Her joy turned bittersweet. When he resumed his travels, the postmark would be from some remote country. Would this be the only way for them to connect?

She opened it and laughed at the cartoon reindeer. Inside, in bold ink, David had written, "On Dancer! Your speech went well, even without the tutu."

"Oh!" She gasped and covered her mouth as realization hit her. "You knew I was Dancer all along!"

"I'm going to miss the reindeer in a tutu." He smiled and chucked her chin. "She brightened my day every time she twirled."

"And I'll miss the Christmas festival. No more Bedford Falls of the South. Just another dull old field."

"Yeah. It'll be hard to drive by there day after day, remembering the great times we had."

She sat up straight and looked at him. "What do you mean, day after day? You're leaving soon, aren't you?"

"You ready to see me go?"

"No!" She grabbed his waist and squeezed.

"I've decided to stop traveling," David said.

"Oh, *that's* great." Although thrilled to be able to hold on to David for even longer, Gabi raised her hand in mock disgust. "Just when I was about to tell you I'd follow you anywhere."

"Why, Gabriella Archer, are you proposing to me?"

She tilted her head. "Maybe I am."

"Then I accept." He pulled her into a deep kiss, and she returned it, sealing her commitment.

When they parted, she said, "Oh! I have something for you, too."

"A ring?" He clapped his hands.

"We'll go shopping for one later."

He snapped his fingers, feigning disappointment.

She entered the house and returned with a greeting card. "I was going to mail it after you left, but since you aren't leaving now. . . ."

As he opened it, she sat by his side. He smiled when he saw the angel blowing a trumpet.

"It's a thank-you card," she said.

"For what?"

"For seeing me as God sees me. I had withdrawn so far away from the world, I don't know how I ever could have made it back without your help."

"Oh, my Angel Gabriella. You always had the wings, you just needed to learn how to use them. Just promise me one thing."

"What?" Gabi thought she'd never feel more right than at that moment.

"Don't fly too far away from me." He kissed her again. And again. And again. . .

 Kathleen E. Kovach and her husband, Jim, raised two sons while living the nomadic lifestyle for over twenty years in the Air Force. She's a grandmother, though much too young for that. Now firmly planted in Colorado, she's a member of American Christian Fiction Writers and leads a local writers' group. Kathleen hopes her readers will giggle through her books while learning the spiritual truths God has placed there. Please visit Kathleen at www.kathleenekovach.com.

You're a Charmer, Mr. Grinch

Paula Moldenhauer

DEDICATION

Dedicated to Jerry who waited for me
to figure it out and to all my friends who
"bazillion-dupled" my joy of a first book contract.

Special thanks to Loretta Milleman, acting postmaster of Fair-
play, Co, and Niki Nowell, who once served as a rural carrier in
Buena Vista, Co. Your expertise in helping me understand the
workings of a small town post office were invaluable.

Chapter 1

Edie Hathaway loved the rush of the cool air flitting through the car and playing with her short, curly hair. She pulled her sweater closer and cranked the Christmas carols on her radio. December in Florida afforded her this pleasure, though the evening air was nippy this time of year. Still, the freedom of the open windows fit her mood. With her grandson, Michael's, present secured, the house decorated, and her handmade crafts delivered to the festival coordinator, she was free to enjoy the holiday season.

Edie's stomach rumbled as she turned onto State Road 50. She put the window up and turned down the radio. No sense looking like a wild teenager now that she was back in familiar territory. After the long day at the Christmas, Florida, post office and the mad dash to Titusville to catch the one-day sale at Walmart, she looked forward to a quiet evening alone. Her little home, neat as a pin when she left this morning, would be a haven. She'd curl up with a cup of soup and her latest novel. Soon she would be whisked from her often harried but predictable life and transported underneath the Tuscan sun.

Her back twinged, and Edie shifted. Though she didn't work

the front most of the year, the busyness of the holiday season made it necessary. On top of running operations and supervising the holiday volunteers, postmaster Edie polished up her customer service skills, smiled at the visitors, and sold stamps.

The memory of Rick's grin as he stood across from her that morning crashed through her comfortable thoughts like an ocean squall. He came regularly to buy prestamped postcards the city of Christmas used as a promotional. Today he had leaned down—all six foot four inches of still-toned muscle—and rested his arm upon the counter, following that intimate move with the audacity of a wink from his baby blues. Would that man never give up? It didn't help that half the town schemed to get them together.

Maybe she should be flattered—after all, most gray-haired retirees had a flat tire about their middle. At least the one chasing her was handsome. Then again, maybe those good looks were the problem—teaching Rick Stanton to charm his way through life . . . just like Frank.

Edie frowned as the car behind her honked. Glancing into her rearview mirror, she saw the driver, who looked like Tom Flanders, motion toward her hood. Was that smoke? She opened her window and leaned her head out. *Hissing.* She moaned and pulled to the side of the road. To her surprise the other car kept going. With a huff she flicked open her cell phone and dialed her daughter. Twilight was deepening, and she had no desire to be left alone as dark fell.

❄

Rick glanced at the number on his cell before answering. "Hello."

"It's Tom. Thought you'd want to know that Edie Hathaway

broke down just east on 50. Saw steam coming from the radiator."

"And you didn't help her?" Rick grimaced at the growl in his voice.

"Simmer down. Figured you might like being her knight in shining armor. But you'd better hurry. If she recognized me she'll be as mad as a hornet I drove by without stopping."

Rick hung up the phone, threw his tow chain into the back of his pickup, and climbed into the cab. How could the man leave Edie stranded? He headed toward 50, frustrated, when his cell rang again.

"It's Randi. I'm sorry to bother you, but I got a call from Mom, and she's having car trouble. It'll be a few minutes before someone can take my shift here at the festival, and I hate to leave her waiting. She probably worked all day then rushed off on errands without any supper. She'd starve before spending a few dollars on fast food."

Rick assured Randi he would take care of her mom and tossed the phone into the seat next to him. The whole town knew of his infatuation with Edie, but this was the first time her daughter had stuck her nose into it. Could Edie be softening?

Their encounter at the post office made him doubt it. All business, Edie's dangling jingle bell earrings had tinkled as she tossed her head in that irritated way of hers. Didn't matter how much he laid on the Southern charm, she didn't bite. If the woman were a largemouth bass he'd have hooked her long ago.

Rick slowed as he saw Edie's car at the side of the road. Good. She was inside with the windows up. You couldn't be too careful on a dark night. Rick flung a prayer upward, hoping the good Lord would grant him even the smallest bit of favor with the stubborn but beautiful redhead waiting in the car. He tapped her window and pasted on a smile as the glass descended. "Good evening, ma'am." Using his best professional protector voice, the one he'd used before he'd retired from the force, he continued, "Looks like you are in need of some assistance."

A flicker of something—irritation, maybe—passed over her gaze, but to his great relief she smiled. "I guess I am. How'd you know?"

"I, uh, got a couple of calls about a stranded motorist"—Rick rubbed the back of his neck—"and headed right over."

"Tom Flanders should have called the station if he weren't man enough to help me himself."

"Yes. Well. . ." Rick took a step back from the smoldering gaze and shone his flashlight toward her hood. "Care if I take a look-see?"

"I'll pop the hood."

It only took a moment to assess the problem. "Radiator hose. I've got my chain. We'll pull her on over to the garage so Jason can look at her tomorrow." Rick rushed to his truck and grabbed the chain and his tool kit, pleased to get about the business of helping Edie and to escape the evaluating gaze of those big green eyes of hers. He whipped out duct tape and wrapped the hose then put a couple of gallons of water into her radiator. Good thing he was always prepared. When the car was ready, he gave careful instructions about how to steer as he pulled it with his truck. He released a pent-up sigh when they reached the garage, safe and sound.

Rick stepped out of his pickup and over to Edie's car. She greeted him with a tired smile. "Thank you." Her stomach growled and she colored, looking cuter than ever.

The weariness on her face and her rumbling tummy strengthened his resolve. "Let's get a bite to eat and then I'll take you on home."

She stiffened.

"Aw, now, don't get your dander up. It's obvious you're hungry, and I haven't had my supper either. It's not a date."

"You've done enough. I don't want to inconvenience you further."

"Edie Hathaway." He leaned closer and lowered his voice. "It's time you dropped your pride long enough to let a guy be gentlemanlike. I am not inconvenienced."

She hesitated, and he stood up straight and winked. "But I am hungry as a bear. Don't make me eat alone after I took the *trouble* to tow you back to town. Come on, Edie." He met her eyes. "Just this once."

He didn't miss the softening in her gaze, but when she opened her mouth to speak he feared another refusal, so he placed a finger on her lips. "Shhh, now. I'm not takin' no for an answer." Surprised he'd allowed himself such an intimate gesture, he stepped away quickly, strode to the pickup, and then opened the door for her.

It was all Rick could do not to yell out, "Hallelujah!" when she turned toward his truck with nary a word and climbed right in. She might not have opened the door to that walled heart, but she'd let him push it back a crack. It'd taken all the willpower he possessed not to kick the whole blamed thing down after years of pursuing Christmas, Florida's favorite single grandma. But patience had its virtue. Now all he had to do was make himself irresistible so she'd let him give that door another nudge.

❄

Edie fought back a sigh as Rick climbed in next to her. How had she let him talk her into this? She glanced at her watch, hoping it was late enough that the café wouldn't be too crowded. All she needed was to prime the rumor mill. She could hear it now. *Looks like that Edie Hathaway ain't as tough as she acts. Maybe that poor love-crazed man will finally win her over.* She shifted on the bench seat and cleared her voice. "Maybe you'd rather come to the house for a can of soup. Don't have anything homemade, but it would be hot."

"Ah, Edie. Let me treat you right for once."

When Rick pulled into Rudolph Restaurant, her heart sank further. She wanted to jump out of the pickup and rush ahead of him, but Rick expected her to act like a lady. She waited for him to open her door.

"Nice, warm night." He took her hand and helped her out of the truck.

She let go as soon as appropriate. "Yes. Good for attendance at the festival."

"I suppose you made doodads to raise money for the church."

She raised an eyebrow. "Doodads?"

"What-cha-ma-call-its."

"They are beautiful, handmade snowflakes, crocheted with great care out of glittering white yarn." She frowned as he opened the restaurant door.

"Never said they weren't pretty." He flashed that million-dollar grin. "But how's a guy supposed to notice the doohickeys with the one who made them standing there looking like beauty herself?"

"Rick Stanton, either you lay off the flirting, or you take me home."

"Yes ma'am." Rick swallowed hard, and Edie felt sorry for him. But couldn't the man just have a normal conversation?

They entered the restaurant in silence. Relieved that none of their circle was there, Edie sat in the chair Rick held for her. When he encouraged her to get anything she wanted, the simple decision threw her into a tizzy. The poor man had taped her radiator hose, towed her car to the shop, and insisted on paying for her meal. She hated for him to spend his money. How much could a retired policeman have to live on? She might offend him by getting something small. Still, she didn't want to let him buy something expensive. Might make him think she would go out with him again.

"Should I order for you?"

Had he read her mind? "Um. . .I think I'd like wings. I hear they're good here." Instantly a picture flashed through her mind of being covered in sauce and making a fool of herself.

"You've never had them?"

"I don't eat out much." Now that all her debt was paid off, she was working on a nest egg for retirement. Never again would she do without the basic necessities.

Rick ordered wings for both of them. "You'll enjoy them more if we're both fighting the sauce," he said with a wink.

Hmmm. . .reading her mind again? She couldn't help but grin at him.

"Tell me about your day at the post office."

"Busy as usual." Edie unwrapped the silverware and put the napkin in her lap. "It never ceases to amaze me how far people will drive just to have *Christmas* stamped on their letter."

"It's a good thing they do. There's not much in this little town to bring in revenue anymore. I'm glad we've started the festival."

The ease of their conversation surprised Edie, as did the way Rick anticipated her needs and made the experience relaxing. Before long, they chuckled together over the sauce that spread all over their faces, and she felt a little flutter in her stomach when he leaned across the table to wipe a spot off her nose. When he paused, hand in midair, and looked at her with a peculiar expression, Edie racked her brain for something to say to redirect his attention. "I suppose you spent the day in your Grinch suit."

"Sure did. It takes a real man to be secure in his masculinity while wearing green tights. Besides, I get a kick out of putting the lights on top of the pickup and pulling over unsuspecting tourists. Sometimes I can't resist saying, 'Do you know how fast you were traveling, sir?' " He chuckled. "You should see the confusion when they look up to see a green face and red Santa hat!"

"I can't believe you tease total strangers."

"They loosen up when they get a gift bag of prestamped postcards and coupons instead of a ticket."

"I'll bet." Edie breathed easier now that his attention was off her.

"Sometimes I try Dr. Seuss speak on them. 'Take off that sour, grinchy frown. You're now in lovely Christmas town!' "

Edie groaned as Rick's booming voice raised a few notches and the other patrons looked up from their meals.

"No garlic in this Grinch's soul,
Not a mean Mr. Grinch on the go.
So, take this bag full of coupons and happy wishes;
Sample our festival's delights and dishes.

Sing folks! Sing, sing on this jolly day;
Celebrate Christmas, Florida's way!"

Edie chuckled. "You don't."

"I do." He waggled his eyebrows.

A jingle from the bell over the door caught their attention, and Edie couldn't help narrowing her gaze as she recognized the patron. "Thomas Flanders."

Rick glanced up. "He should've stopped to help, Edie. But it worked out, didn't it?"

"I think we'd better go." Tom had set her up, and she'd fallen for it.

Rick nodded and motioned for the check, but Edie couldn't wait. If she didn't escape Tom and the amused look in his eyes, she would say something she would regret. Edie rushed outside and climbed into Rick's pickup, watching through the window as Tom gave Rick a thumbs-up and Rick frowned. By the time Rick joined her, Edie could barely look at him.

"You all right?"

"Just take me home, Rick." She turned from his pleading gaze. This whole thing was a bad idea.

Chapter 2

The aroma of fresh coffee brushed against Edie's senses. Keeping her eyes closed, she allowed the soft morning light to caress her face. Most people covered their bedroom windows in full curtains, but Edie loved to awaken to the sun's hello. Her curtains were two tiered, high enough on the window for modesty but leaving an open space between the top and bottom sets for the sun to shine through.

Breathing deeply of the fragrance of her favorite hazelnut blend, she sank deeper into the covers. "I love You, too, Lord, and I invite You into this day. I know You're always here, but please make me aware of Your presence. Guide my steps in the adventures You have for me."

She pushed back the comforter and climbed from the bed. Immediately her hands went to the task of pulling the sheets taut and smoothing the wrinkles. "And, Jesus, I don't know what I was thinking last night, allowing Rick Stanton to buy me dinner. Please don't let him get his hopes up." She pulled the bright daisy comforter over the sheets and covered her pillows with matching shams. "And help me hold my tongue next time I see Tom Flanders."

Edie pattered to the kitchen and pulled a piece of leftover

pumpkin bread from the freezer. Randi had sent the treat home with her after the Thanksgiving meal. She popped it into the microwave before pouring a full cup of coffee. How she loved that coffeemaker. It wasn't just that she could set a timer the night before, it was that it had come from Michael, two Christmases back. Her grandson might have an edge to him, but she saw the tender heart. Glancing at the clock, Edie knew she couldn't linger over her coffee. With no car, it was going to take a while to walk to work. She frowned then pushed aside the complaints rising within. She had two good legs, didn't she?

It wasn't long before Edie shouldered her purse and stepped onto the front porch, reaching down for the newspaper. She tossed the paper inside, locked the door, and turned toward the street.

Oh, no.

"Mornin', Sunshine," Rick yelled. "Swung by in case you need a ride to work."

"How long have you been here?"

His shrug told her everything. She could only hope the neighbors hadn't seen him leaning against his old F-150. She frowned as she walked toward the street. No way was she falling for this. She turned down the sidewalk and began her walk to the post office.

"Aw, come on, Edie. You're not still sore about last night, are you? I didn't tell Tom Flanders to leave you on the highway, and I didn't invite him to Rudolph's."

Edie kept walking.

"You have a full day ahead of you, with the Christmas rush and all. You don't need to be all tuckered out before you even get to work. Why don't you quit being so dad-gummed stubborn and let me be neighborly."

Stubborn? She wasn't the one who'd waited for heaven knew how long in front of the house of a woman who didn't want to see him. She lengthened her stride, relieved when she heard Rick's door slam and engine start.

❄

Never in his life had he met a more pigheaded woman. Why couldn't she just let a fella help her out?

Two could play this game. He allowed her to get about half a block away before he followed behind, the diesel engine of his truck rumbling at the embarrassment of such a speed.

What was it about Edie Hathaway that made him engage in such tomfoolery? He enjoyed the thrill of pursuit as much as any man, but after years of repeated rebuff, had he lost his mind?

She stomped down the street ahead of him, not even giving him the benefit of a backward glance. Still, he loved the way she tossed her curls as she marched. Some of the irritation rolled off.

He'd seen the real Edie, the woman who'd scrubbed his house top to bottom when his wife took sick, the woman fiercely protective of her grandson, believing the best when others wrote him off, the lady who took extra shifts so the workers under her charge could enjoy their kids' fieldtrips or a day off. It wasn't just her cute little wiggle as she treaded on, determined to ignore him. It was that big heart that drew him. There was a world of joy there if she'd only let him in.

He pulled next to her and lowered the automatic window on the passenger's side.

"Go a"—she huffed—"way."

A flicker of guilt coursed through him. He'd meant to help,

not push her to walk faster than was good for her. "Let me drive you, Edie."

"No."

Years of rejection pressed on him. It was time to end this thing once and for all. He'd give it every ounce of effort he had. If she couldn't see how much he loved her, he'd take his aching heart and move on. "I'll follow you all the way there, Edie Hathaway."

"You wouldn't dare." She stopped, hands on hips.

He revved his engine. "Just imagine the talk around town when the story circulates 'bout how I follow you to work each morning with your pretty little nose upturned and feet stomping the sidewalk."

He almost relented as a flicker of fear rushed through her eyes. She'd endured the worst of the gossip mill when that rascal of a husband piled up gambling debts and abandoned her. It wasn't fair to play on an old wound.

He opened his mouth to apologize but snapped it shut as she climbed in. Who would blame him for doing what *worked*?

She stared straight ahead, tension in her posture. His every attempt at small talk was met with silence. She didn't speak until he pulled up to the post office. After she climbed from the truck she pinned him with a glare. "Randi plans to take me home after work."

He nodded. "I'll be at your house in the morning then."

She didn't reply—stared straight through him, her gaze an arrow. He swallowed hard as it hit its mark, but there was no way he was backing down. As angry as she was, she wouldn't speak to him for a month if he didn't see to it she had no choice.

❄

"How nice of Rick Stanton to give you a ride this morning."

Edie bit her lip to hold back the snarl as she pushed the door open and headed for her little office.

Charisa followed. "I heard your car broke down last night. Tom Flanders said Rick rescued you. It's so romantic!"

Hot words churned, and Edie counted to ten. She glanced at the young woman, wishing again that Charisa would take a little more care with her appearance—and her life for that matter. Her hair hung limp and lifeless to her shoulders, and her uniform was pulling at the front, confirming Edie's suspicions. *Oh, Charisa. . .*

Edie pulled the large metal cages into the middle of the room and began sorting. "We have work to do."

Charisa trailed after her as they put out the bundles for the rural deliveries and sorted the parcels, magazines, large envelopes, and other flats. There was twice the normal amount. At this rate, bulk might have to wait a day. Still, it soothed her to organize the stacks. Mindless work was the perfect rhythm to slow the pounding in her chest.

"Did he really take you to Rudolph's?"

With a sigh Edie turned toward the young woman. "It was. . . kind of Rick to help me out last night. But not a bit romantic." Suddenly an image of the look in Rick's eyes as he wiped the sauce off her nose flitted across her mind. She swallowed hard. "He was just being. . .neighborly."

Charisa rolled her eyes. "Everyone knows the man is crazy about you. If someone as hot as Rick Stanton was falling all over himself to get my attention, I'd give him a chance."

Edie didn't like the way Charisa turned a cold shoulder and gathered the mail for the post-office boxes.

But lovesick Charisa didn't know how infuriating the man could be.

Chapter 3

Rick took a long gulp from his thermos, watching the sun rise in the sky. He'd barely slept. Kept thinking of the fury in Edie's eyes and the way he played her weakness. He should apologize. He stared at her house as the lights flickered. Looked like Edie rose with the sun every day. Too bad she hadn't come out, found him waiting, and watched the sunrise with him.

As if she'd have been in any mood for that.

Oh, man. If she knew what time he'd gotten here. . .if he was still on the force he'd have taken himself in for loitering—or stalking—or something.

Lord, am I just making a mess of things?

He fingered the yellow rose on the seat next to him. Rick had only been inside Edie's house once, but its bright, cheery walls made an impression. She'd like yellow. He bit into his doughnut and glanced at his watch. Picking up his travel magazine, he flipped through the pages, pausing at the glossy photos. He should be getting his passport any day. Applied for it nearly a month before. Had to put some kind of action to his dreams.

What would it be like to travel the world with Edie? Would

she want to see the wilds of the Australian Outback, the cathedrals and castles of Europe, or the colors of the Orient?

Rick imagined the light in her eyes and longed to bring her such happiness. He'd seen the novels about exotic places peeking out of her handbag—and the glimmer of excitement anytime she experienced something new. Some women's sense of adventure died as they aged but not Edie's. If she would give him a chance, he'd give her the world.

The front door opened, and Edie descended the steps. Even with that air of weariness draped around her, she was striking. He hurried out to open her door. She climbed in without a word.

Rick got in then glanced her way. "Beautiful morning. Did you sleep well?"

No reply.

The silence stretched as he started the engine. Another cold drive with Ice Woman.

"I talked to Gary down at the shop. Should have your car ready by tomorrow afternoon. He had to wait on a part."

She didn't even nod.

Silence as he pulled onto Christmas School Road. Silence as he turned onto 50. Silence as he pulled into the post office parking lot.

Edie reached for the door. He touched her arm, encouraged when she hesitated.

He picked up the rose and held it out to her. "A peace offering?"

She looked at him. Finally. But she didn't take the rose.

"Please, Edie. I'm only trying to help."

He saw the struggle within her and hated himself for the game he played. But hadn't he tried everything else? He thrust the flower toward her. "You have a ride home tonight, right?"

With an exaggerated sigh, she nodded. He held the rose steady as she climbed from the pickup. At the last minute she turned and—glory of glories—reached for it.

"I'll see you in the morning, Edie. Gary should bring your car 'round here tomorrow afternoon, and then you'll be able to drive yourself to work."

The only answer was the slam of the door.

❄

Edie pushed the rose into her purse, glad no one else was there yet. She unlocked the post office door and slipped into her office. Pulling the rose from her bag, she frowned. She leaned toward the wastebasket then hesitated, the clutched flower dangling above the empty trash can. Then she lifted the rose to her face and inhaled.

What was the man's crime? Driving her to work?

He was right—her days were long and walking all the way here would have stretched her reserves.

But he was just so. . .pushy. Tenacious. Calculating. Rick Stanton knew exactly what he was doing, making her take a ride, how she hated gossip.

Fingering the soft petals of the cheery flower, she noted the friendly color. Not passionate red or romantic white, just sunshiny yellow.

Edie reached for the water glass she kept on hand, went to the bathroom, and filled it. But after putting the rose in it, she didn't know what to do. She almost put it on her desk, but at the sound of voices entering the building, she reconsidered. Glancing around the room for a hiding place, Edie quickly hid the flower between the filing cabinet and the wall then joined Charisa and Jason, who'd already pulled the metal cages into place to begin sorting. She frowned as they whispered together, Charisa's dishwater blond mop next to Jason's salt and pepper.

A look passed between them. Here it came.

"How'd you get to work today, Edie? I noticed your car wasn't here." Jason's deep voice was a little too casual, and Charisa snickered.

If she was defensive or secretive they would only read more into it. "Rick dropped me here. He's up early anyway and offered to help me out."

"I'll bet he did."

Edie did not like Charisa's saucy tone. "What is that supposed to mean?" Edie raised an eyebrow and pinned Charisa with her best "boss" look.

Charisa lifted her hands in surrender and returned to work. The rural carriers arrived and began casing, systematically organizing their mail to prepare for their route, while Charisa stuffed the post-office boxes and Jason began the routine to open up the front. Troy, the retired G. I. who obviously had eyes for Randi, and the other volunteers sat at a table, stamping Christmas, Florida's happy message on mounds of envelopes. Everything was running like the well-oiled machine Edie insisted it be. She turned toward her office, dreading the mound of paperwork that only seemed to increase with the computerization of the US Postal Service. From her desk she noted Charisa's frequent trips to the restroom, and her heart ached for her. She'd hoped the young woman would talk to her without being prompted, but if Charisa didn't speak soon, she'd have to confront the situation. *Lord, give me wisdom.*

At eleven thirty Charisa poked her head in the office door. "I need to use the restroom, and there's a line out the door. Everyone's getting tense waiting, but I gotta go. Could you help out?"

Edie stretched, almost glad for the interruption. She trotted to the front and opened the drawer she used when extra help was needed. When she looked up there he was—tall Grinch hat, pasty green face, and red suit. Rick in all his grinchy glory.

Setup. Again.

It was all she could do not to lean over the counter to see the green tights everyone talked about.

"Good morning, Edie. Did you sleep well?"

She didn't miss the twinkle in his eye—or the fact that he asked the exact question she'd ignored in the pickup a few hours earlier. His eyes dared her to disregard it a second time—in front of everyone.

"Actually, no. I had a lot on my mind." Her words were harsher than she'd intended.

He winced.

"Postcards?" She softened her tone. "Stamps?"

"Not this time." He lifted several boxes onto the counter. "Presents for the grandbabies."

She gazed at the pile. "I thought you had only two grandchildren."

He shrugged and flashed that stunning grin. "Aren't they for spoiling?"

Edie looked down to hide her irritation. It wasn't her business how much he spent on his family. But the postage alone!

As she weighed his boxes, Rick bantered with Jason and the line of patrons, silly Seuss-esque lines rolling off his tongue. She felt the corners of her mouth turn up as the grumpy atmosphere in the post office lifted, people chuckling at the towering sixty-six-year-old Grinch.

Transaction completed, she looked at Rick. He paused and reached into a deep pocket, pulling out a tiny, stuffed Grinch. He winked at her then looked toward the crowded room.

"Some say Grinch is as cuddly as a cactus and as charming as an eel."

His low, resonate drawl bounced off the brick walls. He gave Edie a pointed look.

"And I'll admit this Grinch sometimes acts the heel."

Edie felt her face warm as he turned back to his audience.

"But you need to be sure to judge him well and fair,

Mr. Grinch just struggles to express his deepest care.

So when you're tempted sorely to turn and walk away,

Just pause a tiny minute, think of him, and stay."

He turned toward her again and plopped the stuffed toy on the counter between them. "Remember Mr. Grinch. Don't forget his heart of gold,

And give the poor man a chance, before he grows too old."

He waggled his eyebrows at her, took a deep bow before the impromptu audience, who expressed their appreciation with cat calls and applause, and walked out the door.

Silly, sentimental man! Face aflame, Edie grabbed the toy and rushed to her back office.

As she plopped the stuffed Grinch on her desk, she noticed a tiny piece of paper rolled and held to its hand by a rubber band.

She took a shaky breath and pulled the paper out. Rick's masculine scrawl spoke from the page.

> *Edie,*
>
> *I have acted the heel. Forgive a clumsy old man for pushing too hard. Please see past my fumbling to my honest heart.*
>
> *May I please have the pleasure of your company tomorrow morning?*
>
> *Sincerely,*
> *Your salty old Grinch*

The tears that sprang to Edie's eyes were so unexpected she let them dust her eyelashes before blinking them away.

Crazy, silly man.

She put the toy into the big drawer at the bottom of her desk and forced her attention back to her paperwork, fighting down the emotion wreaking havoc within. The phone rang, and she cleared her throat before answering.

"I just heard about Rick's poem." *Randi.*

"Already?"

"The school secretary made a run to the post office. Listen, Mom. I think I should tell you. Um. . .I was the one who called Rick when you broke down that night. I couldn't find anyone to cover my turn serving hot chocolate at the festival, and I was so worried about you sitting alone on a deserted highway. I knew he'd make sure you were safe."

"Randi!"

"I didn't mean to cause you problems. All I thought about was who I could count on to take care of you."

"No wonder he's been so attentive. He probably thought I put you up to it! You got the poor man's hopes up."

"I don't think so, Mom. And. . .you're going to have to face it. His hopes have been up for a long time. You just keep shooting them down. Hey, I've got students waiting. I just thought you should know the whole story."

Edie held the phone in her hand even after the click died away.

Chapter 4

He felt like he had back when he'd asked Mary Ann Clements, the prettiest girl in school in Tallahassee, to homecoming. A man never forgets those moments—when he bares his heart in front of God and everyone, setting himself up to face the twin mercies of rejection and acceptance. This time the whole town watched for his triumph or demise.

The sun continued its steady ascent, rising behind Edie's little cream-colored house, lighting the flowers that bloomed in the window boxes, painted green like her shutters. It bathed the cozy place in God's holy light, and Rick asked the Lord to give her peace and confidence and to heal any hurts his determined actions had caused. He prayed she would open her heart fully to the love of her Creator.

And I wouldn't mind if she'd open her heart to my love as well, Lord.

He watched a light come on in the back of the house and wondered what it would be like to sit across the kitchen table from her. Was she a morning person like he was? She had to get up at the crack of dawn as postmaster. Would she be animated—or

278

would it take a while for sleep to release her quick wit?

The ache that welled inside was more intense than usual, reminding him of the hard months right after he'd lost Bertie. More than his wife, she'd been his best friend and lover. He grimaced as he thought of their untouched nest egg, how they'd planned to travel as soon as she got well.

Only she never did.

He'd known loneliness was a feeling, but until his wife's death he hadn't understood that loneliness could be a state of being. He sighed. Eventually he'd learned to live outside of the loneliness, but this thing with Edie, this allowing himself to fully invest and hope, carried risk. Not just the good-natured teasing of the townsfolk or even their barely veiled sympathy for him. It carried the risk of another great loss.

Besides Bertie he'd never loved anyone but Edie. Even when Mary Ann showed up and tried to dig her claws into him after Bertie's death, he'd merely felt an old infatuation distracting him from the pain of loss. It hurt when Mary Ann pumped him for money and then disappeared, but not like it would if Edie put him aside once and for all.

A movement at the front door caught his eye.

Here goes nothin'. He stepped from the truck and strode up her sidewalk, meeting her before she came down the steps. "Good morning, Edie. May I offer you a ride?"

He rubbed the back of his neck as she hesitated. When she gave a slight nod, he offered his hand to help her down the steps. He thought his heart would fly out of his chest when she took it. Of course she dropped it as soon as she was on the sidewalk, but he'd take what he could get.

He helped her into the pickup. "Beautiful sunrise this morning."

She nodded, and his heart lifted when she offered a tiny smile. "How'd you sleep?"

She hesitated. "I had a lot on my mind, but once sleep came, it was peaceful."

Was *he* on her mind? "How's Michael these days?"

"Still trying to figure out who he is, I suppose."

Creases marred her forehead, and he wished he could soothe her worries.

"He's taken a liking to Troy. You met him at church, I think. My Michael has a heart of gold—but learning to be a man without a father—or grandfather—to show the way has made his road harder. But it seems Troy is getting through to him."

"You Hathaways have been through a lot, Edie. A whole lot."

She turned away. Never was one to like sympathy. He tried to think of something else to say, but small talk eluded him. He drove in silence until he parked at the post office. "Thank you for allowing me to drive you to work, Edie."

Her eyes sparked. "What could I do after you made a fool of yourself in front of half the town?"

He felt the grin slip into place but sobered when he saw a serious expression come over her.

"Your note of apology was gracious, Rick. I haven't made things easy for you over the last couple of years."

"Edie, I. . ." He pushed the words through the thickness in his throat. "I like to tease and flirt with the best of them, but I play for keeps. I'd be honored if you'd give me a chance."

He hated the shield that covered her eyes. "I'll think about it."

He supposed that was a start.

❄

Edie watched the light flood the dark post office as she flipped the switches inside the door. If only her own questions could be illuminated so easily.

Invite Me into this.

Edie swallowed. *You're always a part of my life, Lord.* But she hadn't talked to Him about Rick, really, other than to beg Him to make Rick leave her alone. A prayer He didn't appear to be answering—and the blustering flirt had been much easier to ignore than this new, softer Rick. Dare she trust he was for real?

She flipped on her computer. Did it matter? Wasn't one failed love story enough? She had Randi, Michael, her job, and a safe routine. And when she was bored—she read about faraway adventures.

The old longing surfaced, and Edie frowned, surprised as desire struck her full force. Frank had promised her they'd see the world—before he gambled away every penny she saved. They hadn't even vacationed at the beach, unless you counted the afternoon picnics she insisted upon. Even then there was barely enough money for gas. She'd made her best out of nothing, cutting peanut butter sandwiches into starfish shapes and stretching the dollars by making Kool-Aid instead of buying soda.

But her efforts were never enough.

Edie stared at the computer as it went through its start-up routine, but the mindless task wasn't enough to halt the flow of bad memories.

Frank's thirst for adventure led to gaming debts, which led to

Frank's flirtation with women who could finance his habits. Even now the knife twisted in her belly when she remembered the first time she caught him with another woman. He hadn't come home, and Tom Flanders had hinted that she might want to check out the casino in Cape Canaveral. He'd even loaned her his car and given her gas money—since Frank had disappeared with theirs.

She really should forgive Tom for his part in setting her up with Rick.

Jesus, I don't know that I'm ready for another relationship.

And how many years had she been saying that?

Steps in the hallway broke into her reverie, and when Charisa entered the office and closed the door, Edie prayed for wisdom.

Charisa hesitated. "I know there's a lot of mail to be sorted. I won't take much of your time."

Edie nodded toward the second chair.

Charisa sat, twisting her hands, more pale than usual. "I might as well come out with it. I'm pregnant."

"I know."

"You do?"

"All the signs are there, Charisa. Does the baby's father know?"

Tears welled in the young woman's eyes. "He. . .left last night—when I told him. . ."

"Oh, Charisa."

The young woman began to weep, and Edie walked around the desk and knelt before her. She pulled the child into her arms. She'd watched Charisa grow up, ignored by her father. She'd grieved at Charisa's search for someone to love her—how others took from the girl but never gave back. Edie had hired her hoping a job would give Charisa a little self-respect. But old habits die hard. The latest live-in boyfriend had been worse than the previous.

Charisa's sobs turned to hiccups.

Edie held her tighter. "You'll make it through this, Charisa," she whispered. She pulled back and lifted the girl's chin. "I know you will."

"How did you do it—when Frank left?"

Edie sent a prayer up before answering. If there was one thing she'd learned, it was that the Lord wouldn't waste her pain. "It wasn't easy, sweetheart. I did a lot of crying. And felt sorry for myself. But I had a sweet little girl who needed me, just like this baby needs you. So I asked the Lord to help me make the best out of a bad situation. And He did."

"It's different. Everyone in this town loves you. All they do is talk about me—none of it good."

"Don't you believe for a second I haven't endured my share of gossip. But what they say doesn't matter. What counts is what God says and what you believe yourself." Edie frowned. Her advice hit a little too close to home.

Tears welled again in Charisa's eyes, and Edie glanced at the clock. The mail was waiting. "Why don't you take the day off, sweetie? I get home about six. Come on over. I'll feed you a bowl of soup, and we'll figure this thing out together."

Charisa's hug was fierce. "Thank you, Edie. But I'm going to help you sort first. I don't think I can face the public, but you need me in the back."

Edie smiled. "That's the spirit."

Charisa and Edie worked in silence as the others drifted in. After Charisa filled the post-office boxes, Edie inclined her head to the doorway. Charisa shot her a grateful glance and left.

"What's wrong with Charisa?" Jason pulled out his drawer and prepared for the day.

"She's not feeling well. I told her to leave after sorting. I'll help you up front."

Jason raised an eyebrow, and Edie flinched. The gossip mill would soon start. How would Charisa survive its brutal onslaught? As customers arrived, Edie pasted on a smile. Life was hard, but in the struggles God revealed His love and faithfulness. She prayed that would happen for Charisa.

❄

It felt good to be behind the wheel of her car, but Edie wished the short drive home was the last task of the day. December at the post office was exhausting. All she wanted was a huge bowl of popcorn and to curl up with her latest novel. Instead, she'd make grilled cheese sandwiches, a salad, and tomato soup. Not fancy, but a comforting—and reasonably healthy—meal for the new mother.

Her sigh filled the quiet car. Charisa had made other bad choices in her life, but this one would turn her world upside down. One thing was for sure: no matter how conceived, a baby was never a mistake.

Lord, help Charisa receive the little one as a gift. Turn her heart from chasing after love that never heals to seeking You.

At six fifteen Edie wondered if Charisa would show. By six thirty she contemplated clearing the table, but just as she reached for the extra place setting, she heard a tentative knock. She hurried to the door. "Come in, sweetheart. I've got supper waiting. Nothing fancy, but it'll fill an empty spot."

The raw fear in Charisa's red-rimmed eyes broke Edie's heart. It was the same terror she'd felt when Frank abandoned Randi and her, and she'd faced a life of being both mother and father to her precious daughter. Her fear had escalated when she realized the full extent of the bills Frank left. It took years to climb out from under the financial mess. She hoped Charisa and her boyfriend had separate checking accounts and no joint credit cards.

Edie forced a light tone as she ushered Charisa to the table, doing her best to put the girl at ease. The aroma of toasted cheese combined with the tang of tomato welcomed them.

"This smells really good." Charisa motioned toward the bright red cloth napkins and multicolored pottery bowls. "And it's pretty, too." A hint of a smile came to Charisa's lips.

Edie thanked God again for her garage sale finds. The bright bowls did make the table cheery. After they seated themselves, Edie smiled at Charisa. "I usually say a prayer before I eat. Do you mind?"

At Charisa's nod of acceptance Edie offered gratitude for God's provision and a blessing for Charisa. When she looked up, the young woman seemed a little more comfortable.

As Charisa relaxed, Edie found herself truly enjoying the company. Charisa was interested in everything—from the books in the pretty basket beside Edie's favorite chair, to the bag of yarn and the half-finished afghan. Soon Edie found herself doing the unthinkable—opening the door to the one space in her house she never showed anyone.

"This place is a mess!" Charisa covered her mouth with her hand. "I mean—"

"It's true!"

"I didn't intend to insult you." Charisa's face flamed bright red. "It's just out of character for you. I've never seen you do anything that wasn't perfectly organized."

Edie glanced around the cluttered room. Bookshelves piled two deep, an overflowing basket of quilting material, and a messy table full of scrapbooking paraphernalia met her gaze. She laughed. "If you look closely, the chaos is actually organized. It's my dream-and-create place—where I let it all hang out."

Charisa pointed toward the back wall. "What are the maps for?"

Edie cringed. Charisa *would* notice those. "I like to read about places I've never been—and I've been nowhere outside of Florida." She shrugged. "I hung a map of the United States and a map of the world, and I put a pin on each place I've visited through my books."

"Do the different colored pins mean anything?"

Edie swallowed hard. "The red ones are for places I read about in novels. The orange represent locations I've studied further."

"What about the purple?"

She would ask. "Those are the places I would most like to visit in person. It's rather eccentric."

"No way. I think it rocks." Charisa plopped on the chaise lounge Edie had re-covered in a fabric that boasted red and orange gerbera daisies. "Let me guess. This is where you escape and read about those faraway places."

"Oh, I read everywhere. But yes, I often read there."

A sudden shyness came over Charisa's features.

"What is it, honey?"

"I've never had dreams like that—and I wouldn't know the

first thing about quilting, scrapbooking, or any of this." Charisa lifted her head. "Though I own at changing channels, especially when I can find the remote."

"Now there's something." Edie chuckled at Charisa's attempt at humor.

Charisa cleared her throat. "I've been trying to work up the nerve to ask you to help me with something."

Edie pulled a chair next to Charisa. "What do you need?"

"I. . .uh. . .heard your husband left you with a lot of debt."

Oh, the joys of a small town. "Yes."

"Please don't tell anyone, but. . .Jimmy drained our account. Both our names are on several credit cards. I'm not sure how I'm going to pay my bills this month, and I have no idea how to protect myself financially."

Edie stiffened. "First thing we do is get your accounts separated. This can't wait, Charisa. We have to cancel the credit cards now. I'll follow you to your place."

It was going to be a long night.

Chapter 5

Rick shook off the melancholy. He'd gotten used to seeing Edie every morning, which made him even lonelier today. His spirits lifted when he pulled next to the restaurant housed in the old school bus, climbed out, and ordered coffee and a mouthwatering cinnamon roll, covered in their famous butter rum sauce. He was glad the Old School Coffee Stop was parked and open for business. The restaurant's eco-friendly coffee cups and highfalutin causes were beyond him, but they made a good pastry.

Not ready to face his empty house, he meandered through the streets of his little town, starting on Blitzen then Comet then Cupid—which only made him think of Edie and how he wished he could shoot Cupid's arrow straight into her heart.

The woman was infuriating. She promised to think about going out with him then avoided him. She disappeared into the back when he dared step into the post office. At church she arrived late and departed early.

After a left on Bartholomew and another left on St. Nicholas, he weaved through the Gospel streets, going east on Mathew and then west on Luke, and finally went north to cruise down Antlers before heading back to 50. It used to be his beat—if you could call it that.

He headed toward the post office for a few more postcards to pass out to the tourists. Maybe this time Edie wouldn't run off at the sight of him.

Rick checked his post-office box and grinned, opening the envelope as he got in line to buy postcards. His heart lifted further at the sight of Edie. It was busy as a beehive today. She'd have to keep her post at the counter. He nodded at friends. As they took their turns, he calculated the least obvious way to end up at Edie's station. He was about to back out of line when Brick suddenly turned to him. "Please go on ahead of me. I need to find an. . .ad-dress. . .on my phone."

Rick tried to act casual as he took the muscled contractor's spot—which put him next for Edie. "Thanks." He directed his attention back to the envelope to hide his embarrassment, and joy burst within as he pulled out the contents.

Brick clapped him on the back and smiled. "Anything to help a friend." He glanced meaningfully toward Edie.

She glanced up. "Next."

"Hi there."

Edie smiled but didn't reply.

"Need about three dozen of those prestamped postcards."

She pulled a bundle from underneath the counter. "We thought you were probably getting low." She typed in the transaction. "What else can I help you with today?"

❄

Surely Rick wouldn't put her on the spot in front of everyone. Then again he had embarrassed her publicly. Dr. Suess love poems. Sheesh. *Don't do it, Rick. Don't ask me out yet.*

A silly grin spread over Rick's face.

Oh no. Here it came.

"Look at this." He flipped something open on the counter.

She glanced down. A passport.

Rick leaned forward, his blue eyes searching hers. "Come away with me, Edie." His usual swagger was gone, and he spoke softly instead of to the whole room like before. "I'll give you the world."

A gasp to her right made Edie and Rick turn their heads.

"Edie, your purple pins! You could—"

"Focus on your work, Charisa."

At Edie's sharp reprimand the young woman's eyes widened.

"Rick, please. . .these. . .crazy schemes of yours. . ." Edie kept her voice low. "How could you afford. . . ? Just. . .stop. . . ."

He snapped his passport shut. She'd never seen Rick Stanton look anything but poised. That's why it cut so deep when he recoiled as though bitten by a snake. In a flash the old Rick was back as he joked with the other patrons and made his way out of the post office. But something told her she'd probed a spot she wished she hadn't.

Edie did her best to push Rick's pained reaction out of her mind, but as the morning went on, her concern for him was replaced by frustration. What was he doing with a passport? There was no way the man could afford to travel the world. Bertie's medical bills would have been enough to wipe out the savings of any normal couple—how much could a retired policeman make anyway?

Ridiculous man, dishing up outlandish invitations.

As soon as the lobby cleared, Edie rushed to her office and pulled up statistics of the retirement for the average small-town cop. She sighed. Just as she suspected. There was no way he could chase those dreams without a slew of credit cards.

Foolish, foolish fancy.

❄

That Edie Hathaway beat all. Shooting down his dreams.

He frowned. The last many years of his marriage he'd been a nurse. All Mary Ann wanted when she showed up after Bertie's death was a purse. How he longed for a companion to share his final days that wasn't looking for either.

He sighed. News of his inheritance was all over Tallahassee when Rick's grandfather liquidated his estate and gave him a generous portion. But no one in Christmas had known, and he kept it that way.

Their travel money.

He and Bertie had scrimped and saved and lived off what they made so that in retirement they could play together, carefree. He hadn't even touched the bundle for medical bills. Worked extra hours to pay them off rather than give up their dream of world travel.

But Bertie had the gall to die before they could use the money.

There was no way he was telling Edie Hathaway his decade-long secret. Mary Ann showed him how easy it was for women to want him for the cash. The woman he chose would have to love him without knowledge of his money.

So Edie thought his dreams were crazy. Well, crazy was letting his emotions carry him away and inviting Edie to travel with him.

But. . .there for a moment it had seemed so. . .possible—her standing across from him, his passport in hand.

He drove out past the Jungle Adventures Nature Park, opening his windows and letting the air cool his hurts. He'd been so sure the good Lord was putting Edie and him together to fulfill the dreams that had been stripped from them both.

But he'd travel alone if he had to. Maybe it was time to quit chasing after Edie Hathaway and find his path without her.

❄

Edie rushed home. It had been all she could do to hold it together after Rick's ridiculous offer. She stomped into her dream-and-create room and grabbed every single purple pin and flung them into the trash one by one.

Hot tears burned as she flopped onto the chaise lounge. *Why, Lord?*

Why did a good God allow a foolish old man to waltz into her life, quoting bad poetry, no less, and promise something she could never have?

It was a mockery of her deepest secrets.

How the enemy must scoff, enjoying trampling her heart, dragging up old wounds she thought she'd long buried. She had to find a way to get rid of Rick Stanton before things got worse. Before she broke in half—or was stupid enough to give in to his fancies.

Chapter 6

Edie stepped from her office. "Charisa, can I speak to you?"

"Is something wrong?"

"I just want to talk with you."

Charisa plopped into the chair opposite Edie's desk. "I know I've run a little late, Edie. Mornings are. . .harder. But I'll get up earlier—try to settle the nausea so I can get out the door sooner."

"This isn't about that, honey. I know you're doing your best. I wanted to ask a. . .personal favor. I'm proud of the changes you've made." And she was. She and Charisa had set her finances in order. Charisa's love for the little one inside had propelled her to change her habits. With less late nights at the bar, the young woman's eyes were clearer, her appearance neater.

Edie shrugged. "I need your help."

"Oh."

"I. . .showed you a room in my house I don't show anyone. Besides you, only Randi and Michael have been in there. I would appreciate it if you kept the map and pins a secret."

"But I think they're wonderful."

"I took the purple pins down last night." Edie sighed. "I can't let dreams cloud reality. I've saved a nest egg so I won't be a burden to Randi after I retire. God will see to my needs whatever years I have left, but I'm not going to make foolish choices I can't afford and jeopardize my security as I age."

"Is this about Rick?"

"Just promise me."

"I won't tell." Charisa gave her a pensive look. "But I'm sad you took the purple pins down."

"Me, too." Standing, Edie opened the door. "Better get to the front. I'll finish up the parcels. With Christmas just over two weeks away there's only going to be more."

Charisa nodded.

Edie worked in silence, lifting and sorting. She rolled her shoulders. The work got more demanding with each birthday. Frowning, she eyed a large package at the bottom of the cage. She leaned to pull it out.

The spasm was immediate and the pain through the roof. Edie collapsed. Instantly Jason and Charisa were there, one on each side.

"What is it?" Charisa rushed to her.

Biting hard against the agony, Edie forced the words. "My back."

"Call an ambulance." Jason nodded to Charisa.

"No! I'm not paying for such extravagance." Edie gritted her teeth. "Call Randi."

Charisa pulled out her cell.

Edie groaned. "Forget it. She's gone all day on a field trip. Just"—she gasped as another sharp pain stabbed her back—"help me off the floor."

Her friends lifted. Every movement shot unbearable pain through her back and down her legs. "I just. . .need. . .to get home."

"I have the wife's minivan today." Jason gave her arm a squeeze. "I'll drive you."

Edie glanced at the clock. The lobby would soon fill, and they would need Jason here. "Just get me to my office." Hanging on to her friends, she shuffled forward. "Not the chair with wheels." She measured her words. "The other."

She yelped as they tried to lower her into the chair. "Can't." Edie swallowed hard. "I'll hold the back of this taller chair for support. You take care of the lobby."

"We can't leave you!" Charisa's face was white.

"Neither rain nor sleet nor gloom of night. . ." Her joke fell flat. "I'm the boss. Go." When they shuffled out, she heard a rumble of voices. Probably discussing her. A tear slipped down her cheek, but she didn't dare let go of the chair to wipe it away. Excruciating minutes dragged by.

A sound at the door caused Edie to turn her head. She didn't know whether to cheer or moan as Rick's strong form filled the doorway. For all her mutterings of last night, she was glad to see him, the one man who knew how to take control and make things right.

❄

Emotion gripped his chest at the sight of spunky Edie Hathaway clinging to the chair for dear life. And the way she looked at him—finally—like he was her hero made his heart drop to his toes.

But he'd worked enough traffic accidents to know the glazed

look of pain, and judging by the way Edie clenched her jaw, hers was off the charts.

"Take me home," she croaked.

"Can you walk?"

"If you help me."

"Anything you need to take?"

Edie nodded toward her desk. "My purse is in the bottom drawer."

"Do you have any ibuprofen?"

"The side pocket."

He opened the drawer and pulled out her purse, noticing the tiny stuffed Grinch. At least she'd kept it. He glanced at her, gauging her weight, and pulled out four of the pain relievers. He helped her swallow them with a glass of water. "You ready for this?"

She nodded. He slipped his arm around her back. "We'll take your car. It will be easier than you stepping up into the pickup."

With each miniscule step he saw her determined effort—and how much it cost her. He would gladly take her pain—just as he would've taken Bertie's.

He eased her into the car. "I've been through this sort of thing before, and you need help. Don't fuss with me. I'm taking you straight to my chiropractor. The ride will be difficult but necessary."

She didn't even argue.

He thought they'd never get there. He could see her pain in the white-knuckled way she gripped the door handle. At the office, the receptionist took one look at Edie and stepped in to help.

Edie colored. "Could you. . .assist me to the restroom?"

Rick stepped back, relieved to have a female helping Edie with the personal stuff.

After her treatment, he took her home.

"Where do you want to lie down? The floor or the bed?"

A flicker of something, embarrassment maybe, passed through her big green eyes. "If you'd give me a hand getting onto my bed."

They shuffled toward the bedroom. He'd never been in the back part of her little house before. Neat as a pin. And full of color. He passed a closed door. "Here?"

"No!" Her answer was a little swift, and he cast a sideways glance her direction.

She stared straight ahead. "That one."

The door was open, and he felt out of place stepping in to all those flowers. The walls were some sort of deep orange, and the bedspread had a huge red daisy on it.

"I'm gonna need to move some of your pretties." He glanced at all the pillows, covered in flowers and stripes. "Can you hold on to this here post?"

Edie nodded, and he led her to the wooden post that rose from the footboard. She clung to it while he moved all the pillows but one.

It took a while to get her onto the bed. He fluffed the pillow under her head and put several others underneath her legs. "Do you have an ice pack?"

"Freezer."

He strode from the room. He'd do what he knew to get the swelling down. Randi would have to spend the night. He glanced at the bathroom and hoped Edie didn't need anything. . . personal. . .before reinforcements showed up.

It hit him then. He'd fallen right back into nurse mode—and he didn't even care.

Chapter 7

Edie's days fell into a rhythm. Charisa spent most nights, with Randi helping out when she could, and Rick showed up like clockwork each morning, on duty except when he needed to fulfill his Grinch obligations. Her neighbor, a stay-at-home mom, came over when she needed help to the bathroom.

Edie was shocked by Rick's ability to take care of her. It wasn't just the cooking, cleaning, and running her to the chiropractor. It was his thoughtfulness. On the first day he showed up with a small TV for her bedroom. The next morning it was a stereo system, which he insisted had been "collecting dust." He'd rigged it up to the TV, placing tiny speakers around her room in inconspicuous places to create surround sound. Later he brought her a new travel novel, served her buttery popcorn, and spent a whole hour reading to her. On day four he installed a thick wooden handrail down her hallway so she could hold on to it and walk by herself.

When Randi showed up that night, she noted the extra touches. "Rick has been a godsend."

Edie gazed at the ceiling. She was lying on her back on the living room floor, her feet elevated against the couch, her head on the pillow Rick had placed there before he left. In her mind she saw his huge form bent over, leaning on one knee making sure she was comfortable. "I think I've had a glimpse of the last year Bertie was alive. He knows just what to do—and when."

"You must be talking about Rick." Charisa walked in without knocking—a habit all of them had developed since Edie couldn't answer the door. She held a bouquet of brightly colored gerbera daisies. "These were at the grocery store. They match your bedroom."

Edie bit back the reprimand springing to her lips. "They are beautiful, Charisa." But she should have put the money toward bills!

"Where'd you get your bedspread? I've never seen anything like it."

Randi grinned. "She made it. Pieced it together from scraps of material left after last year's church quilting bee. You'll soon learn my mom doesn't waste anything." She reached over and squeezed Edie's big toe. "But she does create beauty out of other people's leftovers. Do you like the colors of her walls? Mom wouldn't spend money on paint, but Michael and I bought it for her Christmas present last year."

Charisa plopped on the sofa, flowers still in hand. "How do you guys do that?"

"What do you mean?" Edie lifted her head slightly so she could get a better look at Charisa's face.

"Make a real family."

Randi cocked her head to the side. "I think you already know."

"I do?"

"Families take care of each other—which is what you've been

doing with Mom." Randi squeezed Charisa's shoulder then looked at Edie. "What do you think? Should we let her in on the secret?"

"Yep, she should know." Edie knew where Randi was going. "See, Charisa, you're now an honorary Hathaway—you've become part of the family as you've loved us."

Charisa blinked hard, and then a twinkle came into her eyes. "So. . .if family helps each other out, does that mean Rick is officially *in*, too?"

Edie moaned, grabbed a small cushion next to her, and chucked it at Charisa.

"In what?" Rick pulled back the screen door and stepped inside, dressed in his Grinch costume and holding a bouquet identical to the one Charisa brought.

❄

Rick stood there like an idiot as three female faces whipped toward him. Charisa looked like she was about to burst out laughing. Randi seemed amused. But it was Edie's expression that thrilled him. Her face flushed a pretty pink, and the look in her eyes took his breath away.

He cleared his throat. "Looks like Charisa beat me to it." He raised the bouquet. "But a woman can never have too many flowers. I'll just put these in water. Come on, Charisa. We'll get a vase for yours, too."

The task allowed him to process Edie's gaze. If only it meant what he thought it did. He filled two vases with water—Edie kept them on top of her refrigerator, a fact he'd noted when he had cleaned the kitchen and given the top of the appliance a once-over.

Charisa put her flowers in one of the vases and gave him a feisty look. "I think someone is softening."

He put a finger to his lips and gave her a warning glance, but he couldn't help the grin that spread over his face.

Charisa laughed. "I'll put my offering in the bedroom. Why don't you take yours back to the living room?"

Rick returned to the living room and set the flowers on an end table.

"Thank you." Edie lifted her gaze to his face, and boy did he like that soft, moist look in those beautiful green eyes.

Kneeling next to her, he traced a finger lightly across her cheek. "You need to hurry and get better, Edie. It's time for that date."

He didn't trust his voice when Edie's eyes widened, full of an expression he'd only dreamed about.

"I'll work on that."

He stood and glanced at Randi, who was not a very convincing actress as she pretended to read an upside-down magazine. "Well, hi-ho, hi-ho, it's off to work I go."

Charisa reappeared. "That's Snow White's dwarves, not Mr. Grinch."

Rick grinned and lifted his Santa hat to them before leaving.

❄

"Not a word, you two." Edie gave them a pointed look.

"I'll be heading home then." Charisa raised an eyebrow. "Since *somebody* doesn't want me to state the obvious."

As the young woman left, Edie turned to Randi. "I should've talked to you first."

Randi laughed. "You're of age."

"I don't want to do anything that would make you and Michael uncomfortable."

"Relax." Randi grinned. "I think Rick's good for you. In fact, my only question is, what took you so long?"

Edie shook her head. "I haven't been on a real date since—"

"Before I was born."

"It wasn't that bad."

"But you've never truly given anyone a chance since my father left. I never understood why. You have so much love to offer."

Edie sighed and rubbed her eyes. "At first I was focused on raising you and surviving. When I could finally breathe again, I guess I never found anyone I trusted."

"You know, Mom, maybe the Hathaway women should work on that trust thing."

The weight of Randi's words fell with a thud on Edie's heart.

"Don't look so worried." Randi patted her on the foot. "Come on. Tomorrow starts early."

Randi helped Edie move her feet off the couch, but Edie held up her hand when she started to help her off the floor.

"Let me try." She maneuvered next to the couch and, using it for support, slowly found her way to her feet. It was only a few steps to the hallway lined with the rail Rick had hung. "I plan to be at work Monday morning."

"Sounds a little ambitious."

"I won't lift anything—and I'll take breaks."

Randi rolled her eyes.

"Don't start with me, young lady."

"Uh, Mom, I'm past forty. Remember?"

Edie treasured the kiss on the cheek her daughter offered after she helped her into bed. Edie relaxed against her pillow as Randi flicked the light off.

"Mom?" Randi's voice was soft and sweet in the darkness. For a moment the years fell away, and Edie remembered the little girl who once called out in the night.

"Yes?"

"Rick asked my permission to do something special for you as an early Christmas present. He's bringing it tomorrow. I hope I didn't overstep."

Edie swallowed hard. Only God in heaven knew what Rick Stanton was up to now. Sleep wasn't going to come as quickly as she'd thought.

Chapter 8

Edie awakened to hammering, followed by Randi's soft knock. "What's going on?" Edie stifled a yawn.

"I guess Rick's getting an early start with your present."

Relief washed over her like a waterfall. Her gift was something Rick could hammer—not something in a tiny box to be pulled out of his pocket. It had been silly to waste good sleep worrying. She'd agreed to a date—not a lifetime.

But she and Rick both knew what he wanted, and it wasn't one date. Which was part of the reason it took her so long to say yes. And maybe the reason her relief had the slightest tinge of something else. . .disappointment?

Preposterous.

"Mom! Did you hear me? We've got to get you in the shower. I have to leave for work soon."

"Of course."

The steaming water flowing over her was pure luxury. Rick had hung a strong metal handle about chest high, and by holding on, Edie had the great joy of a private shower. Funny how easy it was to take the little, ordinary things of life for granted—like shampoo and the fragrance of jasmine shower gel.

She even dressed by herself. By the time she made it down the hallway, hanging on to her new rail, Rick was in the living room.

"Good morning, Edie."

Was it her imagination, or did she detect a new shyness in the towering policeman? "Good morning."

He grinned. "I couldn't wait for you to be well enough to go on our first date. So I brought it to you. If you'd allow me to help you with your jacket." He bowed and motioned toward the door. "It's a beautiful morning, but the air is a mite chilly."

"I thought we weren't going anywhere."

"Not far."

Rick went to her coat closet, pulled out a warm jacket, and helped her shrug into it. She took his arm, enjoying the feel of strength underneath her touch. He opened the front door and then held the screen for her. She stepped onto her porch and gasped. To her left hung a long wooden swing, painted the exact forest green of her shutters and boasting a big red bow. To her right two green chairs graced the sides of a little round table draped in a white cloth.

"Oh!" Edie stared at the grape juice glistening in goblets and the pretty glass plates filled with eggs, bacon, and a cinnamon roll. "It's. . .beautiful." She glanced at him then back at the single white rose in the center of the table.

"Your breakfast is served."

"How did you manage it?" She lowered herself onto the chair, noting the soft pillow he'd placed there. "You've been here, helping me."

"You. . .like it?" Rick sat across from her, an almost childish eagerness in his handsome face. "I was afraid to hang the swing without your permission, but Randi said to go ahead."

"I love it. But I can't figure out how you pulled this off."

He looked sheepish. "I'm a man of action, Edie. Even though you didn't respond to me, I had to give something to the relationship—so I made you gifts and hoped for the day you'd receive them."

Her forehead creased. "I've. . .always wanted a porch swing."

"I know." He reached for her hand and gave it a squeeze, sending tingles up her arm. "I overheard you tell Randi last year at the church bazaar. I started building it that night."

"Maybe you could bless the food." Her voice came out in a whisper, and she hated that a tiny tear began to trace its way down her cheek.

Rick came to her side and knelt in front of her. "Don't cry, sweetheart." He brushed the wet away with his thumb.

"You made my gift a year ago? I can't believe you waited all this time."

"I believed God ordained a relationship for us. So I worked off my frustration by building things while I waited—and prayed. Not just that you'd learn to love me—but for the things I watched you go through. I pray best when I'm doing something. And"—he grinned up at her— "when you resisted my attention, I pounded those nails harder and prayed louder."

The tightness in her chest threatened more emotion, and she took a deep breath. "I can't thank you enough for all you've done, Rick—the nursing, the things around the house. . ." Another tear brushed against her eyelashes. "And this—"

"Shh, Edie. It's okay." He wiped the second tear as it fell, and she felt herself reeling as he kept his steady gaze upon her.

❄

Rick's heart pounded as he watched the truth dawn in her eyes. After two years of waiting he couldn't keep it inside. "I love you, Edie." His words came out stronger than he'd meant then hung, too loud, in the air.

She stared at him, fear and joy doing a stumbling dance in her eyes. "I know, Rick." Her voice was breathless. "You've spent the last week showing me. And. . .I believe someday soon I'm going to know what to do about that."

It hit him then—the knowledge that she loved him back. He only had to wait for her to figure it out. Sweet, headstrong Edie.

Her intense gaze begged him to understand. He ran his fingers under her chin, traced the soft lines of her face.

Edie's eyes widened, flickers of fear replaced with sparks of longing.

"You're beautiful, Edie Hathaway." He moved toward her. "And don't tell me to quit flirting. I'm just speaking the Gospel truth." He brought his face closer and paused.

He wouldn't push it if she pulled back.

She offered the slightest forward motion, and he thought his heart would burst into kaleidoscope colors. His lips pressed gently against hers, thrilling as she yielded. Everything in him wanted to move closer, to deepen the kiss. But he pulled back. He mustn't rush Edie Hathaway.

Chapter 9

Edie enjoyed being the first to arrive at the post office after her days of convalescing. She flicked the lights, grinning as the dark fled. The quiet of the empty building seeped inside and soothed her. She hadn't had much alone time since hurting her back.

An image of Rick kneeling next to her on the front porch flashed through her mind. The one soft kiss had stirred something she hadn't felt in years—maybe ever. But, to her great disappointment, Rick hadn't done it again, even though he'd stayed with her on Friday and driven her to church over the weekend. She laughed, the sound echoing in the empty place. The tongues were wagging now—after she and Rick entered Nativity Community Church together. And she didn't even care. If he were simply the charmer she'd assumed all these years, he wouldn't have done dishes, hung railing, and heated chicken soup.

The only thing that held her back was concern for how he spent his money—but didn't God often put opposites together? She'd teach Rick how to hang on to his cash, and maybe, with him by her side, she could quit squeezing the blood out of a turnip, as Randi often accused her of doing.

Jason and Charisa arrived at the same time, chatting. They greeted her, and as the three worked together, Edie liked the way Jason didn't let either of them lift anything of consequence. Edie took a couple of breaks to rest her back but was pleased with how well it did as the morning progressed.

At lunchtime, when the lobby filled with customers, she joined Jason and Charisa. "Only five more working days until Christmas."

Charisa glanced at the winding line and sighed. "I'm not sure that's encouraging!"

The crowds never slowed. At four thirty Edie began watching the clock. Her back was growing tight, but she hated to leave the crowd to the others.

Edie spoke to a man whose back was turned. "I can help the next person here."

She heard Charisa's moan at the same time she recognized the drunken swagger of the girl's father.

Instead of walking to Edie, the man stumbled to Charisa's station, pushing the customer in front of her away. "You little good-fer nothing." His slurred words burst into the room. "I knew you'd never amount to anything—come up pregnant."

Charisa gasped.

Edie nodded at Jason, who slipped from behind the counter and strode toward the man, and then she addressed Charisa's father. "Sir!"

He turned toward her, his bloodshot eyes squinting.

"You need to leave." Edie kept her voice low and firm. "Now."

"I ain't doing no such thing. That low 'count daughter of mine needs to be taught a lesson, and I aim—"

"You will leave, Mr. Daniels." Ignoring the trembling in her limbs Edie stood taller. "Jason will help you find your way."

Jason touched the man's arm and gestured toward the exit sign. Edie glanced at Charisa and jerked her head toward the back of the building. The distraught woman rushed out of sight.

Jason grasped the man's arm. "Come with me."

The drunk suddenly burst into tears as he stumbled to the exit sign. "I did my best by the girl. . ."

The hushed lobby awaited Edie. She cleared her throat. "I can help whoever is next." As she worked she noted Jason's return. Then Charisa came back to her station, eyes rimmed red but head high. Edie nodded her approval and squeezed the girl's hand. Four forty-five. Almost there.

Jason locked the door at five o'clock, and they served the last few customers. Edie longed to rush home and lie down, but she looked to Charisa as soon as the room cleared. "Are you all right?"

Charisa's chin trembled. "I will be."

"Oh, honey. I'm so sorry." She put an arm around Charisa. The girl was stiff and unyielding.

"I'm heading home. Need some space."

"Call me if you need to talk—or come over."

Charisa nodded but didn't speak as she rushed from them. Jason stared after her. "I don't think I've ever been so angry in my life."

"You and me both."

He sighed. "I'm going home to hug my daughters and tell them I'm proud of them—and pray to God I never hurt one of them the way that man hurt her."

❄

Rick's pulse quickened at the thought of an evening alone with Edie. She'd be tired after her first day back at work, so he wouldn't stay late—just take supper over and maybe even kiss her goodnight. He'd given her space after that morning on her porch, in case she pulled away. But if anything she seemed more open.

He was waiting when Edie pulled up. "How's your back?"

"Better than my mood."

Just what did that mean?

"Come inside." She gave his arm a gentle squeeze. "I'm glad I don't have to be alone right now."

Until he exhaled he hadn't realized he held his breath. "Let me get dinner. I picked up some wings from Rudolph's on the way here—I'm hoping it brings back good memories." He winked at her and went to his truck.

By the time he entered her house, she was on the floor, head on her pillow, feet up against the couch. Even in that awkward position, Edie was beautiful. Her reddish-brown curls fanned around her head, framing her sweet face. He sat next to her, leaning his back against the sofa. "Hard day?"

Edie's eyes filled with tears. "Ted Daniels came in—drunk."

"Oh no."

"He belittled Charisa in front of everyone. The poor girl was destroyed."

"What'd you do?" A knot grew in his stomach.

"Told him to leave. Jason escorted him out."

"Where's Charisa now?"

"Home."

"I don't like it, Edie." He sat up straight. "Not if Ted's still looking for a fight."

"Is he dangerous?"

"If he hasn't passed out yet. He's a mean drunk." His hand went to his cell.

"What do you think about Charisa joining us for the evening? She could spend the night. Sleep on my couch."

"Better call her quick."

While Edie called Charisa, Rick dialed the station and suggested they send someone by Charisa's to make sure Ted hadn't come around, causing trouble. Then he readjusted his hopes for the evening.

❄

As Edie watched Rick work his magic, her heart opened in a way she hadn't thought possible. Charisa had arrived looking like a wounded animal, but the haunted look dropped away as Rick served them both wings and hammed it up, making them laugh. Before long, a little color came back into Charisa's cheeks.

As the evening wound down, Charisa excused herself to take a shower, leaving Edie alone with Rick. They sat on the couch, and a little thrill blazed as he took her hand. "You're a good woman, Edie Hathaway."

"I was just thinking you're a good man, Rick Stanton."

A twinkle entered his eyes. "You admit it?"

"You never know what might slip out of this mouth of mine."

He leaned closer. "Have any other secrets?"

"I think I might be falling in love with you." The words poured out before she could call them back. She gasped and covered her mouth.

A slow, lazy grin filled Rick's face as he closed the space between them. "Let's see what I can do to help that feeling along." He moved the hand from her lips and replaced it with his mouth.

If his first, gentle kiss undid her, what was this going to do? She told herself to quit thinking, to simply trust this beautiful thing happening between them as he pressed closer, his lips searching her own.

The sound of running water stopped, and she pulled back. Charisa must have finished her shower.

He brushed a finger down her cheek. "Did you mean it, Edie?" His voice was husky.

She paused, but the truth was before her. "How can I help falling now that I see your heart?"

He stared at her a long minute. "I have a special date planned for Friday night, Edie. Are you free?"

She nodded.

"But I don't want to wait four days to see you. I could drive you to Wednesday night service. And we might need to meet at Rudolph's for dinner Thursday night between my shifts as Mr. Grinch."

"You left out tomorrow."

"That's because I have plans tomorrow, and I'm not sure how long they will take."

The pout that formed on her lips surprised her. "What kind of plans?"

He grinned and touched the tip of her nose. "That's for me to know and you to find out."

She stuck her tongue out at him.

He grinned and pulled her hand to his lips. "Good night,

Edie." At the sound of the bathroom door opening he stood. "That's my cue." Striding forward he called over his shoulder, "Bye, Charisa."

Edie loved the way his form filled the doorway, the way her home had felt full and right with him in it. She liked this new, trusting Edie. She just hoped Rick wouldn't move too fast—even if her heart was racing ahead.

Chapter 10

Rick walked the aisles of the furniture store, flipping sales tags on wooden rockers. How a man could treat his own daughter the way Ted Daniels treated Charisa was beyond him. But maybe an early baby present would give her a little self-respect. Show her there were those who planned to walk beside her on the journey into motherhood.

He chose a mission-style rocker with deep leather cushions and a walnut finish. It was a bit of a splurge, but a wise investment. He scheduled the delivery for Saturday afternoon, after the post office closed, and added the brightly wrapped package he'd picked up at the bookstore. A nice tip ensured both would arrive together.

Instead of leaving the furniture store the way he'd come, he exited the opposite direction to enter the mall. A short walk and he was there. Rick entered and strode to the diamond counter.

"May I help you?"

Rick hesitated. Edie was a practical woman—but she also wore those dangling earrings. Must like sparkle. He pointed to the biggest ring on display. "I'd like to see that one there."

The woman nodded. "Ah, the princess cut. You have exquisite taste. I take it congratulations are in order?"

He grinned like a schoolboy.

Pulling the ring from the display, she placed it on a black velvet cloth. "The primary stone is almost two carats—and practically flawless. The smaller diamonds running down the ring on either side are inlaid for longevity of wear."

The rock glistened as light played upon its edges.

"Must be a special lady."

"The very best." And totally unspoiled. Edie would be content with any of the rings, but this one came closest to expressing her value.

❄

Edie snuggled into her covers, reflecting on how two short weeks could change her life. It had taken excruciating pain and helplessness for her to begin to trust Rick. How quickly her heart had opened once she did.

She rolled over and groaned. She was like a lovesick teenager, moping because she didn't get to see Rick on Tuesday then swooning Wednesday as they drove to church together. It was natural for him to take her hand, and she liked riding together, hands clasped, almost as much as she'd enjoyed sitting through church with his arm draped across her shoulder.

Thursday's time was a little rushed, with Rick between shifts as Mr. Grinch—and she still didn't know how he ate without rubbing off that green makeup, but even a little time with Rick was heaven. When he walked her to her car, he'd leaned down and brushed her cheek with a quick kiss. "I love you," he'd whispered.

It felt natural to answer, "I love you, too."

He'd taken a step back. "You sure, Edie?"

"I can't seem to help it."

He drew her close and held her before kissing the top of her head. "I needed to be certain."

It scared her now that she'd spoken such words so soon. A little romance and she went right off the deep end.

Chapter 11

Edie pulled the curtains back and peeked out the front window. She gasped. A beautiful gray draft horse stamped and snorted in front of a glistening white carriage. The top was open displaying rich red-velvet seating. Rick must have paid for the festival coach to come by her house! He stepped from the carriage, dressed in his cowboy boots and a fancy western shirt with navy ribbing that set off his thick gray hair. Her pulse quickened as he strode up the sidewalk. Recognizing the country love song he hummed, she grinned and opened the door to his knock.

He gave a low whistle, and her face heated. Her signature dangling earrings tinkled as she adjusted the rusty-red blazer over a sparkling gold top.

"You rock my world, woman."

Maybe she should pull out her heeled boots more often. Made her legs look longer with her jeans—and her bottom smaller. She took the arm he offered, suddenly embarrassed at her efforts to look good for him and yet thrilled he noticed.

He helped her into the carriage and nodded at the driver dressed in a white tux. The horse began its *clip-clop*, and Edie couldn't help the happy giggle that burst out. As the carriage rolled through the little town, the pink-tinged sky became purple, which deepened to navy and then black. Edie snuggled into Rick's warm side, his arm around her.

❄

"Lookee up there." Rick pointed. "It's the wishing star. Got a wish all ready for it."

Edie laughed, and he wanted to bottle the sound so he could hear her joy any time he pleased.

As they neared the festival, people stared. He tried not to get all puffed up as friends waved and pointed. He'd finally done it—wooed Christmas, Florida's favorite grandma. She was cuddled in next to him for the world to see. He glanced down at her, hoping she wasn't embarrassed by the ruckus they caused. Though her cheeks were a pretty pink, she didn't pull away, just smiled up at him, looking like glory herself. His throat tightened.

"I have a surprise for you." He pointed as they turned the corner. Along the curve ahead two old-fashioned streetlights illuminated falling snow.

Edie gasped. "They got the snow machine working!"

It was even better than he'd dared hope. The soap flakes glistened like tiny diamonds under the lamps, and Edie began singing "Let It Snow" as they drove through the fabricated winter wonderland. Rick motioned for the driver to go around and come through the snow again.

This time Edie was silent as the horses pranced through the shimmering white. The driver pulled over, hopped out, and hitched the horse to a lamppost, just as they'd discussed. Suddenly Rick's tongue thickened.

"Edie. . ." He waited for her to look at him. When she did, his heart thrummed in his throat. "You're quite the woman. You've conquered hardship that would have ruined most. You showed Bertie and me tender kindness when she was sick." He took both her little hands and wrapped them in his own. "I've long admired your faith and the way you care for people around you—like Charisa—showing God's sweet love without judgment."

Her eyes misted, and the softness there gave him courage. "For some time now I've longed to ask you to walk with me through whatever years we have left, experiencing all the joy we can find in this life. I love you, Edie Hathaway."

He saw the *yes* in her eyes.

"Would you—" He reached for the little box and swallowed hard.

❄

Her hands trembled as Rick reached into his pocket. After the years of being alone, after all the heartache, a good man had fallen in love with her. Her eyes searched his, loving the hope and tenderness she found.

He glanced away a moment. When he looked back she was shocked to see moisture in his eyes. "Would you marry me, sweetheart?"

Her pulse raced as he snapped open the velvet lid.

No!

A huge rock sparkled in the glow of the lamplight. Edie fought for breath. Unable to speak, she turned away from Rick's longing gaze.

Why, God? Why?

Fear roared within and blazed forth, consuming her mind and limbs. No debt. Not again.

"Edie?"

"I. . .can't."

"You don't mean that." His voice was thin. "Look at me, Edie Hathaway."

❄

When she raised stricken eyes to his, he wished she hadn't. Gone was the light—the *yes*. Terror boiled in those green eyes. Then the shutters closed, and he couldn't see inside. The devastation hit him gale force. He snapped the jewelry box shut. "Driver!"

The man appeared.

"Back to the lady's home—the shortest route." Rick reeled as the carriage jerked and hooves thudded on the pavement. He turned from her, grasping the side of the coach.

"Rick."

The sweet tingle he usually felt at her touch cut like icicle shards through his shirt and into his skin. He shrugged off her fingers. "You've said enough."

"I—"

"Enough!" He hadn't meant to growl, but he couldn't talk. He had to escape those eyes, those lips that had surrendered to his. She shook beside him. He fought the urge to pull her into his arms.

The horse trotted to Edie's house. He jumped from the carriage and helped her out.

"Rick, please."

He turned from her swollen eyes. He pulled her hand to his lips, kissing it one last time. "Good-bye, Edie."

Chapter 12

Rick paced the hardwood floor, his clacking boots pounding out anguish. The cell rang, but he wasn't talking to anyone. He had to. . .do. . .something.

Rick called his daughter to accept her standing invitation to visit for Christmas. He'd thought he'd stay in town this year with Edie, but things don't always turn out the way a person plans. Thankfully, Ginny was happy to have him, as always. He certainly couldn't sit in the same church with Edie for the Christmas Eve service. He texted the festival bigwigs and let them know there would be no more Grinch this year.

The phone rang again. He checked the caller ID. *Edie.* He threw the phone toward the couch. What could the woman possibly say that he wanted to hear? Rick strode to the sofa, grabbed the phone, and shut it off.

He cranked the volume on the melancholy ballads crooning from the stereo. Hot tears sprung to his eyes. He wiped them, hard.

Plopping onto his leather sofa, he lay there, staring at the ceiling as the deep, rumbling voice sang sob stories. The waves of anger and grief took their turns with him. When the emotion became more manageable, he began to pray.

❄

Sunlight hit Rick's eyelids and he moaned, turning from the window. Must have fallen asleep about daylight—and slept until noon. His body ached from being crammed into the small space on the couch. He unfolded sore limbs and stumbled to the kitchen for strong, black coffee.

After a quick shower, he grabbed his suitcase and threw clothes into a haphazard pile. He frowned when he turned on his phone and saw four missed calls from Edie and another from Charisa. She'd left a message asking him to call. He hesitated, then dialed. If Charisa wanted to talk about Edie, he'd hang up, but if she needed something else he wasn't going to let her down. After agreeing to meet the young woman, he turned down the thermostat and closed up the house.

Who knew when—or if—he'd be back.

❄

Rick pulled into the park and put on his game face. Charisa sat on a blanket near the cross next to the permanent Christmas tree. Their little town's shrine told the age-old story—Jesus came to earth to save the world. There was something to hold on to.

He ambled toward the young woman. "Hey there."

"You don't look so good."

And he'd thought he could pull this off. "I'll be all right." He plopped down on the blanket. "What can I help you with, Charisa?"

She lifted tired brown eyes, and her hand went to her bulging tummy. "I know you sent the rocking chair. I just don't understand why."

Rick caught his breath. "What gave it away?"

Charisa laughed. "I don't know anyone else who would do such a thing. Plus don't you think a set of nursery rhymes—including Dr. Seuss—was a little obvious?"

Rick chuckled. "Didn't think of that. Just thought a new mama needed a rocking chair and books to read to the little one."

"Why did you do it?"

Rick shot a prayer for wisdom. "I wanted you to know that you weren't alone—and to help you celebrate."

Big tears welled and ran, leaving a makeup smear on her drawn face. "I wish my dad were like you."

"Aw, Charisa. I'm far from perfect. Just ask my kids." Rick paused, sensing the Lord's guidance. "But I have quite a Father myself. My Dad shows me His love over and over. He never ridicules or condemns me. When I make a mistake, He helps me see a better way to do things, but He never puts me down."

Charisa squinted at him.

"I've done a lot of stupid things, but He keeps loving—no strings attached." As Rick spoke, calm seeped into his raw emotions. "My Father has never once let me down." He heard the husky tone in his voice, felt the truth of his words.

Charisa sniffed, and he handed her his big red kerchief. "Nobody's that good." She blew her nose.

"You're right. There's not a person in the whole world that perfect. But I'm not talking about my earthly dad. I'm talking about God."

"God?"

"He can be your Father, too, Charisa."

"I'd be an embarrassment to Him."

"He's never embarrassed of His kids, darlin'." Rick pointed to the cross behind them. "You know why this cross is here?"

She shrugged. "It's a Christian symbol."

"It reminds us Jesus came to earth to deal with our sin. Sin hurts us, and it hurts others."

Charisa flinched.

"But the Good Book says we've all sinned and fallen short of God's glory. We—you and me and the whole world—need rescue from our sin. And that"—he pointed to the cross—"is how God rescued us. The Bible says when Jesus died, the agony of the whole world was put upon Him."

"That's awful."

Rick smiled. "It was a hard thing—for God Himself to die for the likes of you and me. But after three days Jesus came back to life. Now here's the good part—because of what happened on that cross, you and I can receive forgiveness for our sins and live forever with God as our very own—perfect—Father."

The tears began anew, and Rick patted her back. "It's the Good News, sugar. Our Creator wants to be your Daddy. He's waiting for His little girl to come to Him."

They sat a moment in silence. "You gonna be okay?" She nodded, and he stood to give her space to process. "I'm gonna be out of town awhile, but if you need something, call my cell."

Her brow furrowed as she squinted at him, but she didn't ask questions.

Rick sauntered over to the truck, the soft December sun on his skin. This thing with Edie hurt like crazy, but God was still alive and working in the world.

Chapter 13

Surely Rick would answer his door even if he didn't answer his phone. As Edie pulled into the driveway, her heart fell. No truck. She knocked on the front door, though she knew he couldn't be there. On the way home she stopped at the festival, but he wasn't there. She swung past his favorite haunts—Rudolph's, Christmas Groceries, and the Circle K. No luck. Edie did one more pass in front of his house. Still dark.

Rick was nowhere to be found.

❄

"Whatcha thinkin', Paw Pa?" Little Ricky put a round chin on his chubby arms.

Rick forced away thoughts of Edie as he grabbed his grandson. "I'm wondering how high you can fly." He tossed the toddler in the air, letting the sound of the bubbling giggles shove away the darkness.

"My turn, Paw Pa!" Four-year-old Ben raised his thin arms, and Rick tossed the boy into the air. Maybe it was time to move closer. Without Edie, there was nothing to hold him in Christmas except the memories. And he had to let them go.

❄

It had been foolish to hope Rick would be in church. Edie stood with the congregation and tried to sing the wonderful, solid words as "Faith of Our Fathers" rang out around her, but they caught in her throat. The beautiful old song stirred emotion. She blinked hard and tried again to sing, but all that came out was a solitary tear. She wasn't going to call Rick anymore. If he didn't answer her first ten calls, he wasn't going to answer. With a quick motion she wiped the tear hoping no one had noticed. Across the aisle Tom caught her eye.

Oh, dear.

She should slip out before she exposed herself. She glanced toward the back. *Charisa?*

She motioned for the young woman to join her, giving Charisa a determined smile. Charisa squeezed into the pew. There was something new—and good—in Charisa's shy gaze. Having her young friend near gave Edie the courage to stay.

After service Edie introduced Charisa to her friends, even though most had met casually at the post office. Edie's heart swelled as the church family embraced the young woman. With each handshake of acceptance, Charisa's countenance grew more confident.

"I'm glad you joined us today, Charisa." Pastor's deep voice held genuine welcome.

Charisa's gaze was clear. "I'd like to come back if that's okay."

Pastor's booming laugh caused several people to look their way. "My dear girl. This is one place you are always welcome."

❄

Rick frowned as Tom Flanders's name flashed across his cell phone. No way was he answering. Look where it got him last time the schemer called.

When it quit ringing he sighed and dialed voice mail.

"I don't know where you are, but I'm wondering what you did to poor Edie."

Rick cringed at the tone of Tom's voice.

"Her eyes were puffy at church this morning—and I caught her crying. I don't want to see her hurt again now that she's finally trusting you."

Edie trusting him? Ha. Edie trusted no one but herself.

❄

"And then Rick explained to me about God's love." Charisa's eyes shone. "After he left I told God if He was there, I wanted Him to be my Father. And I. . .feel different now."

Edie pulled Charisa into a big hug. "Oh, sweetie, I'm so happy for you."

"Nobody's ever told me much about God before you and Rick. Can you—would you help me learn about Him?"

"Of course." Joy soothed Edie's ragged emotions. She and Rick had made a mess of things, but something good had come out of all their bungling.

"Why's Rick going away?"

Edie swallowed hard. "What do you mean?"

"He told me he was leaving town."

Edie fought to control the welling emotion.

"What happened?"

The tears she'd fought since Friday won the battle once again. "Rick proposed, and I said no."

Charisa brought her the tissue box. "Why?" The incredulous look on Charisa's face was a knife, reminding Edie of her cutting decision.

The tears started again. "He flashed this huge diamond, and I—panicked."

Charisa laughed. "You said no because the ring was too big? There's a first."

"It's not funny." Edie grimaced. "After all those years underneath Frank's debt, I can't marry someone who can't manage his money."

"You think Rick can't manage his money?"

"He's a retired policeman from a tiny town with little revenue. His wife didn't work most of their marriage—and her medical bills had to be astronomical. How's he going to afford a huge diamond and world travel?"

"You don't trust him."

Edie hugged herself. "I was so sure Rick was God's gift to me."

"You're not anymore?"

Edie shrugged. "I've pinched every penny till it turned blue so I can have security in retirement. I can't chase after fantasy."

Charisa shifted in her chair. "I don't know much about this God thing yet, but it seems to me you don't trust Him either."

"How do you think I made it through all those hard years?" Edie paused to steady her rising voice. "I depended on God for my very survival."

"And now you're depending on your nest egg."

Charisa's words hung in the air between them.

"You've been a mother to me, Edie, and I respect you more than anyone I've ever known—with the possible exception of Rick. But. . .may I tell you how I see it?"

Edie wasn't sure she wanted to hear Charisa's opinion, but she gave a curt nod.

"You've been through so much difficulty you can't believe in the good. You trusted God when things were hard, but instead of believing God might give you your dreams, you pull the pins off your map and tell the man you love the opposite of what you wanted to say."

Edie sensed Charisa's hesitation. "You might as well finish."

"It's just. . .if it were me. . .I'd quit clinging to that nest egg like it's my security and trust God to bring good things into my life. The God Rick told me about is not just a God to hang on to when the going is tough, but a Father who loves His girl and wants to give her good gifts."

Edie couldn't speak.

❄

The phone vibrated in Rick's pocket. Was all of Christmas, Florida, going to call him? Sunday night Charisa had left a voice mail saying Edie had told her what happened and that she could tell Edie was missing him. Monday morning Jason sent him a text suggesting that Edie might need his attention. Monday afternoon it was a voice mail from Randi inviting him to share their family's Christmas celebration. It was strange to be on the receiving end after all the years he'd watched the town push Edie toward him. But they would just have to learn that he'd cut his losses and moved on.

Chapter 14

"I'm glad you're with us, Dad." Ginny favored her mother so much that Rick caught his breath.

"It's good to be here." He reached down and pulled little Ricky into his arms. Ben, looking a little stiff in his collared shirt, walked between Ginny and Dan. The church was in an old warehouse and strains of praise music, complete with drums and guitars, met their ears as they entered the building. Rick had never heard "O Come O Come Emanuel" quite like this, but he liked it. He slid into a folding chair and held Ricky close. The little guy clapped his own haphazard rhythm to the beat of the prelude.

Strange how a man could feel so full and so empty at the same time. Rick's heart swelled as his grandson bounced on his knee, but when Dan brushed his hand across Ginny's back and she shot him a loving look, the ache burned within. Just a few days ago Edie had looked at him like that. *Oh, God, please help me handle this hurt.*

The worship leader asked everyone to stand.

Somehow he found his voice and lifted his bass. "Joy to the world, the Lord has come. Let earth receive her king! Let every heart prepare him room. . ."

"Let my heart give You room tonight," he whispered as the others continued to sing. "Help me let go of my pain and worship You."

His phone vibrated in his pocket, and he sneaked it out for a quick peek. MAY GOD BLESS YOUR WORSHIP AS YOU WELCOME THE CHRIST CHILD TONIGHT. PLEASE FORGIVE ME FOR THE HURT I'VE CAUSED AND GIVE ME A CHANCE TO EXPLAIN.

Edie knew how to text? He tried to process the words backlit on his phone. As he slipped it into his pocket, the voices around him broke into his thoughts. "No more let sin and sorrow grow, nor thorns infest the ground. He comes to make His blessings flow. . ."

❄

Edie silenced her phone and put it in her purse as she stepped into the hush of her sweet little church. The pianist bathed the room in worship with her rendition of "What Child Is This?" Edie slipped in next to Charisa. She missed Randi's presence but figured the service would be too hard for her with Michael's recent departure How would they survive Michael's absence now that he'd left for boot camp? Michael and Rick gone in one dreadful week. Oh, she'd made a mess of things. But Charisa was right. She had to trust God had good things for her. She closed her eyes, letting the gentle music seep into her emotions. *Lord, You are the King. Help my heart to rest at Your throne.*

As the congregation stood and joined in carol after carol, Edie worshipped. She chuckled as the children put on the annual pageant—enjoying the way the crowns tipped sideways on the tiny kings who brought glitter gifts to the doll lying in the horse trough.

When the lights dimmed and everyone stood to strains of "Silent Night," she lifted her voice, "Sleep in heavenly peace. . ." The hopeful little flicker began in the back row and was passed, hand to hand. "Son of God, love's pure light. . ." She tilted her candle to Charisa's to catch the glow so she could pass it on to Tom in his usual spot across the aisle. "With the dawn of redeeming grace. . ." The union of the flames pierced the darkness, and Edie embraced the hope. "Jesus, Lord at Thy birth."

❄

Rick tickled feet through footed jammies then carried the sleepy little boys to their bedroom. In hushed tones he recounted his personal adaptation of *A Christmas Carol*, just as he had done every Christmas Eve when Ginny was home. As their eyes began to flutter, he kissed foreheads and pulled covers beneath chins. Then he slipped to the living room where Dan and Ginny sat cuddled in front of a fire. "What time do you expect the boys to be up?"

"Too early." Dan laughed.

"After breakfast we'll head to Dan's parents for lunch and visiting then back home for a quiet evening." Ginny smiled up at Rick.

"I'm not sure I'll make it to lunch." Rick cleared his throat. "And I think we should talk about those evening plans."

Chapter 15

The ringing startled Edie awake. Who would call at eight in the morning on Christmas Day? She propped her pillows behind her then lifted the phone.

As she recognized the rumbling bass on the other end of the line, her heart pounded. When he asked her to meet him at the Exxon station in Titusville, she thought it would burst. Two hours later, she pulled into the station and saw Rick leaning against his Ford. She hesitated, trying to judge the angle of his head, the slump of his shoulders.

❄

Rick questioned his wisdom as Edie stepped from the car. His broken heart shattered anew at the sight of her, but he couldn't help hoping they could fix things. When she came to him and lifted those sorrowful eyes to his, he could do nothing but open his arms. He held her close, breathing in the scent of her hair, making a memory of how it felt to be close to her. Hoping it wouldn't be his last. When she pulled away he felt the loss with the force of a tropical storm. "Let's drive down to the beach."

Once he picked a spot, he grabbed a quilt from behind the seat, and they walked side by side, so close, but not daring to touch. In the distance the ocean stretched before them, a gray expanse next to a ribbon of sandy shore.

"Here?"

She nodded.

Edie prayed for strength to say what she needed to as Rick spread the quilt on the sand. *And, Lord, would You open his heart to me once again?* "Thank you for meeting with me, Rick."

He nodded but didn't speak.

"I'm sorry I hurt you."

The nod again.

"I want to explain why I refused. . .the ring—and to offer a compromise."

His eyes narrowed. He wasn't making this easy.

"Most people know Frank left me with gambling debts. What they don't know is it took me almost twenty years to pay them off. Then I began saving—every penny—so I could be prepared for whatever comes in retirement."

He looked confused.

She touched his arm, hurt when he recoiled. "When you first began your. . .proposal. . .I was ready to marry you. I. . .I do love you."

The flicker of hope that came into his eyes made her fight for composure.

"I panicked when you pulled out the ring. All I could see were dollar signs and credit card bills. I couldn't—can't—return to living underneath a mountain of debt."

"Edie, I—"

She held up her hand. "Please let me finish. This issue is part of the reason I resisted your attentions for so long. You talk about travel and all sorts of expensive things as if they have no price tag attached."

He leaned forward. "Can I—"

"Please, Rick. I'm not done."

He sat back, a stunned look on his face.

"I've realized that I haven't trusted you—or God. I believe He gave you to me, and I want you more than anything. I also want to see your dreams come true. I have a nest egg." Edie clasped her hands to keep them from trembling. "If we're careful, we could probably live off our combined retirements, and. . .we could use my savings to travel for a while. There's not enough to take you around the world like you talk about, but we could go a few places. That is. . .if you'll take me back—and be willing to work through the money issue."

❄

Realization hit like a crashing wave. He'd been so eager to give extravagantly he hadn't thought how it would seem to her. What a fool he'd been to keep his secret while flaunting his wealth. "You're saying my spending habits are keeping us from marrying."

"But I'm willing to—"

"My turn, Edie girl." He reached for her hand. "You're willing to give up your security, the money you've been holing away for years, so I can travel." His voice came out husky. "Oh, my sweet Edie." He lifted her hand to his lips. "Always sacrificing."

Her eyes glistened.

"Do you believe me to be an honest man?"

"Of course." She gave a half chuckle. "A little ostentatious maybe, but honest."

"Call me an optimist, sweetheart, but I've got a ring in my pocket. If I were to tell you that it's completely paid off, and that I still want to share the rest of my days with you, do you think you could trust me?"

Her green eyes widened. "Yes." Her word was barely a whisper.

He reached into his shirt pocket.

❄

Edie gasped as he pulled out the ring he'd first offered her. The sun broke through a cloud as he raised it to her, and the diamond danced in its rays.

"Sweet, beautiful Edie, will you marry me?"

"Yes! But I don't—"

He silenced her with a gentle touch to her lips then slipped the sparkling diamond onto her finger. "I promise to explain, but let me enjoy your *yes* first, okay?" He swept her into his arms, and the kiss he gave left her trembling.

When he leaned back, she brought a shaking hand to the breathtaking ring. "It's fabulous."

"There's not a diamond in the whole world big enough to express how valuable you are to me, but I bought a big one to symbolize your worth." He looked her in the eye. "Edie, I'm a wealthy man."

She nodded. "Our love makes us rich."

"True." He chuckled and took her hand. "But you're not quite following. I'm talking stocks, bonds, greenbacks. Enough to travel the world in style. Enough to buy this ring and more."

She felt the blood drain from her face. "You're rich, rich."

"I am."

She wept then, thinking of how she'd underestimated all Rick—and the Lord—offered her.

"Don't cry, Baby Doll." Rick smoothed the tears from her cheeks, pulled her into his arms, and then kissed her again. "I hope you don't need a long engagement."

She chuckled at the huskiness in his voice and shook her head. As she nestled into what was quickly becoming her favorite place, she giggled. The Giver of good gifts had outdone Himself this Christmas.

Chapter 16

Edie led Rick through the busy post office lobby. First thing that morning, the day after Christmas, she had given her two-week notice then took the day off. Now she and Rick were taking care of business.

"What's that rock on your finger, Edie?" Jason gave a long whistle. "I can see it halfway across the room."

She tossed her head, enjoying the tinkling of her dangling earrings, and held up her hand, wiggling her ring finger for everyone to see. The room burst into applause.

"Three cheers for the happy couple!" Tom Flanders called from the back of the room.

"Praise God, you two finally figured it out!" Pastor's voice boomed from the front.

Charisa laughed. "I can help you two here."

Edie glanced around the room, loving each familiar face. Rick squeezed her hand then winked at her. He stood tall and turned to the crowd.

"Without my sweet Edie, in my heart there was a hole,
But thank the Good Lord she finally let love grow.

And once she made her mind up things happened really fast,
I moved right quickly to ensure that yes would last!
On Christmas we roused the preacher, our friend the county clerk, too.
And, relying on their favors, we began our life anew.
In front of our sweet children that night we tied the knot,
I can't believe Edie Hathaway finally let herself get caught!
So cheer your pretty postmaster, who has a brand-new name,
And let the news of Stanton matrimony spread in happy fame."

Edie rolled her eyes as everyone cheered again, and Rick gave his signature bow. Then he turned to Charisa. "Think you could help my beautiful wife apply for a passport?"

"I thought you'd never ask." Charisa took a gift bag from under the counter.

"What's this?" Edie pulled out the tissue paper. On the bottom of the small sack was a package of pins with purple tops. "Oh, sweetie."

Charisa grinned. "I've had them since I learned you'd pulled the pins off your maps. I was waiting for the right moment to tell you to keep dreaming."

"You, my dear, are a keeper."

The grin Charisa gave her lit the room. "Let's get that passport picture."

Edie smiled for the camera and filled out paperwork while Rick towered near, chatting with everyone.

Edie felt a tap on her shoulder and turned.

"Heard you were here, Mom." Randi gave her a hug. "Just had to watch you apply for a passport. After all those years of traveling from your chaise lounge, you're going for real."

Edie thought her heart would burst as she gazed at her daughter, the ring on Randi's finger, and Troy beaming nearby. Then Edie looked around the room at the myriad of smiling faces. The old saying said friends doubled your joy—well, she thought they bazillion-dupled it. God was *so* good.

Rick leaned over. "We need to do one more thing." Rick glanced at Charisa and back at Edie. "I have a very special letter addressed to Mrs. Edie Stanton. Could I buy one of those forever stamps?"

Charisa laughed and pulled out a stamp. Rick put it in the top right corner of the envelope. "Now, Mrs. Stanton, I know you're off duty today, but I'd really like this letter postmarked by Christmas, Florida's own postmaster before she retires."

Edie grinned and reached for the hand stamp as Charisa held it to her. With a flourish she postmarked the letter "Christmas, Florida."

She gazed into Rick Stanton's lively blue eyes and whispered, "You're a charmer, Mr. Grinch."

Author, speaker, and mom of four, Paula Moldenhauer wrote over 300 non-fiction pieces before receiving her first fiction contract for this
novella. She lives in the Denver area where
she homeschools, cooks mounds of food for
her teenage boys, and serves as Colorado Coordinator for the American Christian Fiction
Writers. She loves hanging out with her husband,
sharing girl-time with her recently engaged adult daughter, eating
peppermint ice cream, and walking barefoot. Her greatest passion
is intimacy with Jesus. Visit her: www.paulamoldenhauer.com.

JOIN US ONLINE!

Christian Fiction for Women

Christian Fiction for Women is your online home for the latest in Christian fiction.

Check us out online for:

- Giveaways
- Recipes
- Info about Upcoming Releases
- Book Trailers
- News and More!

Find Christian Fiction for Women at Your Favorite Social Media Site:

 Search "Christian Fiction for Women"

 @fictionforwomen